Dirty, a novel by David Lineberry
Published by Ashen Pawn Publishing, 2016
Baltimore, MD

www.ashenpawn.com

To contact the publisher for any reason, including requests for book signings or special events, write to: ashenpawn@gmail.com

ISBN: 978-0692697009
1st Edition, 2016
REV042216
Also available in eBook formats wherever sold.

Edited by Anna Wroten
With contributions from D. A. Gibbons
Back Cover Photo by Maria Kelly

Printed by CreateSpace, An Amazon.com Company
Manufactured in the U.S.A.

*This book is dedicated to
my friends and family.*

*Thanks for humoring me
and putting up with my nonsense.*

A NOVEL

DAVID LINEBERRY

ASHEN
PAWN
PUBLISHING

You want to settle for being a mouse?
Spend your whole life fighting for scraps of cheese?
I'd rather be the cat who watches the mice compete to
stick their neck in the trap before he feasts on the losers.

Tim Prose

Prologue

It was the oddest birthday gift she received and given in a most unorthodox way. Belated by necessity, served by strangers, surrounded in an air of unsettling secrecy. The potential of a brighter future in exchange for the clarity of a darker past.

Two weeks after turning eighteen, all she wanted to do was enjoy the rest of her summer before her first college semester began. She'd already quit her job to pack her things. Being a waitress sucked anyway. Now having more free time than obligation, the day belonged to her. Regardless, she started it the same as any other, just as prescribed, with a brisk run along a scenic route. The stable routine of exercise, the intimidating freedom to vary her course, the release of endorphins—all aids she'd been utilizing to drive back depression and relieve her anxiety. And it had worked until she realized she was being followed.

The sun was out but the breeze kept it cool, especially in the shadows of the trees along the paved walking path. That's where she first noticed him. It's not that he looked like he had any malevolent intentions. He was well-groomed and decently dressed, obviously not one of the wandering homeless that slept in the park. At first he appeared to be having breakfast on a nearby bench under the canopy of an old oak, throwing leftover scraps of his sandwich to the birds. But it was clear that he was watching her as she passed by.

She continued on the windy trail, knowing it looped around to branched forks in several locations. The next time she saw him, he was waiting where she'd emerge, staring right at her.

"Hey lady, you got a minute?" he said.

But she wouldn't stop. There was nobody else around. And she was a pretty girl. She could feel panic take her breath away as she sprinted down the route leading to the only exit that didn't require scaling a tall fence or wading through a muddy ditch. The inclination to flee was deep-seeded, overwhelming.

It didn't make a difference. The stranger had cut around, somehow. He was waiting for her at the gate, next to a hot dog vendor serving patrons. He patiently stood there, resting his hands on his hips as he watched her approach. She swallowed her fear and stared right back, having remembered that eye contact often dissuades potential miscreants.

"Hold up," he said, calling her again.

She tried to ignore him as she came nearly close enough to hook sharply around the chain-link fencing and run away.

"Amanda Lloyd, will you please stop?"

She turned to look at him, surprised to hear her name on his lips. A cop waiting in the nearby line for food made her feel comfortable enough to pause, if only to hear his pitch. The stranger walked toward her and reached inside his jacket. As his hand emerged, she quietly gasped before immediately feeling relieved—and a little silly—to see him holding out an envelope. It wasn't the first time she'd overreacted. She had grown accustomed to dealing with undue panic.

"This is for you." The letter he gave had her name on it, with a return address of a law office just inside the city limits.

"What is it?"

"I just deliver 'em, lady." If his dry, grisly voice didn't indicate his disinterest, his expression certainly did.

"This could have just been mailed."

"It was, twice. There was no response," he said. "He wanted to make sure you actually got this one."

"Who?"

"The attorney who wrote it. Maybe you should check your mailbox for holes." Then he walked away with as much enthusiasm as he used to vocalize his words.

It was the first time she'd ever seen it. Her parents certainly hadn't mentioned it. Amanda had never suspected that they would filter her mail, as overprotective as they could be. God knows she was still receiving every piece of junk from everyone else on Earth. She still decided to keep it to herself. At least until she could see what this was all about.

The law office of Theodore O. Kemp was a small outfit in a strip building sandwiched between a pawn shop and a free clinic. The outside window was covered with brightly-colored signs advertising help with malpractice cases, criminal defense, divorce settlements, debt collection and a wide range of other legal matters that no single lawyer could effectively master. The inside was just as tacky with badly aged carpet and wood paneling lining every wall. As dated as the place appeared, it seemed reasonably clean.

There was no receptionist to greet her, just a chest-high counter with a handwritten note taped to the surface behind a small button. *Press for Assistance* it read. She'd never seen a lawyer's office before, not in person. That being the case, movie cliches and common sense were enough to make her question the legitimacy of the whole operation. Amanda had brought the letter, even worn a pantsuit to present herself as professionally as possible. She felt overdressed.

The button echoed a harsh buzz from down the lone hallway but that seemed pointless. There was no response. She stood there and waited, trying to calm her nerves by flipping through pages of an old news magazine that sat on the counter though she never read a word.

With a flush, he emerged from behind the door closest to her.

"Oh, hello. Can I help you?" he said.

"I received a letter from this office and I don't know what it's about."

He looked down at the envelope in her hand and back up at her face with a smile.

"So, you're Amanda Lloyd. It's *so* very good to finally meet you." He extended his hand, visibly showing no sign of moisture.

"I don't mean to be rude, but I'm somewhat of a germaphobe. And I heard no running water."

"Excuse me?"

"Running water, like from a faucet. I heard a flush and you came out immediately."

He chuckled as he put his hand down and leaned on the counter, still showing a toothy grin. "Everything isn't always so obvious, young lady. See, I wash before I flush, using the paper towel to touch the handle. It probably doesn't matter, though in my mind, I feel like it keeps me cleaner. But I doubt you came here to discuss my bathroom habits."

"I don't know why I came here."

"Well, let's rectify that. Shall we?" He started down the hallway to a cramped room in the back, turning his head only once to make sure she followed. Theodore Kemp was a young black man dressed in an expensive suit, still proud to look at the Juris Doctor degree hanging on the wall every time he passed by his office. She paid it little attention as she trailed behind him.

"Am I in trouble?" she said.

"I don't know. Are you?" He smirked, then aimed his open hand to the chair at one end of the table as he walked around to sit on the other side. "How are you, Amanda?"

"I'm good."

"No, really. How are you? Any plans for college?"

She was beginning to feel uncomfortable, almost trapped inside the small room. She definitely had no intention of being there longer than necessary.

"Why am I here?" she responded, completely waving away his attempts for chatter.

"To settle an estate," he said.

"I read that in the letter. You mean an inheritance?"

"Of sorts."

"From who?"

"We'll get to that. Before we do though, I want to make sure you realize that you are not my client so there is no attorney-client privilege between us," he said.

"Why would I need that?"

"Everyone needs a lawyer eventually, right?" he said, smiling wider for no apparent reason. "Why didn't you respond to the first two letters I sent?"

"I never received them."

"Because of your parents?"

"I suppose so. They can be quite protective."

"So they don't know you're here?"

"No," she said, immediately regretting her honesty. "Maybe I should I call them and let them know."

He watched her reach inside her purse for a cell phone as he spoke. "You're an adult and that's your prerogative. But if I can make a suggestion, you might want to hear me out before you do."

She kept the phone in her hand, her finger hovering above the speed-dial digit assigned to her father. "Go on."

He got up from the chair and opened a locked closet behind him. With a grunt, he removed a heavy, keyed fire safe and sat it on the table. Then he placed a thick mailer envelope beside it. The envelope was large enough to contain at least a hundred sheets of paper or more, sealed by manufacturer's adhesive and several strips of packaging tape. The tape was illegibly signed and dated with a black sharpie to show it hadn't been previously cut open.

"Are these for me?"

"Indeed, they are."

She tried to lift the lid of the sturdy box before realizing it was locked tight.

"What's inside?"

"I don't know. And it's important that I keep on not knowing since, if I did, I would have a binding obligation to inform the appropriate governing bodies," he said. "See, Maryland has inheritance tax of ten percent if it contains anything of value, not to mention what would most likely be an exhaustive exploration into the origins of... whatever might be inside. Right now, I'm willing to bear witness that it's simply a fire safe. That's if anyone would even ask, of course."

"Where is the key to open it?"

"At the risk of sounding useless, I must admit that again, I don't know. My guess is that all your answers can be found in here," he said, pointing to the thick, padded envelope.

She picked up the package, intending to tear it open.

"Whoa. Not so fast," Theodore said. Then he dropped several pages of legal documents in front of her along with a pen. "These need your signature before you can break the seal."

"What is this for?"

"Nothing to be concerned over. This one simply states that you received the two items noted in the description. It also declares that they were both in good shape, signed and sealed upon receipt and that, to the best of your knowledge, it would be impossible for me to know what is inside either of them."

"And this one?"

"This is what's called a non-disclosure agreement," he said, ready to gloss over its purpose and smiling like it was standard practice for an inheritance.

"I'm sorry. A what?"

"Non-disclosure. A confidentiality agreement. At it's core, it means that any information you obtain from that envelope will never be shared. With anyone."

"Or what?"

"Or you'll be financially accountable for any damages that result."

"What if someone happens to find it after I open it? I can't accept responsibility for that."

"According to the agreement, that envelope doesn't leave this office. Once you're done reading, it will have to be destroyed. I'll need to witness you doing it."

She looked down at the papers, trying to make the first big decision of her adult life. "And if I don't sign at all?"

"Then you get neither the box nor the envelope. And you can walk away as if we never talked."

Amanda put the pen on the table and skimmed through a few paragraphs of legal jargon trying to make sense of it as best as she could. Then she slapped them down in her lap. "I really want my parents to see this before I sign. I don't feel comfortable doing it without them."

"Like I stated earlier, that's your prerogative. But they can't be in the room when you open these items and you'll be bound to keep knowledge of the contents to yourself. How relentless will they be once they *know* there's something they *don't* know?"

"I feel like you're pressuring me. I think I should go," she said, as she pushed her chair back.

"Wait, please." He sighed as he leaned on the table, pausing to organize his words. "My client hired me many years ago to make sure you received these items. He was adamant that you would be able to appreciate what he left for you and I promised him that I would get them in your hands."

"Your promise isn't my concern."

"And it shouldn't be. But you *should* be concerned about passing up on this opportunity. Somebody went through a lot of trouble and expense to make sure you could have these items," he said. "Now, I understand that you're intimidated by being legally bound to anything, but please trust me, no one is trying to trick you or take anything from you."

"Trust you? I don't know you."

He sat back and spread the pages out.

"You're right. Tell you what, we can go through the documents line by line until you're completely comfortable. I'll explain anything you don't understand and we can amend them if necessary."

"You contacted me. You did your job. What difference is it to you if I accept these?"

He looked in her eyes with what appeared to be genuine concern. Despite the exterior of his office looking like a used car lot, Theodore Kemp's motives seemed honorable.

"I already told you. I made a promise," he said. "I keep my promises."

Against her instinct, Amanda sat back down and once again began to read through the text. She asked him about sentences that seemed unnecessarily wordy and confusing, occasionally zoning out to ask herself if she had made the right decision to stay. In the end, nothing appeared to be harmful. And after the better part of an hour, she signed her name, firmly understanding the requirement for silence.

"You made the right decision." Theodore said as he stacked the contracts and tapped them on the table to even the edges.

"Take your time looking through everything. You're welcome to split it up into multiple visits if it's too much for one day."

He closed the door behind him as Amanda tore into the envelope. Reaching her hand inside, she slid out a thick, hand-written stack of papers from between the bubbled-plastic lining. Turning it open-end down, a key fell from inside and clinked across the table. It easily slid into the fire safe lock and turned.

With the heavy lid cracked open, she peered at the contents with disbelief. Stacks of one hundred dollar bills lay waiting at her disposal. She picked up a large pile to flip through the bills, then dug her hand to the bottom and lifted the stack to see it was the same the entire way down. It would be enough to pay for college, a car, a house. Immediately, beginning adulthood didn't seem quite so frightening. She closed the lid, then opened it again as if confirming the reality of it. It took two more iterations before she locked it back to its former state and buried the key in her purse.

Her mind changed gears in an instant. She started to plot how she'd get it home or in the bank. She began to worry about transporting the large sum in her car and explaining it to her parents. A debate bounced back and forth in her thoughts about whether to hide it or to lie about how she acquired it. *Could I have won the lottery? No, that would require proof and paperwork. Could I have found it? No, my parents will make me turn it in to the police.* Then it hit her that she really didn't know where it came from. In the rush of excitement, Amanda had nearly forgotten about the lengthy letter at her side. It couldn't be ignored.

She calmed her exhilaration enough to sit back down and slide the thick stack of papers closer to her chest. Taking a few deep breaths, she put her eyes on the first page and began to read.

01
...And Dust to Dust

It ain't a rare thing for me to think about blowing my own head off just to get that image of you out of my brain. I need you to know I wanted to be there earlier. I was looking, trying real hard to find you—trying to find *him*. We all were. It just took us time to figure out how to do it.

I wanted to bust through that filthy church door, drag him outside by his hair, and beat his face into a bloody mash. I fantasized about jamming the barrel of my pistol through his lips, hoping it would remind him of every cellmate he ever satisfied to survive in prison. For days, before I knew the truth of it all, I even thought about killing that woman of his while he watched, just to make him suffer. I imagined him cowering in a corner of a seedy motel room, watching her cry for life, knowing the bullet going through her skull was his own damn fault. Then, as I'd have him dangling over the edge of a balcony, choking on the shards of broken teeth in his throat, I'd savor each moment, watching him try to grab at the wobbly iron railing in a panic. And I'd spit in his face every time he'd beg for mercy.

I wanted him dead.

He deserved to die.

You probably think me a dreadful man, some cold-hearted monster with no matter of conscience. I suppose it would be near impossible to argue otherwise. That's assuming you think about me at all anymore. I want you to know that I'm trying to change. I'm working to pay for my wrongs. You have to understand that I would never have really hurt you, never put you in danger if there was any other way. I want you to know I'm sorry and I hope you'll take the time to hear me out and try to understand. I hope you'll have the heart to forgive me for what I done to you. I didn't have much choice.

It all goes back to Ash. He could be arrogant and loud and selfish, but he was my brother. As two white boys growing up in a rough black neighborhood, we had to stick together. He was all the family I had.

Our mom died when we were kids. She couldn't afford cancer treatments or most other necessities but somehow, she still found money for cigarettes. I think she was just too scared to kill herself any other way.

Walt was more of a sperm donor than a father so I refuse to call him anything that implies the relation. When he wasn't in jail, he would disappear for days at a time smoking meth or crack or whatever chemical he could pump through his veins. I was okay with that though. It was better than him shouting at us *stupid little pricks* through whiskey breath or beating us with that damn cane he always carried while he was going through withdrawal. It was a relief when he finally disappeared for good. After a month with him gone, I figured he'd probably just overdosed and was lying in a ditch somewhere. We were afraid his body would be found and child services would try to move us to an orphanage or with strangers, maybe even split us up.

Our biggest fear, though, was him coming back home, higher than heaven and eager to dish out hell. But that didn't happen.

Ash was happier too. Of course, my little brother still went by Stevie back then. Even though we were only three years apart, I was more like a father to him than the bastard that knocked up our mother. I was the counselor who made sure he went to school every day. I was the guardian that watched him go to bed safe at night. I was the caretaker who chopped the ends off of those damn hot dogs that he refused to eat because he said they looked like buttholes. And when we needed food and clothes, I was the provider that dropped out of high school at sixteen to get a job.

That didn't work out so well.

I got fired as a bus boy, carwash waxer, movie ticket-taker. Hell, I couldn't even keep a job scrubbing dried cum from peep-show booths at the local porn shop. Other opportunities would always arise and I couldn't help myself. I'd swipe tips and wallets, tokens and gift cards—anything I could sell at a discount for profit, you name it. Minimum wage with the government rubbing me raw with taxes, it just wasn't cutting it. Electricity had been cut off and water was next to go. We were hungry, cold, and desperate. We were about to be evicted from our shack of a house and I could feel all the responsibility fall on my shoulders. I didn't steal to get rich. I stole to survive.

As much as I wasn't greedy, I wasn't clever either. I was a dumb kid prone to jump balls deep into trouble with no escape plan whatsoever. I spent more than a few days in hiding, more than a few nights in jail. I probably put a hundred miles on my shoes running from police and security guards and pissed-off shop owners. I ain't nobody's hero. Never claimed I was.

Ash looked up to me though. He always respected me, had faith in me. And that boy was sly like no kid I ever seen before. With a little age, he would come up with schemes out of the blue, games that kept us fed and put some cash in our pockets. My kid brother held his own and then some.

Ash invented a scam he called *take out* where we would call in two orders for food delivery. I would have one order sent to a random third floor apartment in a nearby building with no elevator. Ten minutes later, I'd call in another one for whatever we actually wanted and then we'd wait for the delivery guy to show up. While Ash was in the hallway watching the guy trying to deliver the first order to an empty apartment or annoyed tenants who weren't expecting food to begin with, I was going into the delivery guy's car, stealing the rest of the food and whatever cash I saw around. Their cars were always left running and most times, unlocked.

"Don't touch anything you're not taking and don't go riding off, Roy," he'd say. "We ain't trying to get busted."

It was an easy meal and we averaged about forty bucks a pop in change, but he was good at knowing the limits. This was just his first idea. He was thirteen at the time.

Ash may have been my little brother, but with that crafty brain of his, I thought of him more like a partner. If I'm being honest though, when it came to planning our next move, he started taking the lead. He was always the mastermind and I was the trigger man, the guy that did the dirty work. Ash found ways to get us free shelter at churches and gyms and hospitals and occasionally, if we were lucky, even hotels.

We tried copy-shop counterfeiting and laundered the fake bills by buying small items in department stores, getting real cash as change. We set up fake charity boxes at gas stations in the name of scouts or little leagues or sick kids—and only had to cut the store owner in about a quarter of the time. We even found that church goers are such a trusting crowd that women leave their purses unattended when they go up front to pray. While they were finding Jesus, I was finding grocery money.

We ate everyday on scams, usually got a hold of some decent spending cash. Free cake was all over if you knew where to look for it. More times than not, his plans worked without a hitch and they always had backups. And when those backups failed, he had me, ready to fight our way out of trouble.

Then Ash started muling crank. Some guy just approached him one day and asked, out of the blue. It was real small at first: one package, one time, one hundred dollars. A lot of meth cooks and dope farmers—suppliers often being gentle types—like having a go-between so they don't have to meet with shady distributors themselves. And distributors know that even if every dealer they supply is trustworthy, which they ain't, there could be a nosy badge next door with his ear plugged into a wire. Anytime someone in the chain from manufacturer to distributor to dealer thinks it's too dangerous to stick their beak out, they'll send a mule to take the risk and a lot of times, that mule is a kid. Drug peddlers like working with kids because they're cheap and easy to intimidate. And being underage, it's a slap on the wrist if they do get caught so they'll choke down a rap pretty willingly. It beats getting killed.

They especially liked Ash because he was such a bright kid, loyal too. He had real potential to do anything he wanted. He was smart enough to never skim the stack or screw with their product and he never told nobody nothing about it except me. At sixteen years old, he was already working for a handful of suppliers, wearing a backpack filled with thousands of dollars worth of rock and dropping packages all over town on a bicycle. That's about the time he started smoking those damn cigars like some 1920's fat-cat codger. He'd smoke the entire ride, never tapping away the burnt end. By the time he was done his deliveries, the stogie would be a nub the width of his lips and his shirt would be covered in ash. That's where he got the nickname and he liked it.

Nobody local messed with him neither. The people who knew what he was doing also knew the kid with the cigar had connections. And the ones who weren't privy quickly found out he had a big brother with the devil's temper and no reservations about breaking his knuckles open to inform the ignorant.

It didn't take Ash that long to save up enough coin for a car. It was a bucket, but it gave him the ability to start delivering out of the city, even over state lines. I always went with him for the chance to run games out of town. That was perfect because our faces had become a little too familiar in Baltimore and it felt like our small pond of marks had damn near dried up.

On the way to wherever we were heading, Ash would keep conceiving these genius plans, and I would keep making them live. We did this for years. The scams had gotten bigger and better and we made some dough but it was never as much as he made just moving packages from one place to another. Ash was careful to never risk screwing up the drop-offs, but he kept feeding me plans, probably just to keep me happy. Trouble was, the bigger his deliveries got, the more careful he became until he was completely paranoid. That's when I bought a gun, thinking that would make him feel better. No matter, he eventually wanted to stop pulling other jobs altogether. Then he tried to put the brakes on me doing them, even by myself.

We got into heated arguments a few times and tension just seemed to hang around whenever we talked. He still asked me to go with him every time he traveled, even offered to cut me in on the take to be his bodyguard. But I refused. More than a couple of cops had gotten to know my face over the years and driving around with my ass planted on cushions full of plastic-wrapped powder bricks just seemed plain stupid for both of us. No, it was obvious he didn't need me and I didn't want his charity. That's how I saw it anyway. I didn't recognize my jealousy. I couldn't just admit that I felt useless, not to my little brother.

I started doing my own thing, mostly smash and grab stuff. I got one pretty good haul from a high school after they had some PTA casino night—close to two G's in one swipe. I could never do as well solo as I did with him though. I really missed having my partner.

Then I met Trish.

I had saved up a little cash, enough to buy a beer for a skirt anyway. She was only nineteen at the time, but she passed for twenty-one without a hitch. Smoking aged her quickly I guess. She sat across from me at the bar and smiled enough to let me know she wanted me to approach her, so I did. A few drinks was all it took to get her home. Don't misunderstand, I ain't saying she was a whore or nothing. We just really hit it off.

Trish was a crazy one, not just in bed but, yeah, there too. I mean she would bite hard enough to draw blood and tell me fantasies about being raped while we was in the act. She collected baby dolls and named them like kids, then drew tattoos on their arms with permanent marker. And she would only buy second-hand underwear because it had a *history*, especially the ones with small stains. She said whenever she wore them, she didn't feel alone. She said it was like holding hands with a stranger.

Despite her peculiarities, she never pretended to be anything other than herself. Without a doubt, that's what drew me to her. I can't say it was love, but we definitely connected. Trish had no family or close friends and she came in my life at a time when I needed someone to latch onto just as much as she did. So, I kept seeing her.

Once we moved in together, I got to experience her insanity in full swing. She would be depressed one minute, laughing like a maniac the next. Then Trish would cry like a repentant sinner, telling me she'd kill herself if I ever left. I gave her the benefit of the doubt, though. I couldn't say how much of her chemical balance was being screwed up by pregnancy hormones.

Damn, was that a bombshell she dropped.

"I'm having your baby. Don't even be an asshole and ask if it's yours," she said. "It's yours." We had just got done eating Chinese take-out food and she just blurted it out like it was nothing. Then we argued about the beer she was drinking.

I admit, I was scared at first. I didn't know nothing about how to be a daddy. I never had one, not a real one I could model after anyway. But we never talked about abortion, not once. We didn't even consider it. I wouldn't have guessed it beforehand, but the thought of having a kid made me real happy. I might never be someone important, I reckoned, but I was going to be important to someone.

I was there for the delivery too, watched the whole damn mess. As soon as I saw it was a girl, I made a promise right then and there to be a good dad for life, to always be around. Trish picked the name *Nina* and I didn't argue with it none. Years before, she gave the same name to her favorite doll although I never asked why it was her favorite. I guess she just liked the tattoo design she had drawn on the arms. But right after the delivery, Trish looked down at that little face and said she had a new favorite baby doll. And just like that, I had a family.

I tried to go legit and find a good paying job, tried to be a stand-up guy, a family man. I swore I'd be a better person than my old man anyway. I started working construction and it was alright, took some getting used to though. I even passed up chances to snatch tools and copper. I really tried to go straight.

Then Ash called me. I hadn't heard from him in weeks and out of nowhere, he phoned me in the middle of the night, scared to death.

"He's going to kill me, Roy," he kept saying. His voice was shaky. I never heard him panic like that before.

"What happened?"

"I got robbed," he said. "They stole my car and beat the shit out of me. Moreno is going to kill me."

"Moreno?" I said.

"Carmine Moreno. The car was dirty, completely loaded. It was all his stuff," he said. "I'm screwed, Roy. I'm responsible for his stuff, you know? These two spades jacked my car and it's gone now."

"It'll be OK. I'm coming to get you," I told him. "Where are you?"

"The lake trout shack on 33rd and Chester," he said. "Hurry, Roy. Please. Please hurry."

Any animosity we had was quickly tossed aside. My little brother was in trouble and I would never turn my back on him. Not on family. Not ever.

"Stay put and keep your head down, Stevie. Don't worry," I said. "I'm going to protect you. I promise."

Without hesitation, I went to the bedroom and got my pistol, stuffed it into my pants. Trish begged me not to go but I didn't listen. I didn't have a choice. The whole time I'm getting dressed and putting on my shoes, she's fighting me, trying to pull my clothes off and keep me home.

"Don't go, Roy! You'll get yourself killed. Nina needs her daddy," she said, crying loud enough to wake everyone in the whole damn building.

I don't put blame on Trish none since her heart was in the right place but had she not hassled me so much, things may have turned out different. Everything could be different. As it was, between the arguing and fighting, it took thirty-five minutes to get fifteen minutes away. By the time I got there, Ash was nowhere to be found.

I waited there all night, looked everywhere. Alleyways, gas stations, bathrooms, rooftops. I tried calling his cell phone too many times to count. I went to his apartment and likely places within walking distance but he was gone. He was just gone.

Police found his body the next day, hanging out the second-story window of an abandoned row home by a large hook that had been jammed through the roof of his mouth. They had sliced his throat from ear to ear, big enough that they could reach up and pull his tongue through so it dangled out of his neck. Then they hung him there as an example. Usually that's a warning Colombians give to possible snitches, but Ash wasn't no snitch.

I spent the next few hours with my ear to the ground, looking for his killer. It wasn't hard with the words and warnings being spread around the street like a venereal disease. Ash's death order came from the top as punishment for failure and was used to send a message:

You don't fuck with Carmine Moreno or his shit.

The guy that actually took my brother's life didn't even try to hide. He was some low-level dealer who wanted to rise in the ranks, so he bragged about it, let everyone know what a badass he was.

Cops didn't do anything about it. Maybe they didn't know, maybe they didn't care. Maybe they were just paid to look the other way. It was drug business and until decent citizens die, any effort they put in is only for the TV camera. It's hard to imagine the information was difficult for them to come by. Everyone seemed to know. It only took me about eight hours of hunting before I had Ash's killer in my sight.

I remember standing outside, looking at him from across the street, this black piece of shit stuffing his face like he was celebrating. He was sitting at a picnic table in front of some little barbecue stand with two of his wannabe-thug homeboys. The other three tables were filled with bystanders and witnesses and I had no idea how many of them were his associates. I didn't care.

As I walked toward them, I passed a technician working on an air compressor in the back of a pick-up truck. His tools were laying out on the tailgate behind him and he didn't see me grab his pointy flathead screwdriver. The closer I got to the table, the more I could feel rage take over. They were so into conversation, laughing and carrying on, nobody saw me coming. Nobody expected retaliation. Not in a public place, not in broad daylight. I don't know why I didn't use my gun. I guess it just seemed too painless, too humane for an animal like that.

I rushed behind him, wrapped my arm around his head and pressed it against my chest, locking my forearm in front of his eyes. In the same motion, I furiously and repeatedly stabbed him in the neck and face. Police reports would later state that I pierced him nine times before jamming the screwdriver in his temple. As soon as that coon's blood started to spray, people scattered.

Whether they were scared or just stunned, I can't say, but his friends were slow to react. One of them ran away immediately, the other tried to rush me. I pulled out my gun and shot him four times in the hip and stomach. Then I bolted a few seconds after everyone else had cleared out.

That same day, after burning my clothes and scrubbing black blood off my skin, I went to a funeral home while I still had freedom. I gave them the last of my money and arranged for Ash to be cremated once his body was released. It seemed fitting, all things considered, and it was all I could afford. They promised to save his ashes for me. I made them swear on the lives of their families.

I managed to hide for about a day and a half before police arrested me but when they did, I went peacefully. Between the search, the payback, and the trial, I didn't really have a chance to mourn the death of my brother until I went to prison. Then I had plenty of time.

The judge gave me twenty-five years.

02
Foresight

My lawyer had brought up temporary insanity during the trial though he recommended I plead *no contest*. I was found guilty by default, but being as the crime was committed under extreme emotional duress, the judge suspended ten of those years stipulating I complete psychological treatment.

Without exaggeration, all the horrible rumors about prison life are true and just as bad as you'd expect. Maybe even worse. I didn't eat for the first week because what they served was either inedible garbage or decent enough to be stolen by other inmates. It had gotten rumored around the clink that I was racist because I deprived the world of one more nigger. But let me clarify, the bastard I iced wasn't a nigger for being black. He was a nigger for killing my brother. Try explaining that to animals on the inside. I survived two rape attempts, four shiv attacks and one beating by a gang of spooks who wanted to kill me for being too white.

The worst part, though, came eighteen months in when Trish wrote to tell me she'd met someone else, some dyke name Paige. The two became lovers and were running off to start some new lesbian-life together. There wasn't room for a kid in their future. Adoption was Trish's answer. She gave away my daughter to strangers.

Being as how I was serving the greater part of a life sentence and we had no other kin, the judge ruled that an orphanage was the child's best option until foster parents could be found. And just like that, I no longer had a family. I didn't get a chance to fight for custody or even say goodbye. I was stuck in a teal-walled purgatory, spending all my energy trying to survive, alone.

It was around this time of my unraveling that I almost killed a man in prison. He tried to shank me with a broke-off, plastic spork handle in the chow hall. I took two pokes in the ribs before I jumped on him and bit his hand to make him let go. My first instinct was to shove that sharp plastic into his eye, then stomp it all the way down into his head, but I didn't do it. I didn't even touch it. Instead, I beat him to submission, then kept him subdued until a guard could come and take control.

It was this restraint that made the guards trust me. It was their good word that helped me at the parole hearing. The prison was so overpopulated by animals that even with all the scuffles and all the times I had to defend myself, I still got out with time off for good behavior.

Four-thousand, thirty-six days of my life wasted behind bars in a single stretch, forty-nine of which were in solitary. Just over eleven years of hell.

Even with the parole officer up my ass for the first five months, the feeling of freedom was overwhelming. I was an animal uncaged and I swore I'd never go back to prison, no matter the cost. I'd kill first. Hell, I'd die first.

There were three other men living at the halfway house with me. Four strangers, living in a cramped, run-down rancher, waiting everyday for bologna sandwiches to be dropped off by a nun and a bored-housewife doing community service hours. At first, I'd sit around with those clods and shoot the bull but after a couple of months, I was there as little as possible. Between Carl's constant need to jerk off with his door open and Tonto stinking up the house with curry-crusted roadkill, I had to listen to Twinkie croon alongside old country songs that only he could hear through headphones. If I'd remained, I was going to go back to prison for murdering someone else.

Sandman's had become my sanctuary. It was nothing more than a row home basement converted into a corner dive bar, a leftover hole in the wall that was dug out sometime in the 50's. I didn't exactly get a warm reception from the bartender *or* the regulars but it was the only place within walking distance where I could drink myself into a bearable numbness. That particular day, the barmaid had already given me lip for spilling my beer as if I'd purposefully waste a buck-fifty. That was also the day someone had left a twenty note poking out from the tip jar right in front of me.

Now, I know it's no fortune and to people who earn a decent wage, it probably sounds like a stupid risk to even consider. But I was piss poor in prospects, full of animosity and out of shits to give. Plus, as I sat there and stared into the eyes of Andrew Jackson and the free meals he represented, I'm sure the five beers chugging through my veins weren't helping me think straight. I wanted to reach up and nab it, quickly slide it in my palm before placing a sawbuck under my glass and walking out, ten dollars richer than before I strolled in. I was so focused on the cash, I hardly noticed I had company.

"How long you been out, friend?" he said.

I glanced over at the man sitting two stools down unsure he was even speaking to me. Then I looked around and saw no one else close to us.

"How's that?" I said.

"Prison? Or county maybe but I'm thinking state prison," he said. "How long you been out?"

I didn't return his goofy smile.

"Not long enough," I said. "Do we know each other?"

"No, I don't think so. I just noticed how you were eating, hovering over a two-dollar plate of fries like a dog guarding his dish," he said.

"Yeah, well. Some shackles are hard to shake off," I said.

"Oh, no doubt. That's a common behavior for fresh releases. The blurry blue tattoo on your forearm is a dead giveaway too, trademark prison-quality ink. Knowing there's a couple halfway houses around here, I just figured," he said. "I'm not judging you, friend. Really. I'm just good at reading people."

"And yet, you can't tell I want to be left alone?" I said, guzzling my last swig of warm beer.

"Oh, come on, Roy. Let me buy you another one, huh?" he said as he slid one stool closer toward me and signaled the bartender. I gave him the once over and knew he was a fish on dry sand. Everyone else around was wearing dungarees and t-shirts while he was sporting a dress shirt and blazer.

"How do you know my name?" I said.

"Overheard the bartender say it. I don't miss much," he said. "I'm Tim. Tim Prose." Then he pushed over a tall beer as the bartender served it.

"You ever served time, Tim?" I said.

"Me? No. No, thank you. I don't plan on it either. Prison is for those without foresight," he said. "No offense."

I nodded and sipped my beer. Nothing breaks ice like cold beer.

"You know Martin Luther King plagiarized the *I Have a Dream* speech *and* his doctoral thesis? He also cheated on his wife and tried to organize orgies with prostitutes on the church's nickel. I read he battered some woman too," he said.

"That right?" I said.

"It's what they say. Meanwhile, Adolf Hitler was a fantastic leader when it came to uniting people. He completely rebuilt his broken country and stabilized their economy. I mean, hell, he hosted an Olympics and pioneered the world's rocket program. He wasn't a half bad painter either."

"What's your point?" I said.

"My point is that people will only remember you by the most significant thing you do, good or bad. Redemption and fortune are never out of reach for anyone willing to snatch them from the road ahead. Foresight, Roy. You have to have foresight."

"A good plan?" I said.

"That's right. A good plan. A good backup plan too, for however you decide to get back on your feet," he said. "Do you have a plan yet?"

I stared down into my glass.

"I plan on having another beer," I said.

He huffed a slight grin. Then we sat for a few moments in quiet as we drank. I don't open up easily but something about him made me want to talk. I can't say exactly if it was his face or words or voice. He just had this genuine way about him that made me feel comfortable. He made everyone around him feel comfortable. Tim was an easy guy to like.

"I'm going straight, taking it one day at a time. That's my plan. It's just that nobody wants an ex-con," I said. "Nobody will give a repeater an opportunity."

"Then make your own opportunity. You can't get down about doing time, Roy. Once you served it, it's over. Don't let it define you or confine you out here," Tim said. "Giving up is just self-imposing your own form of prison."

As he spoke, the squeaky spring door swung open and slammed shut at the front of the bar. Being predominately older white patrons bred in segregation, everyone turned to watch the young black guy stroll in and sit just on the other side of Tim. While all eyes were on him, I quickly reached forward to grift the twenty from the tip jar. Without even looking directly at me, Tim put his hand on my forearm to stop me before turning his head in my direction.

"One beer don't make us friends," I said. "You want to get your damn hands off me?"

"One crime does violate your parole though," he said. "You want to go back to prison?"

"What are you getting at?"

"You don't think I noticed you eye-humping the former president over there?" he said quiet enough that it remained between us. He removed his arm from mine and leaned close enough to continue softly. "There's mirrors all around the bar, Roy. That's how I saw you and if *I* could, someone else might have seen you too. Glance slightly up over my shoulder, you'll notice a tiny red light in the corner attached to a black box. That's a camera. It's recording us."

I twisted my arm a little as if to shake off his words. Then I leaned forward and grabbed a napkin from a stack beside the tip jar in an attempt to undermine his implications. He could have been a cop or the bar's owner for all I knew.

"Oh, I see. You just wanted a napkin," he said smiling like he was all superior. "And here I am making assumptions and accusations. My, what you must think of me. Well, my apologies, good sir."

Then he laughed at his own sarcasm and shook his head. It was an awkward moment of unspoken understanding. He wasn't buying my ploy. Not even a little.

"Gillian, sweetheart," he said to the older barmaid while pointing my way, "this man's tab is on me."

I didn't know what to say so I said nothing, giving only a nod in return. Imparting gratitude didn't seem entirely appropriate. I returned to nursing my drink, taking increasingly bigger sips to speed it along without being obvious.

Tim leaned over to chat with the young black boy for a few minutes before they made a subtle exchange. I couldn't see it clearly, only getting a glimpse of the small plastic baggie Tim took under the bar in place of a folded wad of cash. Seeing that transaction, it was good for me. It made me feel like this guy, despite his appearance, was no better than I was. Moments later, without even finishing his drink, his dealer had left the place and I started to wear a shit-eating grin of my own.

"It makes sense now," I said.

"What does?" Tim said.

"You. In this place. I get it now," I said.

He smirked from one side of his mouth. "Please, enlighten me."

"You're a smart cat. You obviously have money, I guess enough scratch to buy whatever you're itching for. It makes sense now why you're in this place," I said. "Don't feel comfortable buying cocaine in your own neighborhood?"

He smiled at me.

"Your reasoning is sound but your conclusion is off," he said. "It's good to see you're paying attention though."

"Heroine then? Meth maybe? I may have missed the flavor, *friend*, but it seems like you're hooked on something," I said.

"Only caffeine and women," he said. "I don't do drugs, Roy."

"Yeah, then what's that in your pocket?" I said.

"Oh, it's drugs," he said. "But they're not for me."

Out of what seemed like nowhere, a grisly voice shook the room and made me cringe at the sound. It was familiar like the smell of fresh dog shit and just a bit more awful.

"Dirty Roy Conrad!" he said, standing at my back.

Two old pigs had walked in and immediately headed toward us to jump on my case.

"Well, shit. Who the hell would let you out?" The douchebag elbowed his partner like he just said something worth yucking about. "You remember this guy as a kid, right?" It wasn't the first time I'd bumped into Detective Wallace, but it was the first time in a long time.

The other detective was less familiar, at least at first.

"Of course I do. I mean his back is a little harder to recognize when it's not running away from me, but I could never forget Dirty," he said. "I still have a scar on my arm from chasing your ass over that barbed fence outside Worsley and Greenmount Avenue. You remember me, Dirty?"

"Not really," I said. "I only remember the cops who were good enough to catch me."

"Oooo," they moaned and laughed at me. It wasn't a strong enough jab to get a rise out of them and they wouldn't let themselves show it even if it had been. They were much better at it than I was.

Wallace leaned forward and got close to my ear. "So who you running around with these days, Dirty?" he said. "I mean, it's been a long while since I seen your brother hanging around."

I accidentally knocked my seat to the ground when I jumped off of it to get in his face. He was so close I could smell his foul, old-man breath when it drifted in my eyes. All I wanted to do was grab a nearby fork and jam it in his throat or beat him with the bar stool when he started to insult my family.

"Your brother was a piece of trash, Dirty, and you're more worthless than he is," he said, the arrogant bastard talking about Ash that way. He had no right. I didn't have much in my life to keep me restrained except freedom. I started to shout at him a profane mixture of threats and curses and insults. Wallace returned similarly as he pushed his chest against mine.

Tim immediately came in between us to act as the peacemaker, trying to overpower the venom we were spitting at each other. "Whoa, whoa. Let's all just cool down," he said. "Take it easy. We have other places we can go." To be honest, I don't remember the exact words he used. I was seeing too much red for my drunk brain to record or recall the details. Whatever he said though, it worked.

Wallace began to back off, scowling the whole time as the other piece of shit cop pulled him away. "You're not worth the price of feeding you in jail, Dirty," he said. "You're not even worth the paperwork."

I could hear their mumbling turn into mockery and laughter as Tim guided me toward the door and then outside. Truth is, he saved me from going back to prison that day for assaulting a cop. I would eventually get used to him doing that. I got used to him looking out for me.

"You have to use your head, friend. Control your temper," he said. "What were you thinking back there?"

The adrenaline-fueled rage had nearly sobered me up. My brain wasn't functioning at full power, but good enough to know he was right.

"You don't understand what that pig was making a joke about. You don't know how my brother died," I said.

"No, but I do know that no matter what happened, going back to prison won't help you or your brother. It won't bring him back," he said.

"Just because he's dead, I won't stop defending his memory," I said. "It's worth the punishment."

"You really think so? Think that's what your brother would want? You rotting away in jail over words with some two-bit dick?" he said.

Dark clouds had gathered making it look much later in the afternoon than it was. Sparse but big drops of rain began to land on my head and run down my face. It really helped cool my temper as I listened.

"Look, your loyalty is commendable. But picking your fights until you find one that gives you an advantage doesn't mean you love your brother any less," he said. "He'd want you to be smart, I'm sure."

I nodded as I took a few steps to walk away, thanking him again for the beer. I was honestly all set to head home. Now, under normal circumstances, with normal people, this would have been the end of a short relationship. He needed someone like me though. He needed me more than I needed someone like Ash.

"Tell me, why'd they call you *Dirty* in there?" he said.

I probably should have just kept walking but the thought of heading back to the cretins in that halfway house was good enough reason to pause.

"It's a nickname I guess I earned," I said. "I'm not afraid to get my hands dirty. That's why. They've been dirty all my life."

"That right? It's a good nick name. I like it. Sounds pretty badass even," he said. "So Dirty, you that eager to sleep off those beers or you have some life left in you?"

"I ain't exactly got anybody clamoring for my attention. What do you have in mind?"

"I need a pool partner. You play eight-ball?" he said.

"Not really. I've shot a few games back in the day but unless you're betting to lose, I'm probably not your guy," I said.

"Oh, I think you'll do just fine. If nothing else, you can drink for free. I'm buying," he said.

"I don't need your pity, mister," I said.

"Pity is for the weak, Dirty, and you're obviously not weak," he said. "Come on, you'll be doing me a favor."

I stood there for a second, just trying to figure him out as if it were easy enough to do so quickly.

"You ain't going to slip me one of whatever pills you got in your pocket, are you?" I said.

"Date rape a big problem for you, Dirty?" he said laughing. "I thought nobody was clamoring for your attention?"

He had this way of cracking little jokes and inserting compliments like some damn motivational life coach. The way he spoke and the things he said, always making me feel like I had some worth, it slowly chipped away at my animosity toward life. This was just the beginning of course, but it had already started. My guard was coming down. I had found a partner more clever than I ever wanted.

03
The Scarlet Bedleh

I didn't know what to make of the place. He told me we were going to shoot pool at an offbeat titty bar and I guess I was wrong for assuming I knew what that meant. What the hell did I care anyway? I was getting free alcohol and a good look at some decent tail. I wasn't going to be picky.

The Scarlet Bedleh was completely off my radar though. Instead of stripper poles and barstools, this place—proudly taglined as the Palace of Poon-jab—had belly dancers and pillows. All the girls were Indian, moving around like genies freshly rubbed from a bottle and not a damn one spoke American. I doubt *Cinnamon* or *Jasmine* or *Saffron* understood the theme of the corny stripper names that had been henna-tattooed on their chest. Or maybe they faked lingual ignorance to avoid having conversations. Even still, they were some damn fine-looking brown women. The crowd was a mixed bag of nationality though, everyone seeming to speak a different tongue. I swear going in, I must have heard ten indecipherable languages.

"What the hell is this, Tim?" I said. "Do they even serve beer here?"

"Open your mind, Dirty," he said. "Maybe try a drink that breaks the two-dollar price range."

We walked over to a corner and sat on pillows against the wall. Right away, *Ginger* moved toward us and began to dance the way loose women do when they're fishing for money. She pulled down her transparent leggings so Tim could stuff a dollar in her g-string before he shooed her away.

"Who are we playing anyway?" I said.

"Just a couple of guys," he said.

"Fellow drug addicts?" I said. I was trying to make a joke.

"DEA agents," he said. I thought he was kidding too.

I learned early on that Tim had a habit of keeping important details to himself, details that would otherwise keep people from doing what he wanted.

"That's real funny," I said.

"I'd call it more ironic. But seriously, they're legit. So if that vial dangling around your neck has rock in it, you may want to hide it in the bathroom. I recommend the drop ceiling," he said.

I don't know how he even noticed. It was just a small glass bottle that I always kept under my shirt against my chest. It had popped out for a moment during my scuffle at the bar but I had quickly tucked it back in. He wasn't lying when he said he didn't miss much.

"It's not drugs," I said.

"Regardless, it looks like drugs. If it's something you're not willing to part with, you might want to slip it in your pocket so you're not questioned about it," he said. "No reason to look like a criminal from minute one."

I didn't know what the hell was going on. I did what he suggested just to be safe though.

"So, you're friends with narcs?" I said.

He laughed a little as he looked around the dingy room, lit primarily by spotlights on three round stages to highlight the dancers. One of the girls unveiled small cymbals on her fingers to tap against the snake charmer music while she shook her hips. It was nearly distracting, equally hypnotic and irritating.

"Friends, no. I've never met them," he said. "Not yet."

"Then how do you know they'll be here?"

"Because, Dirty, it's Thursday," he said.

"And?"

"And this is where they come on Thursdays. Well, every other Thursday."

And with that, I suddenly didn't want to be anywhere near there. I wasn't ready to be thrown back into shady dealings, especially with a stranger who was targeting government agents.

"You brought me along to hustle a couple of feds?" I said. "You're out of your damn mind."

"Who said anything about hustling?"

"Why else would you be staking them out?"

He didn't say anything. He simply smiled at a topless barmaid as he handed her a twenty in exchange for two glasses of a milky-white liquor on ice. It smelled like fuel.

"Dirty, all we're going to do is play some pool," he said.

"If you do something fishy, you know they're gonna blame me because of my record. You setting me up?"

He didn't say anything as he sipped from his glass.

"If that happens, I swear I'll gut you before they can take me down," I said.

"Take it easy, tiger. You need to relax. Ever try yoga?" He grinned, making me out like I was the crazy one. "They won't know about your record. They'll never even know your name."

I don't know what made me stay. Maybe it was because I had nobody else. Maybe it's because all the places I had to go were worse than where I was with him. Whatever the reason, I took a chance and trusted him. I followed his lead instead of my gut.

"They're here," he said before he stood up and walked toward a hallway against the back of the bar. I trailed behind him into one side of a small, quiet space containing a pool table and windows that overlooked the main seating area through sound dampening glass. He timed it perfectly so we entered the billiard room at the same time they did, only from the opposite side.

"Oh, you guys playing?" one of them said.

"That was our intention, but there's no reason we can't all play together," Tim said, pausing to read their reaction, "I mean, unless you boys are afraid of getting spanked." Then he smiled widely, showing his teeth in the most chummy way possible. I didn't realize I was watching a predator. Neither did they.

They kindly refused at first but Tim had a way of convincing people to change their minds. He would use suggestions and compliments and witty insults to bend their will to match his own without ever looking desperate, just friendly. Half the time, people would agree to do whatever he wanted not realizing the idea they thought was theirs was his all along. He was a master at this.

"No money. I'm just thinking bragging rights," Tim said, as he continued to bait them without revealing his intentions.

"I guess you have more confidence than cash," one of them said.

"Fine, I tell you what. Let's keep it friendly, gentlemen bets. How about a dollar a ball plus drinks for every game?" Tim said. "I'll even grab the first round."

After less than a full minute of banter, that's all it took.

Now, Agent Hairdo was really resistant to playing with us but Agent Specs perked right up when Tim mentioned the booze. And damn, could that guy drink. They introduced themselves properly but, having my mind distracted with trying to figure out Tim's intent, I couldn't remember their actual names. So I nicknamed them in my mind with the features that stood out most: one had a pretty heinous comb-over and the other had thick framed glasses. Thinking back, I was real bad at paying attention to details at first. I probably should have really tried to remember their names but I was too busy trying to learn my own identity.

"I'm Randy and this is Pete," Tim said as he introduced me. "He's a mechanic-in-training at the dealership." I didn't know the first thing about engines. Lucky for me, neither of them never asked much about it. If they had, I guess my complete and utter ignorance on the subject could always be blamed on me still being in training. I didn't realize until later, but Tim added that tidbit as a safety net. It's those kinds of details that he used in every deception. He was a fanatic about details.

"Dealership? What kind?" Hairdo said as he began to break the rack.

"Carson's Cycles. We deal Harley and Indian, a few sport bike brands. I prefer the cruisers myself," Tim said.

"No kidding," said Hairdo. "I've been riding for years. Got myself a Wide Glide. I've been thinking of getting a new one."

And what do you know? The agent liked motorcycles, the very thing Tim claimed to sell. That kind of lucky coincidence seemed to happen a lot for him.

"Really?" Tim said. "You looking to trade her in or build a collection?"

"Trade it in. The wife would kill me if I started filling the garage with bikes."

"Well, if you're serious, I can get you a deal nobody will be able to beat. I'm off until Saturday but stop in. I'll hook you right up," Tim said. "Unless, of course, you want to play for it tonight?" Then he laughed. Then they laughed. I was the odd one out for not thinking it was funny because I wasn't so sure it was a joke. I smiled anyway.

Just as hustles normally go, we lost the first game of course, and Tim bought a round after putting a few bucks on the table for the difference in balls sunk. He seemed happy to do it though. We lost game after game and every time, he'd put a few bucks on the table, then buy a round. Few bucks, buy a round. Cash, drinks, repeat. He jokingly made comments about losing, subtly veiled to seem like he was tired of dishing out money but wanted to make light of it.

"You guys are taking me broke," he'd say.

"The price of that bike keeps going up," he'd say.

"Could I get a substitute partner over here?" he'd say, suggesting I be replaced by the non-English-speaking dancers as they walked by, getting laughs at my expense. Truth is, he really didn't care that we kept losing. It's exactly what he wanted.

Even Agent Hairdo started chiming in to take jabs at me. "Hope you're better with a wrench than a cue stick."

Asshole.

At one point, Agent Specs began to slur his speech. His drinking problem wasn't evident at first glance but as we continued to play, he started downing his own drinks along with any that the rest of us didn't want. It wasn't until after the second game that I even bothered to try the milky-white liquid from my glass and one sip was enough. I never really cared for sipping hard liquor and whatever that stuff was, it looked like jizz and tasted like feet. I could still see my slobber stain on the lip of the glass when Specs finished it off.

Hairdo started giving his partner the stink-eye every time he'd knock back shots like some pissed-off wife silently scolding her drunk husband. Whenever that happened, Tim became a magician using motorcycles as misdirection to hide his sleight of hand and Hairdo willingly bought into the distraction. Tim did almost all the talking and created whole back-stories for both of us, elaborate enough to be believable, simple enough to be memorable. Originally from Ohio, he was divorced with three kids living in a small townhouse while he gave me a wife and a mistress, both pregnant with my seed. When interest in our personal lives started to visibly fade, he'd fall back on the subject of motorcycles to keep Hairdo's attention away from his partner. I watched him paint a realistic picture with lies, a regular

Rembrandt of bullshit. He almost had *me* believing he sold bikes for a living.

Then Hairdo went to the bathroom and that's when Tim really worked his chatter. I could see Specs slowing down and Tim propping him up, putting an arm around his shoulder and patting his chest in what looked like concern. "You OK buddy?" he said. "Might be time to slow it down. I'm not sure you can handle the sauce like your partner can."

No drunk man likes to hear that, especially a drunk that prides himself on being a heavyweight. His last statement became a challenge, a need to prove otherwise. After intentionally pushing that button, Tim was quick to apologize with yet another drink, one he brought from the bartender himself. And predictably, Hairdo wasn't happy when he came and saw that. He made it apparent, even announcing in agitation that the current game would be their last before clamming up. That's when Tim walked over and put a quarter in the jukebox that, until then, had sat there doing nothing but taking up space. He chose an upbeat song, a perfectly logical thing to do for someone trying to break a tension that had suddenly surrounded us.

I remember watching Tim work, wondering how he was going to make them stay. How was he going to convince either guy to bet more money or that motorcycle they talked up so much? I couldn't foresee any way that he'd be able to get anything at all from them. Specs was just starting to wobble when Hairdo's phone began to ring and, just like Tim predicted, the music was too loud to take the call in there, even with his finger in one ear.

That last drink had pushed Specs over the edge and he was quickly turning into a zombie. There's no way he could have continued standing without Tim's help, just like Tim wanted. Why else would he have slipped a roofie in his liquor? Hairdo was only gone a minute and I'm still not sure who was on the other end of that phone line but Tim knew. He had it set up. By the time Hairdo got back, his partner was a whirly top with no more spin left. Specs swayed back and forth as if a strong wind would knock him on his tail, finally admitting he had reached his limit. Then he dropped. Naturally Hairdo dashed to his side and tried to wake him up, his first concern being his partner's safety.

"I'll grab him some water," Tim said, always the good Samaritan.

He returned two minutes later but Specs had already passed out, not even able to reach the exit without practically being carried. The game was over. Tim helped Hairdo walk him to their car before they exchanged brief pleasantries and phone numbers. Tim even gave him a business card that referenced the dealership, conveniently the last one he had on him.

"He'll feel better after he sleeps it off," Tim said. "And don't you forget to see me about that bike. I mean it. I'll beat any price by ten percent, at least." Then he smiled like a dear, old friend.

We stood quietly and watched them leave the parking lot before either of us said a word. Then I couldn't resist.

"What the hell was the purpose of that?" I said.

"What do you mean?" he said.

"You been creeping on those guys, right?" I said. "For what? So you could swallow their bar tab and toss fifty bucks at a game I warned you I suck at."

"Do you smoke?" he said.

The question was so off topic, it took a second for the words to register.

"Do I smoke? No. Why?"

"It's a good time for a smoke break, that's all," he said. "Maybe we can bum one from somebody."

I was starting to think he was nuts. And it was pissing me off.

"Did you not hear me? I don't smoke," I said.

"I don't either, but it will look more natural than us just standing out here waiting for them, you know?" he said.

"Waiting for who? Can't we just go?" I said.

"We shouldn't. Not yet," he said. "In a few minutes."

"Why the hell not?" I said. "What are we waiting for?"

"To cast off any doubt. Clear our name," he said. "Leaving now, we'll just look suspicious."

I swear no sooner did he say that than headlights beamed me square in the eyes. That black car came barreling back in our direction, quickly turning and stopping with a chirp from the tires against the asphalt. Agent Hairdo jumped out of the car and bee-lined toward us.

"You guys need to stay put," he said. "Don't leave." Then he walked back inside the bar and disappeared on the other side of the frosted glass.

His partner was slumped over in the front seat, completely conked out. I wasn't sure he was still breathing anymore. Then I looked at Tim who was calm as a Buddhist monk. He grinned briefly as he looked back at me.

"Tell me what the hell is going on," I demanded, trying not to let anger raise my whisper to a yell. "Right now."

"You ever heard of a caper fox?" Tim said.

"What?"

"A caper fox. It's the only fox breed that hunts in packs," he said. "They're brilliant."

"I have no idea what you're talking about."

"See, two or three caper foxes will follow other animals while they're hunting and wait for them to go back home to feed their young. Badgers, wolverines, coyote—capers will intentionally pick on animals that are bigger and stronger but slower and less agile than they are," he said.

"What does that have to do with anything?"

"Because while two or three of those foxes are circling the young and getting the attention of the adult animals, there's another fox secretly stealing their food supply right from under their noses. It's what the foxes were after the whole time and those other animals never suspected it. Afterwards, for all they know, their food just up and vanished."

It still didn't sink in. Even when Hairdo came out of the bar, I didn't have a clue what had happened right under my nose.

"I'm sorry to make you do this, but you both need to empty your pockets," he said.

"Excuse me?" Tim said. He looked legitimately surprised. Another great deception.

Hairdo pulled out his badge and ID and flashed them at us.

"You're cop?" Tim said.

"DEA," he said.

No shit. But he truly thought he was informing us.

Tim began to empty his pockets and hold the few contents out in his open palms. Hairdo frisked his pants and jacket pockets before turning to me.

"There a problem, Officer?" Tim said.

"My partner, in his careless overindulgence, seems to have misplaced his badge. It's not on his belt anymore," he said. "But it was there when we got here."

I felt all around my pants pockets, worried that somewhere I'd find a shield planted on me. At the time, I still didn't understand Tim's motives. I didn't trust him completely. I pulled out some change from my front pocket and the cord that usually wraps around my neck, holding the glass vial at the bottom of it.

"What's this?" the agent said, looking at the small white stones and gray dust in the vial.

"A good luck charm," I said.

I'm pretty protective of it and I don't like other people putting their greasy hands all over it, but I didn't argue the case too much right then. I just closed it up in my hand when I felt my empty back pocket. Then I frantically patted all around my jeans.

"Shit. My wallet's gone," I said. "Somebody clipped my wallet."

My look of anger and surprise, now that was for real.

"Your wallet is gone too?" Tim said, before turning to Hairdo. "And *his* badge? Can you take down a report about it? Maybe we can talk to the manager."

"You should call the police about that," he said. "I'm going back inside to look around one more time."

We joined him, obviously. It would be weird if we hadn't. We looked all around the bathrooms and the pool room, the bar and the pillow where we had originally sat down. They even asked about security cameras but being a gentleman's club that values the privacy of their patrons, they didn't use them. I really *was* hunting for that badge. Tim made it appear that he was looking too, but he was just playing a part. It was only about twenty minutes before Hairdo finally gave up and left again, this time for the night. And as soon as he did, Tim sat down to order one last drink for both of us.

"Where's my fucking wallet?" I said. "Did you take it?"

"Relax. It's under the front seat of my car," he said.

"You stole my wallet?"

"Not stole. Hid. Don't worry, your *lack* of money is still inside it," he said. "I couldn't exactly have him frisking your pockets and finding an ID with your real name on it, *Pete*."

"About that, what's going to happen when he goes to that dealership and finds out there is no Ricky and Pete?" I said.

"Randy," he said. "It's Randy and Pete. And they'd be pretty upset to find out they're not real people, Dirty. They exist. If the good agent goes to the dealership, he's going to find out that, as of tomorrow morning, Randy and Pete were let go for selling stolen motorcycle parts below cost."

"How do you know that?" I said.

He gave me only a look for an answer. Just a facial expression that said the details were too involved or unimportant. Or maybe I just wasn't trusted enough to know that information.

"Did you take the badge?" I said.

"I don't do anything for nothing," he said.

"Where is it?"

"Drop ceiling in the bathroom," he said. "I'll come back and grab it tomorrow just in case he's waiting to search us again on our way home."

"All this for a badge?" I said.

"I needed one. A current one," he said. "Overall, it's the cheapest and safest way to get a federal badge."

"I'm sure you could buy a fake," I said.

"I could, but that would require middlemen that I don't trust. It leaves loose ends and I don't like loose ends," he said. "Plus, this isn't some passable forgery. This is the real deal and I strive for authenticity whenever possible. Details, Dirty. It's all about details."

"What makes you think I'm not a loose end? I could've totally screwed you back there," I said. "I still could tomorrow."

He smiled as he took the drink from the waitress and swallowed it in one swig.

"Like I told you, I'm good at reading people, Dirty," he said. "I have a feeling you don't talk to police under any circumstance."

He looked at me for a moment as if holding back something, trying to decide whether or not to divulge more information. Maybe he was just reading me.

"Why tell me anything? You could've come back tomorrow and I would never know," I said.

"Because, Dirty, I'm hoping you might be up to helping me again."

"Helping you with what?"

"Oh, I'll come up with something," he said. "I always do."

I was reluctant but I saw something in him I hadn't seen in years, not since Ash. He was a thinker. A big planner. Maybe even a potential partner. More than that, he was hope and he was guidance. He was a path out of the muddy ditch I was stuck in.

Where that path led I didn't know, but it sure as hell didn't look any worse than where I was.

"I don't work for free drinks," I said.

He laughed as he stood to leave.

"Don't worry," he said. "Help me out and you'll be able to afford your own drinks."

04
Carrot on a Stick

I never went back to the halfway house, not to sleep anyway. I would show up in the front yard occasionally when my parole officer demanded to see me there, then we'd walk up to the corner diner for coffee and twenty minutes of bullshit. That was becoming consistently rare though. I didn't miss that place and I don't imagine Carl or Tonto or Twinkie shed many tears over my empty bed. They probably enjoyed having the little extra room.

Instead, I ended up staying with Tim full-time. He lived in a decent size third-floor apartment, big enough that it had a second bedroom with a pull out couch, one that didn't smell like thirty years worth of piss and parolee sweat. I couldn't remember for sure, but I think his building was one of those that Ash and I had scammed as kids. At any rate, it looked familiar enough that it brought my brother to mind every time I looked at the outside of it.

I had an uneasy feeling the first time I went in that bedroom, the one that would become *my* bedroom. The door didn't have a round knob. It had a fancy, brushed-silver, curved lever handle—the only different one in the apartment, though I didn't give a second thought about that being weird. I had always associated those handles with the big, expensive homes that I never got to live in and as stupid as it probably sounds, it just seemed better than I deserved. Just a stupid door handle and it was somehow above me. And as I turned that lever down and opened the door to see a clean bed sitting underneath a large double window that overlooked a row of trees, I was stunned. I was immediately uncomfortable in a place so well-kept, a place where everything worked properly like one of the hotel rooms Ash and I had scammed for as kids. At the same time, I wanted to get used to this. I wanted this stuff for myself.

From an outside point of view, it probably seems pretty fruity, going from meeting a guy to living with him the same day. There wasn't anything queer about it though, and it didn't seem so odd when I was actually going through it. Our personalities just started to click. He made me feel real comfortable, more at ease with him than anywhere else I had to go. At first, it was, "Crash here for the night, pal. Halfway houses are full of criminals." Three days later, "There's room here, guy. Camp out as long as you need." Finally, we started pulling jobs together and me sleeping there was just a logical given. "We need to get hopping pretty early," he'd say, "I'll wake you in the morning." Before I knew it, that apartment was home.

Even that first week, he started right away teaching me things, showing me tricks and secrets. He was usually blunt and sometimes harsh, but he followed any insult with a recommendation and sealed it with a compliment once his advice was followed just the way he wanted.

"You're wearing dungarees and a ratty t-shirt, Dirty. You're showing off ugly tattoos and your face is in this perpetual state of anger, nothing but a bitter scowl. In the eyes of the world, you're a felon and that's all you'll ever be," he said. "But I see that you have potential to be so much more."

Don't misunderstand his intentions. He wasn't trying to make me a better person, just training me to be a better con man. He was molding me into the person he needed.

"If you want to look like a business man, then dress and talk like a business man. You need to be a cop or a mailman or a bus driver? Act the part and believe it or no one else will," he said. "How you look will state your identity more quickly and effectively than you ever could with your words. People want to believe the world is an orderly place. They want to believe whatever their eyes tell them is truth. Give it to them."

Tim pushed the importance of details in creating a deception. Becoming a genuinely respectable person, building a believable back story, creating a noble motive to hide true intentions— they're all crucial parts of the charade. He talked about how easy it is to break the illusion and once it's gone, the game is over. And I'll be damned if he wasn't spot on in everything that he said.

We would disguise ourselves in business suits and go ring shopping for his supposed fiancée. His suits were mostly too snug on me and a bit too long but he had one that, by no accident, worked pretty well. He actually ended up giving it to me for keeps. And once I put it on, I looked more than presentable and I felt better. I felt confident. I felt important. Dressed up like that, the jewelry salesmen always treated us with respect and trust. They'd look at the watch strapped around Tim's wrist and the perfect fit of his clothes and they never suspected for a second he wasn't some rich sap looking to get hitched. He didn't need to be monitored or scrutinized, not in their eyes. He spoke properly and flashed wads of cash—mostly singles wrapped in a hundred, but they didn't know that.

"You think she'll like this one?" he'd say, holding a large loose diamond in the air as if to watch it sparkle.

"Come on, don't be a cheap bastard. You're a lawyer and she's the love of your life, you frugal shit," I'd say, just like he taught me. "Crack open the spine of your wallet a little."

The salesman would laugh at what I said and pull out bigger gems against Tim's obvious reluctance. Different shapes and sizes, all spread out on a velvet cloth atop the glass case. Yeah, the sales guy always loved me. After all, he thinks I'm doing his job, egging my buddy into a bigger commission for him. They'd talk to me and joke, lightly encourage me to keep putting the pressure on my *colleague* to spend his vast make-believe lawyer riches. When searching for the perfect rock, who's more influential than a brutally honest friend, after all? That was exactly what they thought. Suckers.

Truth is, Tim really *was* searching for the right stones, decent matches that could easily be swapped out with the cheap cubic zirconia he was palming. He'd raise up the real diamond and look at it, then tuck it in the folds of his hand as he dropped the CZ into its place on the velvet liner in one slick motion. Having precious stones wedged in the crevices of his fingers, he'd put his hands in his pockets as if pausing to look over the selection and contemplate. Real diamonds went in the left pocket, cubics came out of the right. It was such a quick switch and Tim was good at it. My added distraction guaranteed they never had a clue we were stealing them blind in plain sight, even if they did re-watch us on security footage. When he was done switching our whole supply, he'd pull out his money clip as if to make a purchase just before having a sudden change of heart.

"You know, this is the first place we looked," he'd say. "I think we'd better shop around, just to make sure this is the right one. I'm confident we'll be back though."

I'd give him another insult, feign some irritation over his indecision and with that, we'd be gone without a trace, them none the wiser. I can't imagine how many months or years passed before they discovered the switch if they even ever did. And diamonds are marked up by such a ridiculous amount, they recover the cost too quickly to make it worth spending the money to investigate.

See, greed is the key. You find out what people want and make them think you have control of it, make them believe you're going to give it to them, whatever it is. Meanwhile, you're really helping yourself to what they have. And make no mistake, we helped ourselves. Tim was showing me the ropes but he gave me a good cut too—twenty percent of the take. That's the same amount he took. The other sixty percent was split between fencing the goods and financing a bigger job that he was keeping to himself.

He never met with the fence himself neither. It's just too damn risky. That's where Colt came in. Colt was a young black kid, smarter than I care to admit but with an attitude that he carried around on his shoulder like an angry grinder monkey. He was arrogant and abrasive, like he was entitled by birth, owed by the world. He looked at me like I was too past my prime to be of any use and even got it in his head that he was somehow intimidating. I didn't like him from the get-go and I never trusted him.

But, he had street connections, and Tim had been using him since long before I came around so what choice did I have but to work with him. Colt knew drug dealers, which is how he was able to get the roofies he bought for Tim, the same sleepers he had dropped off at the bar weeks earlier. He knew guys that sold guns and even one that made explosives. And, of course, he knew some crooked pawnbroker that would buy anything, no matter how scalding hot it was. He would take the diamonds or gold or whatever we needed turned to cash and pass them along to whoever he used. Without fail, we'd always get clean cash in return.

Colt would sometimes help out with the actual stings but usually only as a distraction, at least at first. Say security at a particular place was extra tight, Tim would have Colt show up mid-game wearing his shadiest thug-wear. When a guard sees two Caucasian suits shopping on one side of the store and a young brother in baggy jeans and a hoodie on the other, there's no question who he's watching.

Tim started having Colt and me run some smaller games by ourselves, just to get us used to the play. That's what he said anyway. Maybe he just didn't want his face seen too much. Regardless, we proved ourselves capable, even if the first jobs we ever worked together were really pedestrian.

In one game, I'd go inside a gas station and ask the attendant if anyone had turned in a diamond ring. Of course no one ever had.

"My wife lost my great grandmother's wedding ring," I'd say with Tim's words spilling from my mouth. "If it turns up, please... please let me know."

Then I'd spend twenty minutes looking around the gas station floor and parking lot and bathrooms, whimpering like a scared puppy. It's all part of the show really. It makes it more believable when I go back inside to plead for their loyal help a second time.

"Listen, it's worth way more to me than the face value just because it's a family heirloom. If it turns up, I'll gladly pay a reward for it. A thousand dollars, cash. No, make that two thousand. My wife really wants it back."

Usually, they'd all dismiss me at first, taking the fake phone number I'd give them and tossing it on the side. The ones real interested in making a quick buck would come out from behind the counter and take a look around, maybe even scan the parking lot after I left. They'd never find nothing though.

A couple of hours later, Colt would go in after me and drop his keys somewhere directly in view of the pay window. As he picked up his keys, he'd also remove a cheap piece of costume jewelry from his pocket, puzzled like he just found it on the ground. Then he'd hold it up and look at it with the biggest cock-sure smile his plump lips could form. And more times than not, the cashier would suddenly perk up.

"Did you just find that? Another customer lost that earlier and I promised I'd return it to them if I found it," they'd say.

"Well, you didn't find it. I did," Colt would snap back.

Sometimes they'd try to play on his conscience. He had none. A couple of them even said they'd call the cops and threaten legal trouble if he didn't hand it over. They were bluffing.

"You need to give that to me," they'd order as if they were in a position to demand anything.

"I ain't giving you shit. How do I know you ain't going to just keep it for yourself," Colt would say. "Give me their information and I'll call them. Hell, they might even give me a little something for it."

The cashiers couldn't have that, not the ones blinded by dollar signs. They couldn't hand over the phone number and let him get the money they thought they deserved. One thing they never did was tell him about the reward, at least not the full amount of it. And in the end, it would always come down to money. The more blind they became with greed, the easier it was to dig the hook through their jaw and reel them in.

"How much you want to give me for it?" Colt would say if they didn't come up with the idea themselves. "I bet I could bank some mad cash for a loop like this."

Colt knew they were expecting a two thousand dollar payout so he'd ask for a thousand. After a little back and forth, a few of them actually gave it to him but most talked him down closer to five hundred. I wonder how it felt after they handed over that stack, then called the phone number I'd handed them and got nothing. It was always the main line of a large business, one that had a few thousand employees and an automated answering system. They'd think I'd accidentally given them the wrong number or, in my nervous state, just forgot to leave my last name and extension to get beyond the robot secretary. As long as it wasn't obvious they got scammed, that's all we cared about.

Between five hundred and a thousand dollars, tax-free cash split between the three of us, for a few minutes worth of work. And we would do this six or eight times a day for a week straight before we changed games to keep the noise away. No way a real job could give me that kind of coin, especially one making five bucks an hour after Uncle Sam shoved his fat fingers in my pie to take his slice.

The money was good, better than I ever had, but it was nothing compared to what Tim had up his sleeve. All the cons we were running were just stepping-stones to a larger job, bricks for a house he was building. Only he never shared the address. See, he seemed to have the Midas touch and every scam we pulled worked out just like he scripted it. He wasn't the type to freely share details so we just stopped questioning things altogether. And why not? We'd listen to him and it always paid off.

"Stop swearing so much, Dirty," he said. "Curse to be funny or curse to emphasize anger. Saying it casually and constantly only makes people think you're uneducated."

"Lay off the weed, Colt," he said. "You want bigger cuts in your bank account, I need to trust that your brain isn't coated with a thick layer of bong residue."

He'd say it and after a while, we just followed like disciples because his guidance was always spot on. The games he'd come up with always worked. The advice he gave always made things run better. But these easy little jobs were just to get our appetites wet for more. He had his sights set on something much bigger.

Before we started pulling off even small cons, there was a lot of research to do. Scoping out security guards, employee schedules, surveillance systems, traffic patterns. Tim left nothing to chance and did his homework on every place he had planned for us to make a play. Sometimes he would disappear for hours on his own, plotting the huge grift that he wouldn't discuss with Colt or me. But when the time would come to gather information on a job he wanted us to work, he always took me with him.

At first I thought he wanted to show me his thought process, maybe even wanted my input. I would eventually come to realize he was just keeping an eye on me, making sure I stayed out of trouble. He knew what he wanted to accomplish, he made all the plans by himself. He didn't need or want us crowding his space while he ironed out details and crafted spectacular piles of bullshit from thin air. But there I was, sometimes spending hours at a time in a car watching a building or business or a mark. And while we waited, there wasn't a lot to do together but talk. And damn, he loved to talk.

"Do you like sports? Where'd you grow up? What was prison like?"

It was all pass-time, get-to-know-you jabber and I played along. Before I knew it, he became the closest thing I had to a friend outside prison walls and we got to know each other pretty well, at least on the surface. I kept Ash close to my chest though. He hinted around about my brother a few times, asked directly once or twice. I never wanted to talk about it. Not protecting him was my biggest failure, his death my darkest shame. Tim could always tell when a subject was too sensitive to touch. Usually he would sidestep awkward moments with a joke or some obscure knowledge about an animal nobody had ever heard of, describe their methods of killing prey or their weird mating rituals. The guy obsessively watched wildlife documentaries like an addict. That day though, he wanted me to come to Jesus.

"What would you do if money was no longer a problem?" was how it started.

We had been staking out a big house on Witherspoon Avenue at the time, in the Homeland section of Baltimore. Real expensive digs behind an iron fence and gated driveway. We did this for a week straight, spent hours trapped inside a car with nothing to show for it but chapped asses. Then we went to some country club and parked on a nearby street that overlooked tennis courts beyond the brick walls, trying to see in as much as we could. That's when he pitched his question.

"I wouldn't play tennis with these rich hags, that's for damn sure," I said.

He looked over at me wanting more. I didn't know what to give him.

"Just like I said before, Dirty, you need to have a plan," he said. "What would you do with a big chunk of money. What would make you happy?"

"I don't really know," I said.

"You don't know?" he said. "You never thought about it?"

"Spending make-believe money hasn't been a big priority of mine. Seems like a waste of time," I said.

"Forget the money then, Dirty. You're missing my point here. What do you want from life? What would make you happy?" he said.

I shrugged my shoulders. Sure there were things I wanted. Seemed pointless to think on them though. I might as well wish to fly. Or be invisible. I never was the kind to set my goals very high. Everything I ever wanted, only thing I wanted in recent years just seemed too far out of reach. Thinking about things you can't have just makes not having them that much more miserable.

"We can't do this forever, right?" he said. "You do anything long enough, you'll eventually get pinched and I don't plan on going to jail. One day, we're going to have to retire, use the money we've made to get whatever we want next."

"I guess I ain't gave it too much thought," I said.

"Well, think about it. And decide what you want once you're done with this. A little house on a beach? A sweet little wife in a bikini bringing you drinks? Maybe even a couple little Dirty's running around taking lunch money from minority kids," he said smirking the way he did when he wanted to lighten the mood.

"It's only been a few months for me and I'm just getting used to all this. It's been a long time since I entertained any hope of a future worth thinking about. I guess I have you to thank for that," I said. "As far as what I *want* though, I don't know. What do *you* want?"

He nodded for a moment and began to open up more sincerely than he ever had before. I could tell by the tone of his voice.

"I want my girlfriend back," he said. "That's what I want."

"You got a girl?"

"I had one, a beautiful girl. But, she was taken from me," he said.

"Another guy?" I asked. I figured it was either that or some horrible accident. And I guess I was hoping we weren't going to talk about death.

"No, nothing like that. She came from a wealthy family, very possessive and controlling. Her parents didn't take too kindly to someone like me," he said.

"That's it? They just made her stop seeing you?"

"You sound surprised it's that simple," he said.

"Well, I am. I'm just thinking, if she really wanted to, she would contact you anyway," I said. "What could they possibly do to a grown woman?"

"I guess you haven't dealt with rich people too much. They're assholes. Always used to getting their way, using their money and power for leverage. They moved and took her away to only God knows where, then forbade her from contacting me," he said. "You know, they threatened to have me killed if I ever went near their *little princess* again."

"All to get her away from you? Damn. I wouldn't know what it's like to have parents who cared that much," I said.

"It's the only thing they could do to keep me from her. I loved her. When I made love to her, I tell you, the world stopped moving," he said.

I knew there had to be more to it than what he was saying. Tim and a couple rich people? I was sure as the rising sun that he tried to fleece them and got busted. Up until then, I had never seen his face show those little signs of genuine emotion though. His jaws clenched slightly like he was trying to hold back feelings. His eyes would zone off and stare through the dashboard as he talked. He was remembering her. Looking at her in his mind's eye. Missing her.

He kept going. "Mandy had the softest skin, the sweetest smile. I'll never forget the way she looked at me with those brown eyes the first time I ran my fingers through her hair, guided her mouth down on me. I'm not trying to kiss and tell, Dirty, but I was her first and only."

"No kidding," I said.

"Damn right," he said. "And that's why I'm doing this. That's what I want. After I score enough cash to steal her away, I'm getting her back. I'm going to find her and get her back."

He had a purpose. It wasn't new or fleeting. This is what he was after even before the first moment we'd met. All his planning, all his scheming. Every extra penny he had earned was being saved with this goal in mind. It makes me sick. He was so confident about what he wanted and, at the time, I was aimless. I had little to strive for like that, nothing I thought I could get. I wanted to though. I wanted to want something. I needed a goal.

"Everything you said before sounds good," I told him.

"What?" he said.

"The house and beach. The half-naked woman serving me drinks. That whole thing sounds good," I said. It was the easy answer.

"Even the kids? I never took you as the father-knows-best type," he said. Again with the smirk.

"Yeah, I'd like that one day. I want another kid," I said.

"Another?"

"I had a girl taken from me too," I said. "My daughter."

I told him all about Nina and how good it felt to be her father. I told him how Trish had left me while I was in lock-up, and how much I wanted to backhand her across her rug-eating mouth for giving away my kid. The conversation just seemed to lead that way.

He whipped out a bag from behind the passenger seat and removed a camera with a long zoom lens. Then he started taking pictures of the women playing tennis, resting it on the steering wheel to steady it. He focused on one broad in particular, an older blonde with a huge rack, though at the time I didn't know why. He never shared information before he was ready. It's just how he worked and I was used to it.

"She a friend of yours?" I said.

"Not yet," he said. He kept checking the view finder after every few photos. He needed a perfect shot so he took dozens to choose from. "It's not too late, you know."

"For what?" I asked.

"To be a part of your daughter's life," he said. "What if I can help you get her back?"

"No. It's impossible. The courts wouldn't even tell me who's watching her or where she lives. After I got out, my P-O told me that, *given my own upbringing and the nature of my crime, I'm too much of a danger to her well-being.* Apparently, me not seeing my own kid is in her best interest," I said.

"Bureaucratic horseshit," he said as he continued snapping pictures.

"They'll never let me have her back," I said. "They're probably right anyway, you know. I ain't good to be anybody's daddy."

"You want to see her, right? Be around her?" he said. "You're already better than half the parents out there. I think you have more potential than you give yourself credit for."

There he was again. Building me up, saving me from myself. My life coach.

"The way I see it, Dirty, you can choose to accept what they say, prove the label they've slapped on you and let someone else have your flesh and blood. Or, you get back to what's yours," he said. "I can help you find her."

"And then what? Kidnap her? I'll end up staring at the cold side of prison bars for the rest of my life. And Nina, that would just screw her head up more than it probably already is," I said.

"You're right, but maybe you can visit her, talk to her. Maybe start a lifelong relationship so she doesn't think you just abandoned her," he said.

"I don't know," I said. It just seemed ridiculous to me.

"She's your kid, Dirty. What don't you know?" he said.

I sat there quietly in his subtle rebuke. The sad part is, he was right to shame me, no matter why he was doing it. I wanted my kid back. I wanted to be a better dad than I got. I just needed a push in that direction.

"Maybe there's even a way you can see her with the blessing of her foster parents," he said. "So it's all on the up and up."

And there it was. He had given me a goal. Something to strive for. I would get myself together, save some cash and go straight. Then, I'd get my kid back in my life. Problem was, I had no idea how to do it. Luckily, Tim always seemed to have a plan.

05

The True Nature of Sea Otters

It wasn't all champagne and tits with us. Colt and I constantly had our hands firmly gripped around each others' throats, especially in the very beginning. I didn't like his cocky attitude. He had no respect for my age. We were just different sorts of people and that made it hard for us to unlock horns. Yeah, we'd throw colorful comments back and forth but that was just the easy shot to take for both of us. I'd call him a ghetto rag monkey, he'd call me white-trash trailer troll, then we'd spit every creative slur we ever learned at each other until we were bored. Don't get me wrong, there were a few times I truly wanted to pound him into the dirt but he never would throw that first knock no matter how much I begged. Besides, he was really useful, sometimes damn near necessary.

Being as it was though, he was less than enthused about being involved in the plan.

"You done lost your damn mind," was his exact response.

"It will be quick and easy," Tim said. "We'll be in there for 20 minutes, tops."

"Let me ask you, is there even a slim chance of us looting some papers on this?" Colt said.

"Cash? No," Tim said.

"Is there any possibility of *getting information* that will help put coin in my pocket?"

"No," Tim said.

"Well ain't that some coincidence 'cause it's the same odds you gonna see my black ass raking a courthouse. Why the hell you doing this? Stealing state records. That's a felony and it ain't worth the risk."

"It's only a misdemeanor but that's irrelevant. We won't get caught," Tim said.

"Irrelevant? It ain't to me. I keep waiting for this grand plan you working on to make us bank and instead you bringing me this shit? Want me to risk everything for nothing," Colt said.

"We're doing this to help Dirty find his kid," Tim said. "He would do it for you."

Colt huffed and rolled his eyes at me. We all knew that was bunk.

"I'll give you a thousand out of my own pocket to help," Tim said.

"A thousand dollars?" Colt said reluctantly. I was just as surprised.

"Yes, but not for three weeks. By then, I'll have a score put together that will make us all happy. *Very* happy," Tim said. "But we need you on this."

Colt slumped back into his couch and looked at me like I was a diaper stain. He didn't want to get to know me. He didn't want to get close. He really only talked to Tim, even then.

"What about the cops? This is a court building, right? There's screws in blues pushing everybody through a metal detector at the entrance. If shit goes astray, they right there," Colt said.

"You won't be breaking any laws. Neither will Dirty. I'm the only one taking a real risk here and I got it covered," Tim said.

"What exactly are you thinking?" Colt said.

"This is a state government office and after office hours, the door is locked with a numerically coded lock plus a physically-keyed deadbolt. Now that's within the walls of the courthouse which is already guarded, under constant surveillance and armed with a networked alarm. I wouldn't even think about breaking in when they're closed," Tim said.

"So we go when they're open," I said.

Tim nodded. "Now when they're open, there's always people there. Luckily, the state only hires the most ineffective workers on the planet. Everyday, from noon to one, the entire records staff goes to lunch, leaving only two people in our target office, one of which is the department supervisor. The last Friday of every month, however, that supervisor has an off-site meeting with one of the governor's ego fluffers. That leaves only one long-time staff member guarding the records, a sweet little number named DeShonte Washington."

"Sounds Asian," I said.

"Kiss my ass, Dirty," Colt said before he looked back at Tim, turning his scowl into a cocky grin. "So what? You need me to whip out my hypnotic charms and seduce a sister?"

"Keep your charms in your pants," Tim said. "You just need to tell her that you lost your son when you were convicted for drugs. But now you're clean and you want his address so you can write to him."

"What if she can't find the name?" Colt said.

"She won't even look it up. It would be a sealed record and she legally can't show you. Besides, she won't have time to think about it. She's going to be feeling pretty sick," Tim said.

"How so?" Colt said.

"Every time DeShonte is left alone, she celebrates her fleeting independence from management with a large diet-cola and two chocolate crullers from the bakery next door. Every single time. We're going to slip an eye-dropper full of ipecac syrup into her soda before she gets back into her office."

"What's ipecac?" I said.

"It's a bad afternoon for DeShonte," Tim said. "Now, she can only be gone from her desk for fifteen minutes before her computer automatically logs her off for inactivity and she's busted for breaking protocol. So she's always quick about coming back from her donut run. That means we have to be too."

"Why not just go in when she leaves?" I said.

"She locks the deadbolt behind her. If her keys go missing, all kinds of flags will get raised and they'll have a uniform sitting on the door. We need her to come back and unlock the deadbolt on her own," he said. "Once she's back, the ipecac will get her out of the office within a half hour and she'll be in such a hurry, the last thing on her mind will be the deadbolt, especially since the door will automatically lock behind her, passable only with a numeric-code."

"How do we get past that?" I said.

"The surveillance system is all hardwired but they installed an RF relay so that officers can use a portable monitor while they patrol. They don't use them as far as I've seen, but the tech works nonetheless," Tim said.

"How does that help us?"

"There's a camera pointing at the door from a nearby corner. I can use a RF monitor to watch her while she punches in the code and there's our access. I'll do that every morning for a couple of days before to make sure it doesn't change," Tim said.

"We have to steal one of their monitor things?" Colt said.

"No need. I already have one. It's a nanny cam relay but I already tried it right outside the building and it works. I can see whatever their cameras see," Tim said. "I just can't take it inside. It will look too suspicious should they question it."

"And what about the cameras seeing us?" Colt said.

"I'm going to study them, know where to obscure my face so I'm not identifiable. You won't need to hide since you're technically doing nothing wrong."

"What will I be doing? Specifically?" Colt said.

"After you ask her for the info, get a little more aggressive when you see her start to get ill. Just keep your distance so you're not showered in airborne stomach acid and regurgitated pastries. When she takes off for the bathroom, and she *will*, follow her. Keep badgering her. Don't let her concentrate on throwing up. I don't want her to recover quickly. Make sure she stays flustered and stall her as much as possible if she starts to come back," Tim said.

"And what about me?" I said.

"You'll be in the bathroom," Tim said.

"Why?"

"To keep her from using it," he said. "The closest toilet is a family bathroom right across the hall. You go in and lock the door. She'll have to hike it around the corner and down a long, long hallway where there's gender separated restrooms at the other end." Tim moved his arms to diagram the layout in the air as he continued to explain. "I'll be in the hallway waiting to see Colt chase down a nauseated DeShonte. After they vacate, I'll come knock on the bathroom door signaling you to get out of there and keep watch on the hallway while I head in the office to find the files on your daughter. Our girl should still be logged in so I'll have full access. Hopefully I'll be done quicker than she is, but if I'm not out and you see them coming, just walk by and give a few hard knocks on the office door so I know to bolt."

"I can't let you take that risk for me. This is my deal, Tim. I'll go in and look around," I said.

"We're not raiding file cabinets here, Dirty. How are your computer skills? You going to be able to go in and navigate an unfamiliar operating system?" he said.

I gave no response.

He kept going, "Besides, you've been there before to ask about your daughter. They get one good shot of you on camera and correlate your mug to an earlier visit, they'll link it to your daughter, then you. If you get busted, that's enough to break your probation and could mean serving out the rest of your original sentence. Once I'm out of the building, though, we're free and clear."

It just made sense.

"What if someone is watching the security monitors when you enter the office? They might come snooping right away. You won't have time to leave, much less find anything," I said.

"Well," Tim said. "I guess we'll just have to keep the guards' hands full with other things."

The day came when we were sitting there in the car, waiting to make our move. I remember looking around at the mad blur of suits rushing in and out of the building we had marked. Lawyers, officers, jurors, plaintiffs, defendants, office workers. It stuck with me that hardly a damn one had a smile on their face. Just not a place I guess *anyone* really wanted to go.

"Look at this crowd. It's like a circus," Tim said. "Just more clowns." Then he lowered his eyes back on the little screen where he was watching the broadcast from the security cameras.

"Why are you doing this?" I said.

"I told you, I'm double checking the entry code. It's 2-9-6-1-3-5. They might be hitting a 4 at the end but I'm pretty sure it's a 5," he said.

"No, I mean all of it," I said. "Why are you risking your neck to help me? What's in it for you?"

He put the little monitor down in his lap and tilted his head slightly to look at me. Then he stared out through the window at a small truck filled with gravel parking in front of the building, then toward a pizza delivery guy heading inside. They were both his idea.

"Ever seen a sea otter?" Tim said.

I just shook my head and readied myself for another nature lesson. Fucking Ranger Rick this guy was.

"Adorable little critters on the surface. Seriously, if you could take one for a stroll through a park on a Sunday afternoon, you'd have every vagina within half a mile radius getting moist from the concentrated saturation of cute," he said. "But you know what? Sea otters are assholes. They'll hold their young pups hostage and hurt them until the mama otters bring them fish to eat. They'll rape baby seals until they drown, then hold onto the corpse for days so they can rape it some more. They truly are the uncouth dickheads of the animal kingdom."

"So?" I said, looking back at him right in the eyes.

"So, these same sick little bastards also interlock their paws when they're floating in the water to ensure they don't drift apart while they sleep. They go out in groups and fish together, hunt together, protect each other. They stick together, because even bastards need friends. Even bastards need family," he said. "And maybe helping a friend find his family makes me feel a little less like a bastard myself. I guess in that regard, I'm not so selfless." Then he turned the monitor off and put it under the seat before redirecting his attention outside again.

As much as he'd ever tried to build me up with words, nothing made me feel better than he did that day. He was taking a huge risk, putting himself in danger, spending his time and energy on this scheme, all for me. He was proving he'd become more of a friend than I had believed, definitely more than I had been to him. Tim won my loyalty that day and I wasn't going to let him down. I wasn't going to let him get caught, no matter what.

"And *thar* she blows," he said.

We got out of the car and followed this big moose of a woman to the donut shop, but we didn't walk together. Once outside that car, we were strangers, at least in the eyes of anyone who might be paying attention. Tim walked ahead, fast enough that he entered the bakery first and stood in front of her in line. I lingered around the back like I was looking at the menu, letting everyone get in front of me, DeShonte included.

I was a little nervous about it, honestly. Funny thing is, this was the *only* part that worried me, the part I figured would be the most difficult. Turned out to be simple.

The donut shop had cameras so we had to be careful about that, or at least Tim did. He got his coffee and a large diet cola. She got her fist-sized donuts and an ironically large diet cola. Then as she was getting ready to walk in front of me toward the door, I pointed out a folded ten-dollar bill that I had placed on the floor seconds before.

"Ma'am, you dropped your money," I said, smiling as much as I could. I didn't suggest it as a possibility. I allowed no room for doubt. I told her the cash was hers like it was red-printed gospel. Even people who would ordinarily be honest and look around for a true owner will think twice when a third-party affirms it's OK to claim, that it is *in fact* their property. Hell, maybe some people are dumb enough to not keep track of their own money and really would think it's theirs. Most are just greedy. Predictably greedy. But I didn't care if she kept it. I just needed her to pick it up.

"Oh my, did I?" she said. Her bulbous eyes popped out of her skull and her pupils turned into dollar signs. For ten dollars. Free, unexpected cash. She looked down at the bag in one hand and the large plastic cup in the other and, in a fraction of a second, decided which was going to be most awkward to grip while bending over. Just like Tim predicted, she put the cup down on the island counter next to all the sugars and creamers, right beside where he was fixing his coffee. She couldn't have played along any better if she'd been working with us.

"Oh, thank you, mister. I was wondering where I put that. Thought I done gone crazy. This is my gas money," she said laughing as she quickly stuffed it into a zipped compartment of her over-sized bag.

Tim was a magician but nobody knew what hid up his sleeve. As he reached to get a sugar packet with one hand, his blazer hung like a drape over her soda, just momentarily blocking prying eyes from seeing him switch cups with the other hand. Except nobody was looking, especially not her. His timing with her distraction was perfect. It was so quick, I wasn't even sure he had done it until he walked out. Then she did too, happily carrying a spiked drink that she started sipping before she hit the door.

The front of the court building was becoming a madhouse, courtesy of Tim. We needed the guards to keep their focus away from the security cameras so he gave them other things to deal with. Balloons, flowers, pizzas, copper pipe, gravel. He spent the week before setting up as many deliveries as possible to the courthouse, all addressed to judges, all with stolen credit card numbers. There were clowns and strippers and singing telegrams showing up, each one having to wait in line while officers were dealing with angry delivery men and truck drivers. And that was on top of the crowd of people trying to get in for legitimate reasons.

Colt was already inside prepping our mark when I made my way through the line, hurried by cops running thin on patience. Then I went to the bathroom just like we planned. And I waited.

It was only about ten minutes before I got the knock and walked out to see Tim going into the clerk's office. So I stood around the corner and watched for any sign of Colt or DeShonte. Everything was smooth. But I guess nothing is ever that easy.

"Roy? What have you been up to?" he said. That voice, a familiar annoyance I thought I'd ditched for good. I looked over to see Twinkie walking toward me, his hair slicked to one side in an effort to polish himself up. I hadn't seen him since I last stayed at the halfway house. I definitely didn't miss him.

"I'm waiting for someone," I said.

"Yeah? Me and the guys were just placing bets on what happened to you. Carl was sure you probably skipped town. I figured you just found yourself a lady-friend," he said with a goofy, redneck smile showing vacancies in half the spots where teeth should have been.

I gave every indication that I wanted to be left alone. He just wasn't taking a hint. He kept babbling on and on about having to see a judge for something or other. I didn't pay attention. I didn't care. All I wanted was to see Tim get out of Dodge before my mark came from the other end of the hall. That meant I had to keep my focus so I could give him the warning knock. But that didn't happen.

Apparently Colt had badgered the girl so much, she decided to run upstairs to a different restroom, one on a secure floor for employees only. One where he couldn't follow. And while he waited for her in the stairwell, no doubt holding his crotch, she took the elevator down. When I saw those doors slide open and DeShonte walk out with her face planted in a metal waste can, I didn't have time to think things through. I didn't have time to warn Tim.

"Go away, Twink," I said abruptly before I left him staring at my back.

But Twinkie didn't listen. He followed me while I followed her. In seconds, she had reached the door and entered the code. As soon as she stepped inside that office, I panicked. I needed to make sure Tim didn't get caught.

Now, they say if all you have is a hammer, everything looks like a nail. So I nailed her with the only tool that came natural to me in a pinch. I threw a hard fist to the back of the jaw and her body dropped like a sack of mud. Being as I was behind her, she never even saw it coming. DeShonte's face got buried deep down in the trash can full of vomit, sounding like a gunshot when it banged against the floor. There was no way that couldn't attract attention.

Tim poked his head around the corner to see me standing above her unconscious body, my former housemate standing at my heels. As Tim eyed us both up, I saw a look of worry I'd never seen on him before.

Then Twinkie took off and I did what I thought best. I ran after him.

Tim stayed behind and rolled DeShonte's body over so she didn't drown in her seemingly endless stream of puke. From what they told me, Colt showed up right after I'd left and Tim had him intentionally get one of the officers. After all, guilty men don't purposefully seek the attention of authority.

They claimed they saw her hugging the bucket and watched her faint right as she went into the office. Tim also mentioned that it look like she hit her face on a nearby chair when she fell. He blamed her sickness for her passing out; he explained away the bruise on her face. He had even switched sodas again so there was no trace of ipecac in her cup. And when she came back to consciousness a few minutes later, she had no recollection of what happened. She never saw me. I guess she believed what they said as reality and I assume guards were never suspicious enough to replay the surveillance tape. If they had, we never heard nothing about it and we were long gone before they did. Tim had covered our asses again.

I didn't get to see any of that though. I was too busy chasing Twinkie until I finally caught up to him on the sidewalk outside. He waited for everyone around us to walk away before he uttered a word.

"Don't hurt me, Roy," he said lowly. "I didn't see nothing. I don't want no trouble."

I could see the fear in his eyes when he looked at me. He didn't mean no harm.

"I don't want to hurt you, Twink," I said. Then I looked around before I got closer to him, spoke right in his face. "But I ain't going back to jail neither. You understand what I'm saying, right?"

"My lips are sealed, Roy. I promise. Who you keep company with is your business. Just leave me out of it. Please," he said, nearly pissing himself.

I nodded to the side for him to go and watched him walk away, shaken. At the time, that was good enough for me. Maybe I should have taken a step back and really examined my situation. Maybe I should have been better at paying attention to details. Right then, right there though, I was just happy to not get caught.

06
How to Kill the Pope and Lose Ten Pounds

Tim did some weird things. At first, I always tried to figure out his reasoning but, like I said, he wasn't the type of guy to share anything before he was good and ready. Hell, for that matter, neither am I. After a while though, I realized his bizarre choices would make sense eventually, so I just stopped asking. It was just easier that way. He always revealed the plan when we needed to know.

Like the time he hired a hooker for Colt, paid for the room and everything.

"You have to do it in front of the open window though," Tim told him. "Show us a power bottom." Then he laughed.

We sat in the car and watched them stain the sheets for a good half hour while Tim snapped pictures like some kind of private eye. She was a sexy blonde too, not a typical Baltimore street-walker sporting c-section scars and half of her teeth. Real classy. He found her through an escort website, also probably paid for with stolen credit cards. We couldn't see Colt's face, only his black hands reaching up to grab her white titties while she rode him like a rodeo rockstar. No doubt, he enjoyed himself.

I didn't know what Tim had planned. I just went along with what seemed like an exercise in his own fetish, occasionally making little jabs at him for it. I asked if the photos were for getting his jollies or if he was taking pictures of his sister for the family album. But he didn't take offense. He knew I was just busting his chops and probing for information that he wouldn't give up. Not until he was ready.

After the courthouse fiasco, though, Tim seemed different somehow. We'd gotten away with it and he said he didn't blame anyone for what happened. He swore he was still going to help me reach out to Nina with the address he found. But we pretty much stopped doing small scams and I'd catch him staring into blank walls, zoned-out in deep thought, preoccupied all the time. He would go off by himself more often than before, disappear first thing in the morning and stay away for hours at a time. He kept saying he had a big take he'd been fine tuning but I was starting to think maybe he'd lost trust in me. Maybe in both of us. I'm embarrassed to admit that I had come to depend on him. He'd become my best friend. And I thought he was cutting me out.

That's the only reason I followed him. I used Ash's car, the damn thing still running after all those years. By that point, it was just a cruddy piece of rust held together by luck and my stubborn refusal to let go of my brother. It was good enough to keep up with Tim though, even if just barely. I followed him to a playground, a funeral parlor, and through a few ultra-suburban neighborhoods where I half expected to see Wally and the Beaver walking home from school. He wasn't going anywhere he'd gone before, at least not with me.

I watched him park on the street and get out at one point, binoculars in hand, then walk up a large hill behind a strip mall. I crept behind him all stealthy-like as he stood behind a crowd of trees, staring through the leaves into all of the houses just on the other side the street. He was scanning back and forth in a pattern so he didn't miss nothing. I'd been around him enough. I could tell what he was doing. He was checking for security cameras and motion-sensor flood lights and fenced-in yards with *Beware of Dog* signs.

He'd stop and stare a little longer at one place in particular, one of the larger houses in the neighborhood. Just inside, there was a beautiful brunette walking back and forth in front of the living room window, folding laundry and cleaning. Then a little girl ran in the room and into her arms. I watched Tim's face light up with a wide smile. I had no idea what he was doing or who they were, but this was personal to him. That I could tell.

He reached down into his pocket and pulled out his phone. I was nowhere close enough to see what he was doing with it though. I wanted to hear who he was calling, even considered trying to get closer, but I stayed put. I didn't want him to catch me.

A second later, my phone buzzed in my pocket. I received a text message. It was from Tim:

Next time, let's carpool and save on gas.

I slumped my head down before I stood up and walked toward him directly, taking care to not draw attention from outsiders. I felt like an idiot. He didn't even look at me as I approached.

"I wasn't trying to spy on you," I said.

"Yes, you were," Tim said. "What did you think you were going to find?"

"I'm not sure. I guess I'm just wondering what you got planned for us," I said.

"You were wondering if I was planning on doing it without you, right? Don't worry. I'm not," he said. He paused for a second to look at me. "Finding someone you can trust to have your back, someone who's both willing *and* able to jump in when the fan blades are sufficiently covered in shit, it's essential in what we do. You've got testicles like cannonballs and I need you, Dirty. For this job I'm getting together, you're crucial. You have to trust me on that."

He looked back down into the house. From his position I could see an older guy on the second floor that I couldn't see before. It didn't look like Tim paid him too much mind as he shifted the aim of his binoculars toward the living room again.

"Is the old guy the mark?" I said.

"You could say that," Tim said. "But I won't be touching his money." Then he said nothing else.

I was frustrated. Sick of being fed crumbs of vague information and taught life lessons through nature metaphors. Tired of having an overabundance of meaningless conversations and still being in the dark.

"You gotta trust me too, you know?" I said. "Never telling me nothing. It's like you're afraid I can't keep my mouth shut."

He stepped over toward me and looked me in the eye.

"What's in the bottle?" he said.

"What?"

"The little crack vial that's always hanging around your neck? You're not a tweaker. I know that," he said. "So what is it?"

I'm sure he'd seen me rub it through my shirt a hundred times. It was a habit I'd formed, just something I do when I'm antsy or bored. I didn't respond though, not with words. I just stood there with a defeated look on my face.

"See, Dirty? Some matters are private. Issues exist that are yours and yours alone," he said. "We all have them. This one right here is all mine."

I looked down at the woman playing with her kid. It wasn't hard to figure it out.

"That's your girlfriend, ain't it? The hot sex-bunny you're always going on about."

He turned and looked down too, watching the woman pick up the little girl, blow into her belly and laugh.

"Yeah," he said. "That's my girl. I almost forgot how beautiful she is."

"Is that her kid?"

He glanced at me in a weird hesitation.

"They're sisters," he said.

He was becoming reluctant with responses. For a guy that loved to talk without saying much, this had really strapped a muzzle on him.

"I guess you can't go talk to her until she's completely alone," I said.

He didn't even respond to that so I stopped commenting. I didn't ask anything else about it. And I started to feel pretty bad trailing him like I'd done. From day one, helping me was all he ever did and there I was, annoying him and prying into business that wasn't mine. As I stood there in a restless quiet, wading up to my knees in a pool of guilt and embarrassment, I felt like I needed to give him *something*. It was all I had left.

"It's my brother," I said.

"What?"

"In the crack vial," I told him. Then I pulled it out of my shirt so he could look at it: a small metal-topped, glass container filled with tiny pieces of bone and white ash. "I had him cremated. That's him in there, part of him anyway."

He gave it an odd look for a second, a mixture of surprise and disgust like he'd just discovered a fart in an elevator, then gave me the same look.

"Is that bone? I wouldn't expect there to be bone," he said.

"Yeah. Bodies don't ever burn up completely so they crush up what's left. I sifted through and found the biggest pieces that would fit in the pocket-urn," I said.

"Oh, you even named it," he said before he used a slight mocking tone to add, "patent pending." Then he smiled awkwardly.

"Carrying this around, it's pretty screwed up, huh?" I said. I knew he thought it was demented, no matter his response. Even I did and it was my idea.

"No, no. I get it," he said. "I mean, I don't exactly foresee it taking the fashion world by storm but with death, you do what you must to cope. Where's the rest of him?"

"I still have him," I said. Then I tucked the vial back into my shirt and let it hang by my heart. "I haven't decided where to take him. I thought about dumping the remains in the harbor. He always liked walking around down there. Maybe Fort McHenry. He liked that place too. Then, I think about finding the guy responsible for his death and force-feeding him the ashes. Not mixed in anything. Just straight pouring the whole box down his throat so he can choke on 'em."

"Revenge has its honor if you ask me. I figured that's why you went to prison to begin with," he said, still more focused on the woman than me.

"It was. I only got the trigger man though, not the guy who gave the order. I guess prison broke my spirit. I lost the drive for vengeance," I said. "Besides, he's too hard to get. Going after him would be suicide."

"I'll say it again, Dirty. Whether you want to kill the pope or lose ten pounds, it all requires the same thing: a good plan and a willingness to sacrifice," Tim said. "No one is untouchable. Who is he?"

"His name's Carmine Moreno," I said.

His stare snapped toward me with eyebrows raised.

"Carmine Moreno, the drug lord?" he said.

"Yeah. You heard of him?"

He let the binoculars lay across his chest as he crouched down and looked at the grass for a moment, his mind racing to connect all the dots. Then he quickly stood up and began to walk down the hill with me at his heels.

"You want a kick in the right direction?" he said nodding his head as if to answer his own question. "Come with me. I need to show you something."

✻

I knew Tim had other people who helped him, but not like I did. I was his closest partner. Colt was right up there too. Anyone else he ever used, he kept at an arm's length. They never knew what he was planning, ever. They did their small part, they got their small cut. Fee for services rendered. All the gears driving the machine were kept separate. Tim said that was safer for everybody involved. If one person gets pinched, everyone else is still rolling free.

He used a lot of connections through Colt, but whenever he needed a document forged, he went to Claire. I didn't even know her name until that day. In fact, I may never have met her at all if I hadn't followed him.

Tim drove us to a revitalized city neighborhood where all the artsy free-thinkers live together to mock minivans and domestic beer. *Stella's Pizza Pub* was a dive bar resting in the middle of the block with hardly an indication that there was a business of any kind inside. They didn't advertise or hang signs. It was a word-of-mouth place, proud to be off the beaten path and catered to non-conformist twenty-somethings who all somehow managed to be exactly alike.

The whole place reeked of sweat and condescension. We pushed our way through the sea of thick-framed glasses and weird facial hair to a door in the back that looked like a broom closet. Inside, there was a steep, narrow staircase that climbed directly to her apartment.

He knocked but she didn't answer. So he knocked again.

"You know my rule, Tim," she said through the door at the top.

He looked at me and rolled his eyes.

"Seriously, Claire?" he said. "I thought we had a rapport now?"

"You know my rule, Tim," she said again. "You show up at my door with someone new, my rule doesn't change. It applies to everybody."

He sighed, then turned to me. "Take off your clothes," he said.

"What?"

"Your clothes," he said. "Just leave them here on the steps. All of them." Then he started stripping down.

"We're getting naked together now? In this tiny-ass staircase?"

"What's the matter? You ashamed of your body?" he said. "I didn't take you for a prude."

"That's not the issue. I just don't like being naked around strangers. And other naked guys," I said.

He was already bare-chested and starting unzipping his pants like it was nothing.

"Relax," he said. "Trust me, I'll avoid looking at your stuff as much as humanly possible."

"I second that," Claire said through the door.

With great hesitation, I started undressing while Tim stood a couple of steps above me staring at the door, his naked ass way too close to my eye-level.

"Don't take that personally. She likes girls more than we do," he said, waiting on me. " You almost ready back there?"

I dropped my balled-up pants beside my bare feet. And there we stood, both completely nude. "Done," I said.

The door propped open as much as the chain lock would allow. She looked through and gave us a quick eye up and down before closing it and opening it up unhindered.

"Clitoria Vanderbilt!" Tim said as he walked inside, completely comfortable with all his parts on display. "I'm starting to think you enjoy seeing me wearing nothing."

"Urologically Tiny Tim," Claire replied. "I definitely prefer it over wondering if one of the things you're wearing is a wire."

"You still dating that bodybuilder?" he said.

"No way. The juice made her sprout something that looked like a baby's penis. It freaked me out," she said before looking at me. "Who's the whelp?"

"A colleague," Tim said. "He's Dirty."

"Aren't we all?" she said.

"Amen."

She was a skinny butch with half of her head shaved and the other half dyed red like cherry candy. Her petite frame carried a voice much deeper than you'd think as first glance. Claire was like a chihuahua with a bulldog's bark.

"You can cover up with this," she said. Then she threw me a towel.

"Thanks," I said as I wrapped it around my waist.

"Believe me, it's mutually beneficial."

She offered one to Tim but he held his hand up and shook his head. "Dammit, Tim," she growled. "Can you please wear one this time? You know there's no sitting allowed in here without it."

"The communal terry cloth togas? Not a chance. God knows how many wieners hide under there between washings," Tim said. "We won't be long. We're just here for the pictures."

She shook her head as she tossed the towel on the chair beside him. Then she walked down a small hallway and disappeared to the back of the apartment.

"Where'd you find this one?" I said.

"Don't judge a book, Dirty. Talent is talent, and Claire's my go-to nerd. Seriously, she's good," he said.

The wood paneling walls were covered with obscure rock concert adverts and movie posters. It was surprisingly clean considering the extensive bong collection that filled every inch of shelf space.

She came back wearing latex gloves and handed Tim a large yellow envelope bound shut with a string and button.

"Right now, there's no fingerprints on the envelope or the pictures inside. That changes the second you touch them. You want a pair of gloves?" she said.

"And break your mandatory all-nude policy? I wouldn't dare," he said.

He opened up the envelope and slid out a stack of black and white pictures. He'd look at them, then hand them to me one at a time. The first was a picture of the hotel that we visited to watch Colt get his rocks off. The next shot was the same hotel, only zoomed in on the back of a BMW SUV parked out front.

"I can get extra copies if needed, right?" Tim said.

"For one more week," Claire said.

The next shot was a picture of Colt and the hooker. Only it wasn't the hooker anymore, at least not entirely. The face was someone else though the photo alteration itself was perfect. It took me a few seconds to even notice it wasn't the girl he hired. Another few seconds to remember where I'd seen the transposed face before.

"And you'll erase the original files permanently?" he said.

"One week from today," she answered. "The drive will be reformatted, twice."

Tim smiled and looked at me as he walked toward the door.

"God truly bestowed gifts abundant on you," Tim said.

"Just make sure you do the same," she said.

"You know I'm good for it. I'll have a deposit in your box by noon tomorrow."

I started to unwrap the towel but stopped when she spoke to me.

"Hey, new guy. If you ever see me in public, we never met, never did business and this never happened. Whatever you're doing with that stuff, I know nothing about it," she said.

"You and me both," I said. "And believe me, I've been trying to forget you since I walked in."

She smiled with an air of disdain before she shut the door behind us.

"What is that stuff?" I said.

Tim held his finger up and shook his head before we dressed in silence. I moved as quickly as I could to avoid the possibility of someone walking in on two naked guys getting dressed in a stairwell. Then I waited in the bar for him to finish up, leaving the crumpled towel on the stairs behind me.

We didn't speak again until we were in the car. Right away, Tim looked over at me with a smirk. He held the envelope up and waved it back and forth a few times.

"You know who this is?" he said.

"I definitely recognize the tits. The face looks likes that broad from the tennis club," I said.

"That's right. And that broad from the tennis club owns the SUV parked in front of the hotel. Well, same make and model anyway. Claire digitally manipulated the license tag and window decals on this one," he said. "Now, it looks *just* like the one that tennis-girl drives."

"So who is she?"

"It's Audrey Moreno. She's Carmine Moreno's wife."

His words were like a cattle prod to my brain. It's not that it seemed like an unrealistic coincidence to share a target like him. Far from it. Moreno had certainly made more enemies than friends during his tenure, a fact I discovered soon after I became one. What took me by surprise was fate patting *my* ass for once. Even still, I was too hooked to let doubt have a foothold.

"This is the score you've been working on? The one we're all going to retire from?"

"Yes it is, Dirty," he said. Then he leaned forward and got closer as he spoke. "You want some pay back for your brother? How would you like to hit Carmine Moreno everywhere it hurts?"

I had no idea what kind of plan he had knocking around in that mind of his, but I already liked where he was heading. Out of habit, maybe memorial, I reached up and rubbed Ash's vial through my shirt.

"I want to kill him," I said.

"I figured as much," he said as he sat back and formed a sinister smile, never taking his eyes from me. "Let's take his money first."

07
Cowboy Blue

Colt was the biggest crybaby of any adult man I'd ever met. He'd whine like a teenage girl if something sounded like too much work, or it wasn't the way he thought it should be, or, hell, sometimes just because he had to complain about something. Any minor inconvenience and it was like he was popping his menstrual seal all over again.

Once Tim finally laid out all the details he'd been keeping to himself, I knew for sure Colt would be the one to rise up as chief naysayer. The plan was pretty risky, I'll admit. And it involved a level of violence that went far beyond what we'd ever used before but it felt like I was perfectly suited for it, by no accident I'm sure. Everything we'd done up to that point had only been toned-down practice. Testing and team building and scraping together pennies to buy supplies for the big game. Until then, Tim didn't want us taking any huge risk without a huge reward. This was it.

There was no room for error. Any mistake could mean life in prison but it was just as likely that we could be killed in some slow, painful way. Ash was my motivation. If I didn't have the personal stake in it, I'm not sure I'd have been nearly as committed. I wondered back then if Tim had changed the play after learning my past connections, even though he said he had it planned that way all along. I believe him now.

Tim had locations and routes already plotted out, but we still had a grocery list of stuff to get. Smartphone-style burners, duffel bags, stun guns. I picked up most things with the money we'd earned. Tim pulled a few jobs by himself to steal some car keys he knew were essential. Colt had to get his hands on the riskiest thing we needed though: multiple pounds of C-1.

To my surprise, as we sat there listening to all of Tim's obsessively thorough prep work and lengthy detailed instructions, Colt was quiet. He didn't say one negative word about anything. He seemed excited by it, like this is what he'd been waiting for since the beginning.

It felt strange riding in my brother's car without him. When he was alive, Ash always drove while I rode shotgun. More than a decade after his murder and I was still using it, only now I was constantly behind the wheel. And I had a different partner beside me.

There was a certain smell that covered the seats and the dashboard and carpet. It would bury itself into my nostrils and, on a long enough ride, seep into my clothes. There were definitely traces of his cigars and fast food, maybe even spilled beer and body odor and stale cologne. It wasn't particularly good and not quite offensive, just unique. But it had been there for years and never went away as if the car was a living beast with a scent of its own. To me anyway, the smell was a real part of Ash that stayed alive after he passed. Just breathing it in brought back memories of the person I cared about more than anyone in the world. I guess that's why I was so fond of it. At least until it was tainted with noise.

"Damn, it smell like shit in here," Colt said. He sat beside me with the bottom half of his face buried inside his shirt like a little kid using a porta-pot.

"We could have used your car," I said.

"Hell naw, I ain't trying to get my ride hit," he said. "My car actually has some resale value cause it don't smell like no old person's asshole."

"Then shut your mouth and show some appreciation."

We stayed parallel-parked on a narrow, one-way side street while Tim was in another car altogether. Where we sat, there were tall brick buildings on either side of us and neither had windows overlooking our spot. Directly at my rear bumper was a large pickup truck with two flat tires and a wheel-less axle up on a stack of bricks. It looked like it had been abandoned weeks before. Almost every store and home within a two block radius had been shut down and boarded up, so nobody ever stopped there, not on that street. Traffic was nearly non-existent. I was just waiting for Tim to call before I did anything. I tried to stay focused, keeping a lookout on the driver side mirror.

"You seriously ain't afraid to swallow this air? It smells like you letting homeless dudes workout in here. I know you white people like that yoga shit," he said. He looked at me and rolled his eyes. I think he was trying to irritate me into an argument just to kill time. "I'm just saying, yo, I can't breathe."

Finally the phone rang. We were using disposable burner phones, relatively inexpensive but not exactly cheap. They were capable of anything you'd expect from a decent smartphone, including setting the ringtone to some horrible rap music, which is exactly what was done when they were activated. I don't need to specify who did that. That being so, I was still glad to have any interruption that would shut Colt's mouth.

"She'll be there in about two minutes," Tim said through the handset. "You ready?"

"We're ready." My adrenaline was pumping. I had never done anything like this before. Neither had Colt. The familiar mixture of apprehension and excitement had put an end to his blathering. Finally, I had silence in the car. Finally, I could concentrate.

"OK, she's past the last traffic light. Roughly one minute away," he said.

I watched carefully through the window to the mirror, focused on the road behind me as well as any possible witnesses. There were none.

"No more turns. She's on your street, about a block a way."

I could see her coming up the street behind me, but she couldn't see us. I had even taken the light bulb out of the driver side brake light so she'd have no idea we were about to move. I put the car in gear as she got closer with Tim riding her bumper.

"Get ready," Tim said.

She was coming up quick.

"Now!"

I jammed down on the gas and jutted Ash's car out of the space and into the street, right in front of her. Audrey screeched to a halt just shy of hitting my fender. Behind her, Tim slammed down on his brakes too. He still tapped her pretty hard, but that was intentional.

She sat in the SUV a few seconds before getting out. Tim made no delay and walked to the front of the van he drove, acting like he was inspecting the damage. Colt and I got out too. We didn't want to give her time to make a phone call.

"Dammit! This is why you don't drive right up on people's asses," she said to Tim. She walked toward the rear bumper, whining in her loud raspy voice. "You were on your cell phone too. I saw you."

We came up behind her, just like Tim told us to. Colt had a black cloth bag. I had the stun gun. She was focused on her car and there was nobody else around—I double checked before I did anything. Colt waited for my move, then we hit her simultaneously.

As soon as I shocked her with a half-million volts, Colt threw the black bag over her head. She couldn't control her muscles for several seconds, long enough for Tim to stick her with a syringe full of whatever drug he had. That knocked her out completely. I caught her lifeless body while Colt popped the hatch of her SUV and we put her inside, then covered her up with a blanket like a stiff. Finally, I dropped the stun gun in a plastic bag and handed it to Tim so it could be destroyed with all the other accessories. The whole process took a fraction of a minute.

Before we drove off, he put fake tags on her car. They were laminated prints quickly stuck on with magnets but, from a distance, they looked just like real license plates. If anyone went checking traffic cameras it would take a lot longer to identify it as *her* SUV.

Tim really thought of everything. I hopped back in Ash's car, he took her SUV and Colt drove Tim's minivan. This was the order we followed, part of a strategy for cutting down the possibility of police interaction. If we were to ride past some cops, I'd probably be the first to get pulled over driving a junker with one brake light. Colt would probably be next just because he was last in line and had black skin. His job was to slow down a squad car should we be tailed. But Tim, driving a luxury white SUV and dressed in a blazer, he was a model citizen. He wasn't getting stopped.

It was a long ride to the industrial park but we drove the speed limit the entire way. Tim had secured an empty warehouse and we quickly set up camp in there, parking our cars inside. It was mostly open space aside from some bare shelving units and a few offices in the back. That's where we stashed her.

We tied up Audrey's limp body to an office chair in the middle of the room, then the office chair to a steel beam. Finally, Tim sealed her mouth in duck tape and re-covered her head with the hood. There was no window. She wasn't getting out. He had lined the walls with some kind of sound dampening foam and added a deadbolt to the only door. We just had to wait for her to wake up.

At Tim's suggestion, we left and ate an early lunch to kill time. Just three guys sitting at a diner on break, eating and laughing amongst all the other 9-to-5ers.

We couldn't hear anything when we came back an hour later. The entrance was still intact though. Nobody had gotten in and, more importantly, she hadn't gotten out.

Before Tim opened the door, he gave us the only instruction we needed. "I do all the talking. Let her know you're in the room, then stand behind her. And no matter what I say, don't hurt her."

It wasn't until we went inside that we could hear her moaning and crying. The sound of the door slamming shut only made it worse. Tim removed her hood and pulled up a chair a few feet in front of her.

"I need you to be quiet so you can hear me," he said calmly. She quelled her bawling to a whimper.

The near hyperventilation-type breathing was making snot drip down the tape across her mouth while black mascara tears stained her cheeks. Her face appeared to be melting. I didn't feel any remorse until I saw how much we'd terrorized her. She shook like a scared kid. Then I remembered she had committed her life to a killer and, unlike my brother, would eventually walk away unharmed. That made the guilt a little easier to shake off. But Tim looked ice-cold the entire time. He straightened his jacket and sat with his legs crossed, very relaxed like a talk show host about to conduct an interview. He was either incredible at hiding any trace of sympathy or, more likely, he had none.

"I apologize for bringing you here this way, but it was a matter of necessity," he said. "Now, I'm going to remove the tape from your mouth and I'm going to ask you a few things. We already know the answer to some of these questions so, for your sake, honesty is most certainly the best policy. Can you see the man behind you?" he said pointing in my direction.

Audrey looked back with her peripheral vision and quickly returned focus to Tim. Then she nodded with fear in her eyes.

"We're going to call him Cowboy Blue. If you scream, Cowboy Blue will shoot you in the face. If you lie to us, Cowboy Blue will shoot you in the face. If you fail to cooperate in any way, well, I think you get the idea. You don't have to die today. But if you won't play nice, killing you will be a matter of necessity. Do you understand?"

She started sobbing again. Tim reached forward and ripped the wet duck tape away, then flicked the residual snot from his fingers to the floor. Audrey tried to speak but couldn't get anything out but blubbering.

"Shh, calm down. We don't want to hurt you," Tim said. He swiped away the runaway strands of hair that covered her eyes. "Now, where were you heading?"

"I was just running some errands," she said.

Tim sighed and stood up. Then he looked at me and casually said, "Go ahead. Kill her."

I didn't even have time to cock my gun for effect.

"No, no, no. Please don't kill me. Please don't kill me. Please," she said crying harder again.

"Honestly, we don't want to hurt you," Tim said much louder. "That's why you're here. But we're short on time, so we're short on patience."

"My husband has a lot of money. Please, he'll pay you. He'll pay you whatever you want," she said. "Just let me go."

"Audrey, sweetheart, listen to me very carefully." Tim sat back down and looked into her crying eyes. "Your husband is the *reason* you're here. He hired us to kill you."

Fear merged into panic and overtook her face. In an instant, we changed her world.

"No, he wouldn't do that," she said.

"You sure about that? You can't think of any reason why he might want you gone? I can name a dozen off the top of my head."

She whimpered and cried quietly. She was at least forty years old, but she was in fantastic shape and just naturally beautiful.

"You know he has girls on the side, right?" Tim said.

"No kidding. He's had whores since the day we were married."

That was a swing and a miss.

"He ever mention how much your life insurance is worth?" Tim said.

"Not too much. Five hundred thousand I think," she said.

"A couple of months ago he had it increased to a million. I guess he forgot to tell you," Tim said. "Carmine has been getting this all set up for a long while." He was truly the king of bullshit and he just kept spitting it out.

"No, I didn't know. But I can't imagine he'd care much about that. He doesn't need the money," she said.

"Need it? You're right. He doesn't. I guess that's just gravy," Tim said. He was fishing for information and pulling up empty hooks. It reminded me of a gypsy fortune-teller, extracting information and letting people come up with their own reason to sell themselves a dupe. "There's only one reason that really matters. I think you know what this is about."

Audrey started crying harder.

"He must have found out," she said.

"Found out about what, darling?" Tim said. "I want to hear you say it. I want to make sure you know."

"The affair."

Tim stood up and raised his eyebrows behind her back trying to hide his surprise.

"That's right, Audrey. He knows about the affair," Tim said. "And tomorrow, lover-boy could be pissing himself in this same spot."

It was all lies. He didn't even ask about her boyfriend because we didn't need to know who it was and we couldn't seem uninformed. Knowing wouldn't have changed the plan anyway, at least not his vision of it. She was already buying the facade that she helped create.

He continued, "Lucky for you, we have some personal beef with your husband so if someone has to die, we think it should be him, not his lovely wife. And I believe you can offer us something better than the price he's placed on your life. So, I'm going to ask you one more time. Where were you heading?"

"To the bank," she said.

"You have a safe-deposit box, correct?" Tim said.

"Yes. Carmine set it up for me in case he ever got arrested, but I also use it for spending money," she said. "We deposit cash every week."

"How much is in there right now?" Tim said.

"A little over a million."

I thought Colt's eyes were going to pop out of his skull. His big mouth opened but not a sound came out.

Tim didn't even flinch at hearing the amount. He knew the score was big. But he didn't stop either. "How much is in the *other* safe-deposit box?"

The look on her face was pure ambush. I could see it in her eyes. He knew about something she thought was completely secret to everyone. Somehow, he knew. She was so taken aback, she didn't mumble a grunt.

"Come on," Tim said starting to raise his voice. "You go to the bank every Tuesday morning with Prince Charming. Then you go back every Tuesday afternoon by yourself. The fucking moon phases aren't so predictable. You're skimming money from your own stash."

"Yes," she said.

"So how much is in the *other* safe-deposit box? The one Carmine doesn't know about?" he said.

"A little less than a million," she said.

Tim stood up and walked around her, smiling behind her back like he'd just won the lottery. Then he bent down behind her and spoke into her ear. "Well, congratulations, sweetheart. At roughly two million, the price is right. It looks like you're going to be the one to see your kids graduate."

"So what now?" she said.

"What now? Now we're all going to the bank before they close so we can empty out both of those boxes. In exchange, we're going to kill Carmine in a way that you can still collect the insurance money. You know he increased his own policy at the same time he did yours to curb suspicion? You're going to be a very wealthy woman," Tim said. Total bullshit.

"Don't kill him, please. I'll give you all the money, just don't kill him," she said. "I'll go to the police and get protection."

"Are you out of your mind, lady? Who knows which cops are in his pocket?" Tim said.

"Then I'll take the kids and leave," she said. "I'll run."

"And then what? You don't think he'll have some other crew out hunting you down, making sure you visit the south side of a six-foot pile of dirt? You want your kids to watch men storm your hotel room and murder you in front of them?" Tim said. He relaxed his tone and raised her chin with his finger so she would look at him. "Besides, if you show your pretty face still breathing air, he'll know we lied to him and we'll be next on his hit list. We just can't allow that. Sorry, blondie, the only way out of this is for one of you to die. It's just a matter of necessity."

And that's how he did it. Tim convinced a woman to pay us to kill her husband. She wasn't exactly excited by the idea, but it was her best alternative, her only real option. It was evil genius. But it was just the beginning.

We only had a few minutes to get to her bank before it closed. The manager required identification to gain access to the box so she had to go with us. It was a tense ride in Tim's minivan. Colt rode up front with me while I drove and watched Audrey in the rear-view trying to avoid eye-contact with any of us. Everyone remained quiet until she broke the silence.

"How do I know you're not going to kill me once you have the money?" Audrey said. She had stopped crying as far as I could tell with her eyes hiding behind those large sunglasses. Tim made her wear them along with a baseball cap to mask her identity.

"You don't. But you know for sure we'll kill you without the money," Tim said. "I guess you just have to trust logic. Once we have the cash, we *need* you alive. It's the same logic we'll trust to keep you from ever talking to the cops or Carmine's people."

"How do you figure?" she said.

"Once we walk in here, they'll have video of us together. They'll see us walk in and come out with a big, plump satchel. If confronted later, our story will be that you hired us to kill your abusive husband and all evidence will point to that. If you talk to the cops, you'll go to prison and your kids will be raised by strangers. You tell Carmine's crew, they'll slaughter you and probably your kids too."

"How does that keep you from killing me?" she said.

"There's no benefit to it. As long as you're still walking around, we can make Carmine's death look like an accident. You'll collect the insurance money that *he* set up himself and life goes on, no one the wiser. If you disappear too, suspicions rise all around and the heat goes up tenfold. That just makes things harder on us. We don't want things hard on us."

The four of us looked like a group of misfits pulling up to the bank in a minivan. Tim walked inside with her while we waited, watching them disappear behind the sliding glass doors.

"She's not a bad piece of ass, is she?" Colt said.

"Not at all. I guess that's what money can buy," I said.

"Well, we'll know soon enough," he said. "I wonder if she goes for brothers. Just saying." Then he laughed as he jabbed my arm with his elbow, trying to prod me into amusement. Honestly, it almost made me smile, but I didn't want to give him the satisfaction.

"So, what if something goes wrong in there?" Colt said. "How long before we go in and check things out?"

"We don't," I said.

"But what if they in—"

"We don't go in," I said. "Tim told us to stay here so that's what we do."

And that's what we did.

They came out ten minutes later with a satchel that looked stuffed to capacity. Audrey climbed inside while Tim opened the hatch and put the money in the back. Then we returned to the warehouse. And we were one step closer to completing Tim's plan exactly as he envisioned it.

08
Forcing a Devil's Ante

Audrey wasn't happy about being chained up in the room again. I can't say I blame her. You ask me, she shouldn't have been so surprised though.

"I did what you wanted," she said. She was starting to cry again, pleading to be let free. "Why are you keeping me here?"

We had her handcuffed and leashed to the steel support pole in the middle of the room. She could move around a few feet but she was stuck inside there.

"We can't have you showing your face until we take care of Carmine. He needs to think you're dead," Tim said. He threw a large blanket on the floor beside her. "Get comfortable. You're going to be here a few days."

"A few days? Why?" she said.

He ignored her questions. Instead, he bent down to her level as she sat in the chair.

"Look at me," he said. "When we communicate over the phone, you'll refer to us in one way and one way only. I'm Mayor Red, he's Agent White, and you know Cowboy Blue."

"You're giving me a cell phone?" she said.

"Say our names," Tim said.

"Red, White, and Blue," she said. "I got it."

"No. *Mayor* Red, *Agent* White, *Cowboy* Blue," he said.

"Fine. *Mayor* Red, *Agent* White, *Cowboy* Blue," she repeated.

"No variations, no descriptors, no nicknames, and no indication of our actual identity over the phone," Tim said. "Get used to saying it because those are the names you'll eventually give to the police when they ask who kidnapped you."

He stood up and we walked out, leaving her in isolated confusion. I could hear her asking more questions while the door was shut in her face. After that, we couldn't hear her at all.

Tim removed the satchel from the back of the minivan and walked it over to a large storage locker on the side of the warehouse. Then he tossed sealed padlocks, each with unique combinations, to both of us and started opening one of his own.

"Here's the deal. We'll put the money inside the locker and chain it shut, then we'll clamp it with all three locks so it can't be opened without all three of us here. I don't doubt either of you but this is a lot of money and I don't want anybody getting ideas or suspicions about anyone else," he said. "It's like the Arabs say: *trust in God but tie up your camel*. It's just good sense."

Then he opened it up so we could take a look inside at the stacks of bills lining the bag. The three of us smiled at the sight. Then we chuckled, all of us.

"Damn. I ain't ever seen that much money so close where I could hold it," Colt said.

"It's a beautiful sight, indeed. Almost two million dollars exactly. But we won't touch a dime of it until we're all done and it's time to split it up. I don't want to have to worry about anyone buying stupid shit and attracting attention and I'm sure you don't either," Tim said.

We didn't even get a chance to scoop out a small pile, fan it across our face. He quickly closed up the bag before we could even discuss the alternative and shoved it in the back of the locker. After covering it with a blanket and several boxes, we chained the door securely, each adding our own lock through two of the links.

Tim immediately faced Colt.

"You ready to turn on that charm of yours?" he said.

"Hell, I can't turn it off," Colt said.

"I have a blow up mattress in the back of the van," Tim said. "Take that in and set it up for her. Be nice. Get her some water. Emphasize how this confinement is protecting her. If she were to escape, she'd be running to her own execution. Her husband wants her dead and won't stop until she is. Reassure her that with us, she's going to be OK and very wealthy. Then unbind her hands."

"You want me let her go?" Colt said.

"No, just unbind her hands at the slightest sign of discomfort. After you're with her, we'll lock the deadbolt behind you. Hide the key on you somewhere in case you need to get out but don't let her know you have it. And be nice to her. Really nice. We need her relaxed," Tim said.

"A little while with me, she'll be stress free," Colt said smiling.

"Keep black mamba to yourself, Colt. Don't even try to flirt. Be a perfect gentleman. Play cards with her. Talk to her. Tell her you have a wife and kids and describe them all. Throw in a little tragedy so she'll feel for you. Relate to her," Tim said. "Just don't turn your back on her. She may look like a kitten but she's a lioness."

"Easy, yo, I got this," he said.

"I'm going to call you in two hours. Don't answer it. Give her the phone and let her answer it," Tim said. "When the call is over, take the phone away."

We watched Colt carry the boxed blow up mattress inside the room and shut the door behind him. Then we headed out to change our clothes and buy a large plastic bucket.

"What's with the ridiculous nicknames?" I said. "Cowboy Blue? Really?"

Tim smiled and started the ignition. As usual, he didn't like to answer directly.

"Only two of them are ridiculous, Dirty. But assigning them hides the importance of the other one."

It felt good to be back in a suit, even though it was more confining than what I was accustomed to wearing. Weird as it sounds, it helped calm my nerves which had kicked into high gear at the thought of what we were about to do. I had never been involved in something so grand, so organized. I didn't want to let Tim down. I didn't want to let Ash down.

Tim and I sat in the van right outside and stared at the warehouse door where Audrey was confined with Colt. Then he called her.

"Hello," Audrey said. Her voice sounded fine albeit reserved. At least over the phone, there wasn't a hint of panic or tension.

"It's Mayor Red. How are you holding up?" Tim said.

"I'm surviving," she said.

"Are you alone in the room right now?"

"No, Agent White is here beside me."

"Is he treating you well enough?"

"Yes. He's been very nice," she said.

"Listen, I'm sorry we had to snatch you up the way we did but it will all be over soon. You understand why we have to do it this way, right?"

"Yes."

"Tell me why so I know you understand," Tim said.

"Because Carmine will kill me if you don't get him," she said.

"That's right. Remember that in case you get any crazy ideas.

We're protecting you and as long as you cooperate, we won't hurt you."

"I understand," she said. "I'm cooperating."

"The main reason I called was to see if you're hungry. Want us to bring back some food?" he said.

"Yes, please. Anything vegan," she said.

"OK. We can do that. See you in a bit," Tim said. Then he hung up and looked at me.

"Think that will work?" I said.

"I think that will be just perfect," he said. "Now if you'll excuse me, I need to practice."

I got out and waited in the warehouse. Ten minutes later, Tim walked inside all into character. He wasted no time barging through the office door and demanding Audrey wear the chains. I could see the fear immediately return to her face.

"Why are you cuffing me again?" she said, understandably confused.

He ignored her and continued. She hardly resisted but he was getting rough, pulling her arm like he wanted to intimidate her. I thought at one point he was going to slap her. Colt looked as surprised as me.

"You don't need to keep me locked up. I won't run," she said, her eyes beginning to gloss back over.

"I believe you. I just don't want to have to," Tim said.

"What about food? I thought you were bringing something."

"Ran out of time," he said.

Moments later, he signaled for us to exit the room and we did.

"Wait, wait! I have to go to the bathroom," she said.

Tim held the bucket up and waved it before dropping it on the floor in front of her. The hollow sound of plastic against cement echoed through the room. Then he locked her in again, muffling her cries with the closed-door.

"Damn man, what the hell? A little harsh, don't you think?" Colt said.

Tim stopped walking toward the van and turned to stand in front of him, face to face.

"Don't go getting sweet on her. She's not an innocent here," Tim said.

"She ain't so bad either. Just saying," Colt said.

Tim was calm but direct. He didn't raise his voice or try to argue. He merely stated a truth that was easy to forget.

"She's married to a man who leaves a path of blood and death everywhere he does business and feeds off the lost lives of those unfortunate enough to have crossed paths with him. That doesn't persist without her sharing some of those same mentalities and I guarantee you that, given the chance, she'd slit your throat and watch you bleed out. I'm just making sure she knows her place and you should too. She's not our friend. She's not a victim. She's our payday."

Colt only responded with a grim stare. Maybe he didn't completely agree, but he understood.

"Now get your Poker face on," Tim said. "Tonight, we deal with a devil."

Carmine Moreno never had illegal dealings in his home. I guess it was smart not letting criminal associates know where he rest his head. It had kept him alive long enough. He owned several places around town—a strip club, a funeral home, a junk removal business, some slum housing he used for office space. Every bit of it was established with drug money.

As it were on the night we went to see him, he was set up in a two-story vacant, talking shady business with a few of his fellow lowlifes. I only knew this because we interrupted them. Colt was sitting in a car around the back of the building, staring at the second-story window just as instructed. I went along as support and kept my mouth shut. That was my whole job. Once again, Tim did the heavy verbal lifting.

When we walked up to the door, three Latino hoods popped up and blocked our way inside. Tim puffed out his chest and removed the badge from his belt. It was the one he had lifted from Specs the night I first met him.

"DEA. Tell your boss he *wants* to see us," Tim said.

"I don't know who you're talking about," one of them said.

Tim clenched his jaw and scowled. Then he moved a few inches closer and inhaled a long breath through his nose.

"Carmine either talks with me now or I bring down an army of bulletproof vests and burn this place to the ground using your oil-soaked body as kindling," Tim said. His tone was quietly agitated, controlled but dominant.

One of the others disappeared inside. My heart pounded watching these guys size us up. Adrenaline had me ready to scrap knowing we were screwed if they decided to exchange fire. Tim didn't flinch as he stared them back down though. He couldn't. He was a wooden duck showing crocodile fangs. I inched closer too, not letting them see any doubt in our feigned authority. A minute later, the prodigal thug emerged and waved us in.

He started to frisk us until Tim opened up his jacket and deliberately put his holstered pistol on display.

"Uh-uh. Carmine wants my service piece, he can come get it himself," Tim said. He was unwavering in his attitude. He was committed to selling this.

They walked us through a hallway and up to the second floor toward the back of the building. We must have passed a dozen guys, some of which were packing fully-automatic weapons too big to conceal. Then they took us into Carmine's office.

He had seven other men just in that room. Five of them marched off while the other two stayed, no doubt as protection. The one closest to the window was a tattooed monster with arms thicker than my thighs. This stuck out to me specifically because el gorilla-grande was standing directly where I needed to be.

And in the center of the room, there he was, the bastard that had my brother executed just to send a message. Carmine sat on the other side of a large executive desk which probably cost more than the building it was in. Behind him, a grotesque painting of a crucifixion done completely in a reddish amber-brown that looked like dried blood. It was fitting decor for a monster, no matter how repulsive it was. And that's coming from a guy with the partial remains of his dead brother hanging around his neck.

I wanted to pull out my gun and blow his head off right then and there. If the plan didn't work out, I'd never forgive myself for passing up the opportunity to end his life. But I knew it would be a self-imposed death sentence. And patience promised greater rewards.

Tim held his badge above his head as he looked around the room and sat down in a chair across from Carmine. Then he rested the envelope he'd been carrying in his lap.

"What a shit-hole. Not quite the palace you have over on Witherspoon but if you ask me, it's a throne-room more befitting a king of your stature," Tim said.

"What do you want?" Carmine said.

"Not much on small talk, huh? Must be a hell of a first date," Tim said.

"Time is costly and you're wasting mine," he said.

"Funny you should say that because time is what I'm here to offer," Tim said. "Do you know that the DEA has, not one, but six open investigations that involve you?"

"Say it ain't so," Carmine said. "They must have closed a couple."

His men gave an obligatory smile. Tim laughed too showing no signs of fear or doubt or insecurity. Then he nodded for me to walk toward the window.

"Of course you know that. I'm sure you have at least a couple of my colleagues cashing your checks," Tim said. "So let me tell you something you don't know. After years of watching you slither through the cracks, a witness has finally stepped forward who's more than capable of taking you down. For everything."

I inched closer in front of the glass pane, squeezing in next to his extra-large goon. He was giving me evil stares but I couldn't back away. I had to make sure Colt could see me from his position on the street.

"Is that right?" Carmine said.

"That's right," Tim said.

Carmine maintained a smug look of apathy. This wasn't the first time he'd been threatened.

"And who would this be?" he said.

"Your wife," Tim said. "Audrey wants to go Wit-Pro."

Carmine's face changed in an instant. Any hint of a smile vanished.

"Bullshit," he said.

"She's already singing enough songs to build you an extended record. I hope you like anal sex because once that cell door slams shut, it's still the favored pastime." Tim continued, "Oh, and by the by, the million dollar safety-net that you had set up at the bank, she cleaned it out this morning. Of course, she had her own emergency parachute that was almost as big—a second, equally-stacked box that she was building when your head was turned. That's all gone too."

"You're lying. She would never turn," he said.

"Lying? Your face tells me you have your doubts," Tim said. "Don't take my word for it though. Why don't you go ahead and call her. Right now. We'll wait."

Carmine sat still for a moment, just shaking his head, looking around the room at everyone in it. He held his hands close together and spun one of the giant gold rings around his finger as he processed the situation. Then he pulled his phone from his desk drawer and dialed. There was no answer but voicemail. Then he tried again. Then he sent a text.

"Weird, huh? Try again if you want. Try all night. She won't answer you," Tim said. "Or to save time, how about if I give her a call on speakerphone. Just keep your mouth shut and listen."

Tim didn't make a call. Not right then. He simply started playing the recording he'd made of the incoming audio from the earlier call. It started with the ringtone and continued from where she had answered.

"Hello," Audrey said.

"Hi, Audrey. It's Agent Michaels. How are you holding up?" Tim said, reciting his part to coincide with the recording.

"I'm surviving," she said.

"Are you getting lonely out there?" he said.

"No, Agent White is here beside me."

"He's a good guy. One of our finest."

"Yes. He's been very nice," she said.

"Listen, I'm sorry we have to go through all this red tape before we get you signed up. You're absolutely sure you're ready for this, right?"

"Yes," she said, giving an honest response in a different conversation.

It was amazing. Aside from very slight pauses before her answers, Tim's speech fit along perfectly.

"Then why do you sound scared?" Tim said.

"Because Carmine will kill me if you don't get him," she said.

"We'll get him. We're going to keep you safe until trial. After you testify, we'll have you set up where he'll never find you. I promise," Tim said.

"I understand," she said. "I'm cooperating."

"The main reason I called was to see if you're hungry. Want us to bring back some food?" he said.

"Yes, please. Anything vegan," she said.

"No problem, dear. See you in a bit," Tim said. He stopped the recording, acting like he hung up. Then he looked right at Carmine. "I'll just let that marinade for a second."

Carmine's angry shake had nearly turned into rocking. The spin of that gaudy ring had quickened, like he was trying to unscrew it from his finger.

"So why aren't I in cuffs?" he said.

"At this point, relative to a lot of the other candy peddlers out there, you're small time, Carmine. You aren't the legendary collar you once were. If we go through all the trouble to bring you in, take you to trial, and get a conviction, you know we'll get? A half-hearted *attaboy* and maybe, just maybe, a chance of promotion with a small pay bump. But you've been around a long time and we figure you must have a pretty big stash that you're willing to part with in exchange for your freedom."

"Where is she?" Carmine said.

"In a safe house. That's all I can tell you," Tim said.

"So you never entered her into witness protection?"

"Not officially."

"Then maybe I just kill you now and find her myself," he said.

Tim rested his arm on the back of the chair as if he hadn't a care in the world.

"Boy, that's some token of gratitude," Tim said smiling. "Before we continue, full disclosure, I need you to take a look out the window and tell me what you see."

I slid aside so I wasn't blocking the view, but he didn't get out of his chair.

"Thiago," Carmine grumbled as he motioned to the Mexican muscle who looked out to the road for him.

"There's a black dude in a van giving me the finger," Thiago said.

Tim continued to smile while he spoke. "That *black dude* is another agent. He's a sweet kid but he's not the trusting soul I am. The second he stops seeing one of us through that window, he'll count for a very brief amount of time, then he'll drive off and call in a fleet of flashing lights."

"Bring her to me," Carmine said. "I'll make it worth your while."

"Oh, I don't know. Our while is worth quite a lot," Tim said.

"Then what are we talking about?" Carmine said.

"You know, she came to us a few weeks ago. We kept it under wraps until we could figure out what she was up to. I mean, why after all these years, would she suddenly decide to turn against the man who's been keeping her stocked with diamond encrusted tampons? So we followed her. And we found out," Tim said.

"I guess that's what you have on your lap?" Carmine said.

"See? Right there. That's why you're the brains behind the empire," Tim said. Then he tossed the envelope on the desk.

I wasn't looking at Carmine. I wasn't even looking at Tim. My eyes were planted on Thiago because I was fighting for real estate in front of the window. He was getting irritated. Anxious. I could see it in his face.

Carmine looked through the pictures of his wife, images that showed her naked breasts being fondled by the hands of a strange black man.

"Just FYI, the time between entering the room and full-on, porn-worthy cuckolding was about sixty seconds. This wasn't her first cabaret. So, if you're still racing that filly, I'd get checked for all the typical STDs—HIV, HPV, Jungle Fever. I'm not sure *that* one is transmittable, but I hear once you get it you never go back," Tim said.

He was goading him to anger, almost mocking him as he made light of the whole thing.

"Now you're looking mad, like you might want to kill her," Tim said. "Am I wrong?"

"Take me to her," he said. "Now."

"First off, the information is free. The rest will cost you. A lot," Tim said. "But we have to be smart about this. What do you plan to do to her?"

"That's my business," he said.

"No. It's our business too. Let's say we take you to her. You have mercy and merely beat her half to death, to the point that you think she'll never betray you again. She could eventually rat *us* out for giving her up. The other agents and I can't have our careers forever in her hands because you suddenly get sentimental," Tim said.

"That won't happen," Carmine said. "I guarantee it."

"So you kill her? The strange disappearance of your wife will open up another investigation, one that links us. Now that we're involved, we can't have that either."

"I know how to take care of it," Carmine said.

"Call me paranoid but I just can't have faith in a man who's proud to have six open investigations against him. And, forgive me for the lack of camaraderie I feel with you just yet, but once you have her, you might try to give us nothing but a flurry of high-speed slugs. You've already suggested this very thing a few minutes ago," Tim said.

"So what do you propose?" he said.

"She has to die, Carmine. It's the only way to know she won't ever betray you or sully our good names. We can do it for you.

Or, if you insist on doing it yourself, we need to be there with you. But just you by yourself. None of your minions. And we want to get paid," Tim said.

"How much?" Carmine said.

"A million, unmarked cash," Tim said. "That pays for silence from the only four agents who know about this. And we'll keep her safe until it's time for you to deal with her however you want."

Carmine scoffed, "You got some set of balls."

"For freedom, that's a bargain. And you'll probably get it back when you make her return the stacks of cash she milked you for. Even without it, I'm sure a conscientious fella like yourself has life insurance on her but that will require a dead body," Tim said.

It wasn't an immediate response. Carmine wasn't the kind of guy that was used to being strong-armed. Even still, he knew he had to play along, at least until he could find a means to wiggle away. We just had to fill all those escape routes.

"Fine. Take me to her."

"Not so fast. See, we want to enjoy this money without concern. After some brainstorming, we could only think of one way to make sure we get our money, you get a dead trophy wife, *and* you're completely exonerated. That, in turn, frees us from worry of an investigation, " Tim said. "You need to hide in plain sight. Treat your wife like a car you intend to use for criminal activity."

"You want me to report her stolen?" he said.

"Exactly."

09
Thimblerig

It was the most uncomfortable I've ever felt in my life. Laying in a dark, closed coffin with four pounds of C-1 plastic explosive on my chest, the stability of which depended on the competence of some toolshed terrorist that Colt knew. I ain't never been afraid of enclosed spaces before, but that was suffocating. The thick air lingered with the smell of wood sealant and embalming fluid from the corpse we'd tossed out. I was baking in my own body heat. Sweat was oozing out of my pores so much I could hardly keep the earpieces attached. It didn't help that the only protection I had between me and the home-brew bomb was the locked briefcase that concealed it.

I cracked the lid of the coffin for air. I had to. I knew I'd be waiting a while and I'd pass out if I didn't let some oxygen inside. I was just trying to get used to the confined space before Carmine showed up. Occasionally Tim would check on me, just a quick word to make sure I was still conscious. I could talk to him through the earpiece in my right ear but I kept my words to a minimum. I didn't want to use any more air than I had to.

Carmine welcomed the idea to report the abduction of his wife the way sheep receive wolves. You would have thought we asked him to shove hot coals up his ass. I can't say I was surprised though. The history he maintained with police was mutually and entirely hostile and nothing would ever change that. He'd never used them for retaliation, certainly never for help. Exchanging assistance either way would only make him look weak to his crew and every other thug with his eye on the crown. In the end though, he finally caved. It took more than a little heavy-handed convincing but that was Tim's specialty. And as long as Carmine believed our story, he really didn't have much of a choice. He wanted to keep his freedom. He wanted to find his wife. From where he sat, we were the only way he'd get either.

Tim plotted the course and Carmine called it in. I'm sure behind closed doors the police had a field day with it, FBI too. Despite his social standing, every civil servant collecting a paycheck to carry handcuffs had an interest in protecting the very thing Carmine was targeting: the life of his beautiful wife. Being an abduction case, there was no press at first, but everyone knew the spotlight would flip on soon enough. I imagine some of them wanted to spite Carmine, to rescue the distressed damsel he was desperate to have returned, maybe show they could piss a little further than he could. Others probably wanted to be part of the media frenzy and enjoy the notoriety and accolades that were bound to follow. We just wanted them to keep Carmine in line. And after they were involved, he was forced to abide by the rules. He had to know this. He wasn't stupid.

Tim didn't give him much time to get the money together. Carmine didn't need it, despite trying to argue otherwise. He just wanted time to look into us, go through his people to find a back door to the safe-house and cut us out. Then he'd have the upper hand. We couldn't give him that. He'd kill us.

The second earpiece started to ring in my left ear. It wasn't for me to answer though. That one didn't even have a micro-phone because I'd never have to say a word. It just allowed me to listen in so I'd know what was going on between Tim and Carmine. I could prepare for when it was my turn to jump and if plans went south, I could opt out at any time. But like most ideas Tim set in motion, everything was going perfectly.

"Go ahead. I'm here," Carmine answered.

"You have the money?" Tim said. His voice was modified, deepened and warped, an effect he applied as it went through his phone.

"Yeah, I got it."

"One million in unmarked hundred-dollar bills?" Tim said.

"I said I got it," Carmine said. "Where do I take it?"

"Are the police with you?"

Carmine didn't know how to answer. Of course we knew the feds were with him, hovering over his shoulder and coordinating everything on his end. It was what we demanded. But the fake ransom note that we gave Carmine threatened him against police intervention. He had to play his role of victim for the uniforms that were surrounding him.

"No, I'm alone," Carmine said.

"Put me on speaker," Tim said.

"What?"

"Keep me on speakerphone and don't take me off. I want everyone in the room to hear this loud and clear," Tim said.

There was a brief pause, then a bit of ambient noise. Carmine was reluctant but police were probably listening in anyway.

"You're on," Carmine said.

"There are two rules. Simple rules. Do exactly what you're told. And don't lie. If you break either rule, there will be penalties," Tim said. "You lied to us, so we're cutting off one of her fingers."

It was bullshit. Carmine probably knew it but he put on a show like he didn't.

"I'm not lying," he yelled after he blurted a few curses in Spanish.

"We know you're lying. We're watching the house and we saw the authorities arrive. That's two lies, two fingers," Tim said.

The more exaggerated his response, the more innocent he looked. That's the crock Tim had sold him.

"Don't do it. They're here, alright. FBI and police are both here. But I'm coming alone with the money, just like you wanted," Carmine said.

"No. Don't come alone. You're going to need some help," Tim said.

I always wonder if that was the moment that Carmine started to feel the screws tighten.

"And who exactly am I supposed to bring with me?"

"The youngest officer in the room," Tim said. "Go out to your car now with the money and *that* officer. You have sixty seconds." Then he hung up.

Tim wouldn't stay on the line very long. He had spit a bunch of gibberish about bouncing ping points and proxy servers and incog-VoIP, whatever the hell that is. The bottom line is he knew they'd be tracing his phone calls, trying to pinpoint his location. So, he was running every call through a computer program that would relocate his call path to places all over the world. Every time he rang, he used different anonymous accounts to make it that much more difficult. It was all over my head. His too until Claire set it up for him.

He called back, still talking on speaker.

"Are you in the car?" he said.

"Yes," Carmine said.

"With the officer and the money?"

"Yes."

"Drive to the parking garage at the corner of Pratt and Light Street. You have twenty minutes," Tim said. "Officer, what's your name?"

"Jerry," the officer said. I'm sure Carmine had his suspicions about him, but he wasn't connected to us at all. He was a just a random pig acting as a leash.

"I need you to make a phone call, Officer Jerry. Do you have a personal cell phone on you?"

"Yeah, I do."

"Call Carmine's house number from your phone and tell them if he's followed, we'll kill her. We're watching you," Then he hung up.

Everything that Tim did had an ulterior motive. Sure he wanted to relay that message, but more importantly, he wanted the officer to admit he had a phone on him so he couldn't lie about it later. Tim was crafty for sure. I was just glad he was on my side.

I sat up in the casket to catch my breath. The air had gotten too stagnant and humid to bear and I knew I only had a little longer by myself. Colt was supposed to pick me up as soon as I was done my part. He was listening in just like I was, only he got to do it while relaxing in an air-conditioned car. That was the plan as I knew it anyway. After hearing him whine about being claustrophobic, I volunteered as the cadaver decoy to shut him up but I had no idea how hot it would be that day. I always felt like I had to pull my weight and prove myself to Tim. After all his effort for me personally, I didn't want to let him down.

Twenty minutes expired.

"We're at the garage," Carmine said as he answered the phone. Formality and etiquette were long gone. He was already frustrated and we had just gotten started.

"Third floor, right below a large sign that reads '3A' you'll find your wife's SUV," Tim said. "Park near it and open the back."

Tim had a cell phone sitting on the dash of the SUV with its camera pointing toward the front seats. Another inside the back with a view of the open hatch. Both were feeding live video streams to his computer. From there on out, he could see everything they did.

Carmine opened the back of his wife's vehicle and found the briefcase we'd left for him. Inside were two thin robes and baseball caps.

"Strip down to your skivvies and put on the outfits," Tim said. He watched them undress to make sure they weren't wired. "Take the money out of the satchel and put it inside the briefcase. Then lock it with the dials and leave it back there in view of the camera."

They did all of it. Carmine would occasionally groan and grumble curses but he did as instructed. He still had to play nice for the sake of appearance in front of the officer. And I suppose he felt as long as he stayed with the money, he had some sense of control. That was just an illusion. Tim had all the power.

"Officer Jerry, I need you to take your personal cell and police radio and drop them in the satchel. On top of that put your uniform and Carmine's clothes. Keep your gun and your cuffs though. Carmine, drop your phone in the satchel and slide it under the car behind you, then get in your wife's SUV," Tim said.

"The phone I'm on right now?" Carmine said. "How will we talk?"

"Do it. You have fifteen seconds."

Tim had them change cars in case they were being tailed and used a garage in case there was a helicopter overhead. He removed any means of communication except for the method he'd prepared and ensured they weren't wired. He got rid of the GPS that was likely hidden in the lining of the satchel and made them put on flimsy disguises. The forethought that went into every aspect of the money exchange was painstakingly thorough.

They got into Audrey's SUV and I suppose that's when they heard the ringing. Then they answered the cheap burner phone we had left in the glove box.

"Now what?" Carmine said.

"Your junk removal place on Keswick Avenue. Drive there. You have fifteen minutes."

"Will Audrey be there?" Carmine said.

"She's waiting for you. Fourteen minutes, fifty seconds."

I imagine police thought it a waste of resources to keep an eye on the buildings of legitimate businesses owned by Carmine or any of his people. They had their hands full enough trying to look after his illegal trades. Besides, who would be stupid enough to use Carmine's own assets in a ransom exchange for his wife? It made sense to do it though. Instead of using cars we'd have to buy or rent, vehicles with paper trails, Tim only had to lift ignition keys. And on account of the situation, his lackey-thug Thiago had closed down all of Carmine's businesses for the day so nobody was around.

Time was passing quickly and my part couldn't come soon enough. I was anxious and tense and sweating like a fat man trying to jog. I was excited too but not just for the money. After years of swallowing that bitter pill, I was finally going to get some justice for Ash. I couldn't wait to press six.

"We're pulling up now," Carmine said as he answered the ringing phone again.

"Then you're going too slow," Tim said. He already knew where they were. The phones we had set up to stream the video feed also had GPS turned on and all that info went back to Tim. Once they got into that SUV, he could pinpoint their location within a few feet. "Drive to the far end of the lot. You'll find one truck with a missing clasp. Back your car up to its rear bumper," Tim said. And that's how they aligned them.

"Is she inside there?" Officer Jerry said.

"Be seen and not heard, Jerry," Tim said. "Put the money in the back, roll the door back down like you found it, then get in the cab of the truck."

He could watch as they opened the hatch of the SUV to get the briefcase. Then they opened the rolling door of the delivery truck. It was full of large boxes and junk, but it too had a camera system set up in the back and another in the cabin. He could see them moving the case from one lens view directly into the other. Tim's eye was on the money the entire time and he made sure they knew it. There would be no trying to sneak it away.

"Enough of these damn games. Where's my wife?" Carmine said.

"She's still alive and waiting for you as long as you make it in time," Tim said.

"What's that supposed to mean?" Carmine said. I could hear the truck doors slam shut as they got in.

"It means get moving. Just try not to hit any kids," Tim said.

There was a momentary pause, just a few seconds of speechless befuddlement from the backhanded jab.

"What did you say?" Carmine said in a voice much softer than usual.

"It was a truck just like this one, right? You probably think you buried that little secret but we know all about it," Tim said. He didn't want to give Carmine time to come up with a plan or decipher his own. He kept them distracted and ignorant. That was the way he manipulated people. "Now drive. I'm getting impatient."

Tim kept calling this setup a *thimblerig* though I didn't really understand why. Basically, he wanted them to get used to separating themselves from the briefcase every time they changed vehicles so it would never seem suspicious. From their perspective, they were always with the money. It was only a few feet away, always within reach. And it seemed acceptable, logical even, that it was out of their hands so it could be guarded by a camera during the entire ride. First the SUV, then the truck. I thought that stopping twice before they got to me was overkill but I was wrong. It was very necessary.

"The ignition key is under the floor mat," Tim told them. "Go to the old industrial park on Rossville. You have twenty minutes or she loses a thumb."

I prepared myself. I made sure the phones in my pocket were all silenced. I pulled the little curtains on the inside of the vehicle so they were closed tight. Then I sat up for ten minutes to take in deep, slow breaths before I laid down and shut myself back in the darkness.

"Dirty, are you in place?" Tim said. "They're coming your way." "I'm ready," I said. And I was.

I could feel my heart pound against the explosive-filled briefcase as it was resting on my stomach and pushing Ash's vial into my chest. The fingers that held it in place would touch the ceiling of the casket every time I exhaled. I tried not to think about what was inside. It's really not that I cared much about dying. In a moment of drunken honesty I'd admit there were times when I sat in a prison cell and felt like death would be a kind release. But as I lay there, being so close to a dozen wrong moves that could get me killed, I just wanted to see a world without my brother's killer before I was taken out.

Then it was time.

"Go left at the corner past the far building," Tim said. "This place look familiar to you?"

"No," Carmine said.

"Maybe you've really never been here. But your crew has. Plenty of times. This is one of the spots they dump bodies of the people you have killed," Tim said.

"I don't know what you're talking about," Carmine said.

"Yeah, I bet you don't." Of course he would never admit it, not in front of a cop.

They drove around and saw a gravel lot that had become a dumping ground for locals. It was littered with old washers and toilets and construction trash. And back behind it all, completely out-of-place, was the car that I'd been roasting inside.

"You know, we found something that belongs to you," Tim said.

I could hear the engine roar and then silence as they pulled up and turned off the truck.

"Is this my hearse?" Carmine said. The night before, we had stolen it from the funeral home he owned using the keys Tim had somehow acquired. I'm sure it seems like a weird choice, but it fit our needs.

"Put the money in the back and close the door," Tim said.

I heard the hearse's hatchback open directly at my head. I stayed as still as I could and held the lid of the coffin shut from inside.

"Why the hell is there a casket in here? Is Audrey inside?" Carmine said.

"Audrey is with me. The coffin was already on board when we borrowed your car," Tim said.

My hand was holding it closed so tight, I couldn't even tell when they tried to lift it.

"It's been sealed already," Carmine said, followed by some rant in tongues that sounded like a gypsy lifting a curse. "You people have no respect. I'm not riding with a desecrated body."

"If you're that afraid of belligerent ghosts, you should probably worry more about Audrey becoming one," Tim said. "Put the money inside and close the door."

I could hear the case being slid in beside the coffin. Then I heard the back door slam shut. The palms of my hands were filled with an oily sweat but I could finally let out the breath I was holding.

"Now look to your right. You'll see an old refrigerator on its back with a washing machine covering the door. It will take both of you to lift it off. The ignition keys are in the freezer section," Tim said.

The keys were obviously hidden to prevent the car from being stolen from an unintended party crasher. But like I said, everything Tim did had an ulterior motive. We needed them away from the car, both of them, even if only for a few moments. The junked fridge was a good fifty feet away, easily allowing me time and space to do my job.

"Do it now, Dirty," Tim said to me. "I just tipped off the press."

The windows in the back of the hearse were tinted to nearly black, then covered with black curtains. I couldn't see outside. They definitely couldn't see me. In the minute they stepped away from the hearse, I opened up the coffin lid and switched briefcases. Only sixteen yards away and completely in view the whole time, they had no idea the money had just changed hands. Still again I laid, hugging *that* case with much greater ease.

Shortly after, I heard them get into the car and fire it up.

"Drive to Peninsula Highway," Tim told them. It used to be the sight of a large industrial area until steel was no longer manufactured in Baltimore. Then it became a vacant stretch of asphalt that people only used when every other road in the area was blocked with traffic.

"I'm done playing games," Carmine said. "Where's my wife?"

"Last stop," Tim said. "You'll be reunited with Audrey before you know it."

I tried to relax but nervousness and excitement were getting the best of me. My muscles were so tense, I was having trouble maintaining control over my body. I even felt my leg kick the top of the casket when we hit a pothole but luckily, I guess it wasn't loud enough for them to notice. Fifteen minutes later we had arrived in the middle of nowhere. It was a short, bumpy ride but it felt like forever before he had them pull over on the side of the road.

"Officer Jerry, get the money from the back and bring it up front," Tim said.

I could hear him follow the instructions within moments as the hatch opened and the rigged case slid against the bed and out of the back. The farther away from me it was, the better I felt.

"Handcuff the money to Carmine's wrist. Do it at gunpoint if he refuses," he said. I doubt the officer would have gone that far but it wasn't necessary anyway. Carmine willingly bound himself to the briefcase.

"Show it to me on camera," Tim said.

They did.

"Now take a walk, Officer Jerry. You're no longer needed."

"Here?" he said.

"Get out of the car. And take your gun with you."

It was a four mile hike to the nearest phone. And he was walking along the side of an empty highway in a robe with a gun in his hand. Nobody was stopping for him and he wasn't talking to anyone, not for a while.

Once alone, Carmine yelled through the phone. "Now listen to me you son of a bitch, I'm done playing around. What was the point of that?" He started making threats and cursing in a mixture of tongues but Tim let him finish his little tantrum before even trying to explain.

"Everyone will believe she was really kidnapped. And now, we're all set up," Tim said. "After you arrive, you'll have plenty of privacy to do whatever you want to her. And once she's dead, you can blame it on the kidnappers. Nobody will know you did it."

Carmine wouldn't say too much after that even though Tim kept him on the line to make sure he didn't call in his crew. Tim withheld a destination, instead giving him road by road directions as Carmine needed them. It led him to the alleyway behind some abandoned row homes in a shady part of town. Then he gave him instructions to walk inside one home in particular. I had chosen it.

Once I knew Carmine was out of the car, I got out with the briefcase and camouflaged it in a plastic shopping bag. Then I walked around the block to the front side of the run-down strip of houses. It was very familiar territory to me, a place I'd revisited every few weeks after I got out of prison just so I wouldn't forget. I stood down the street with the bag in hand and watched the front of the boarded-up row home, just waiting for my cue.

"Head in through the cellar door. It's unlocked," Tim told him. "Then go upstairs."

"Where are you?" Carmine said.

That's when the news crews started rolling up out front. Tim said he was calling five different stations but only two showed up. The other three missed out. I don't know what line he gave them but they were watching the opposite side of the street for whatever they expected.

I was nervous about being shot on camera so I hid out of their sight but I couldn't leave. Not until I saw it. I tried to blend in as best as I could, sitting on a bus stop bench next to a sleeping bag-lady.

"You're almost home. Go up to the second floor," Tim told him.

"I swear if you're fucking with me, you'll never see any of this money. I don't care what badge you carry. I'll use every resource I have to put your head on a pike, every one of you," Carmine said.

"Top of the steps, go to the last bedroom. You'll find all the windows have been covered with plywood," Tim said. "Pick a window and kick the board out. You'll see Audrey on the other side."

As soon as he started banging his foot against the wood, he got the attention of the news crews on the street out front. I guess out of instinct, they turned their cameras toward the window he was clearing. It was the same window my baby brother had been hung from years before.

The slab of wood dropped to the ground and Carmine slid his fat head out through the window. He was obviously confused when he saw the reporters and news cameras focused on him. He never looked my way though, never acknowledged me sitting there, staring at him just like most everyone else. It's probably for the best as the middle finger I wanted to give him was far less grand a statement as I made with my thumb.

I long-pressed the number six and it speed-dialed the phone hidden in the briefcase cuffed to his wrist. It didn't even have a chance to sound a ring. The electronic signal sparked the blasting cap and seconds later, flames shot out of the window directly behind airborne chunks of Carmine. Everyone within a couple hundred feet had bits of a burnt drug lord raining down on them. The smell was vile.

Of the two news cameras, only one captured the footage as the other one had its lens blurred when it was hit by a gooey clump of flesh. Neither channel would air what they caught as it was deemed too graphic, even for national news. The video was released online instead.

I didn't get hit with any of the charred remains that littered the street. The only shrapnel that even came close banged against the bus stop enclosure like a bullet before it clinked down on the sidewalk in front of the old bag-lady and me. It was his gem-covered gold ring, ugly as hell though it was probably worth a small fortune.

The mangy woman and I looked down at the hunk of precious metal, then at each other.

"You saw it first," I said as I tapped it toward her with my foot. "No one needs to know." She quickly picked it up and shook out the glob of meat that was still lodged inside before tucking it inside her jacket. After that, I simply stood up and walked away.

I wasn't nervous as I strolled down an alley and away from the commotion. I hardly thought about the contents of the bag I was carrying even though people had been known to catch beatings over pocket change in that part of town. I was content and relaxed, even happy. It was the best I'd felt in years. I finally did right by Ash and managed to secure a future for myself so I could focus on seeing my daughter. I was the giant carrying a gold-shitting goose with the clouds under my feet.

I never expected just how quickly I'd come tumbling down.

10
Rogue

Chicken and waffles with drunks. That became my victory champagne when Colt never showed to pick me up. I tried calling him a bunch of times, then I tried calling Tim. I got no answer from anybody.

I waited for hours at the spot we chose, the whole time eyeballing a corner pub down the street. I didn't drink a drop of the good stuff though, not while carrying a briefcase stacked with cash. It wasn't all mine and I felt a responsibility, even if it was to cunts who weren't returning my phone calls. I had wandered around for a while until my feet got sore. I'd rested under a highway overpass, tucked away at the top of a slanted support. Finally, I'd walked to a *Waffle Shack* and sat at the diner bar alone before immediately being joined and situated between a couple of drunk assholes.

I had never had chicken and waffles before but, being a new millionaire, I figured I could afford to try new things. So I lodged that damn bag between my feet and ordered the most artery-clogging dish they offered: beer-battered chicken atop a deep-fried waffle and grits, the whole deal smothered in butter and sausage gravy. I emptied my thoughts and dug right in.

See, I fell into the same trap as Carmine. Having that briefcase, all that money gave me a sense of control. I felt powerful. Comfortable. I was resting there on a blue-collar holiday when I should have been watching my own back. I knew there were risks. I knew there'd be guns on both sides of the law looking to investigate and retaliate. A lot of money gets a lot of people feeling real selfish. I should have been thinking things through and maybe I would have foreseen being screwed over. Because all that dough is hard to enjoy while resting on a cot behind bars. Even harder when sleeping in soil.

I sat there for a few minutes after I finished the whole plate feeling like I had a dismembered foot lodged in my intestines. I paid a generous tip, blew off a conversation with the soakers one last time and answered the call that would begin the demise of my perpetually chipper demeanor.

"Where are you? Where the hell is my ride?" I said.

"Don't say anything incriminating, nothing specific, no names," Tim said. "We have a problem."

"Is it the reason I'm walking right now?"

"Definitely. It looks like our third wheel has gone rogue," he said.

"How rogue?"

"Pretty far removed," he said. "You know that missing dog we found? If I had to guess, I think our boy tried to force some unwanted petting on her and she bit back. Looks like he put her down."

I knew Colt was taking his long glances at Audrey, but I never thought he'd try to rape her. I definitely didn't think he'd kill her. My temper was flaring.

"And the locker?" I said.

"Untouched as far as I can tell from a distance," he said. "But I can't get close to it. Too many spinning lights. It's only a matter of time before they break it."

"So what's the game-plan?" I said.

"Find a cool place in the shade," he said. "I'll call you when it's sunny outside again."

"And this box of cake, when are we eating it?" I said.

"Put it in a freezer for now. We're not eating it. Don't even lick the icing," he said. "It might be poisoned."

I didn't know what that meant. Not exactly. I imagined maybe the bills were marked or a tracking device was somehow slipped in the stacks of cash. Then I thought maybe, just maybe, Carmine had the foresight to plant explosives in our bag like we did his.

I hadn't even peaked inside the briefcase at that point. I couldn't, not easily. Carmine had rotated the lock digits when he put the money inside, maybe even altered Tim's combination altogether. If I'd broke the latch, it wouldn't have stayed closed again and that would have just been too risky. I wanted all three of us to open it for the first time together so suspicions would never fall on me if the count was off. Like I said, I felt a responsibility to my partners.

"Poisoned? You want to clarify that a little?"

"It's what I said. Just put it away," Tim said.

I couldn't decipher Tim's damn code, but for whatever reason, he was afraid to say too much over the phone. Those lack of details made me a little uncomfortable holding the bag. And that was before I really considered it could be a bomb.

"Look? Can you just come get me?" I said. But he had already hung up.

I immediately started walking. Ain't no way I was waiting stagnant at a bus stop right out in the open. And in that area, there wasn't much better a chance of finding a taxi than sasquatch. I kept to alleyways and side streets, cutting through secluded areas to avoid main roads as much as possible. Then I stole the first bike I saw.

It had been years since I'd ridden one but, despite it being a bit too small for me, it came back almost immediately. For miles I pedaled and pedaled that thing until my legs felt like rubber. I knew exactly where I was going, a place I hadn't thought about too much since I was a kid.

During Walt's drunken fits of rage, Ash and I would disappear. We'd start walking, knowing we'd have to be gone for hours until the toxic elixir finally rendered our "dad" unconscious. Cops would pick us up if they saw little kids wandering around at night so we had to stay off the streets. A favorite spot of ours was Double Rock Park, a huge plot of woods protected by the state. Little kids loved it because they could climb on the boulders and slabs of smoothed stone formations surrounded by a small endless stream that went on for miles. Teenagers loved it because at night, the trees made it secluded enough to toke or drink and have it off. We loved it just because it was safe, more so than our home anyway. It was the closest thing to a safe haven the state ever gave us.

Ash and I always preferred the small trail, the one that went around the perimeter of the park. It was always empty, away from the giant rocks and streams that attracted everyone else. And at the back, there ran a fence separating the state-run park from a privately-owed cemetery that was restricted from using the land too close to its neighboring edge. The chain-link fence sat only five feet high and we could easily climb it, even as little shits. Still, someone at some point found it necessary to cut a hole in it big enough to walk through. That just made crossing easier.

Our go-to spot became a small circle of trees a half-mile north from the damaged section of fence on the border of the cemetery—limbo between the secluded public trail and usable private land. We would hang out there and talk and just enjoy being alone. Sometimes we'd hike far enough to watch people mourning at graves or we'd walk through to read the tombstones. Whether avoiding the wrath of Walt or running away from people we'd ripped off, that enclosure of trees was the place we'd meet to find each other whenever we got separated.

That's where I headed.

I could hardly walk by the time I got there. I dropped the bike, then made my way down the path and across the rocky stream in dusk's diminishing light, bag in tote. Memories came rushing right at me. There was more trash and graffiti than I remembered, but the clearings, the trail, the markers, they all looked untouched by time. The fence had been patched but not replaced. Just one five-foot section of silver steel chain-link in between rusty neighbors.

I hopped over and walked to that circle of trees. Then I stood there and spun around slowly so I could take it all in. It was like a familiar childhood friend that you'd recognize after decades of heading separate ways and growing apart. Like me, the spot had aged, not with gray hair but overgrown vines and branches and foliage. I looked at the large tree roots that jutted out of the ground, the ones we'd each claimed a lifetime before. I sat down on mine to rest and I was twelve years old again. But this time, no matter how long I'd wait, my brother wasn't coming back.

I know it sounds stupid, but I spoke out loud to Ash that day, like he was sitting right there beside me. I don't know what I believe about ghosts or souls or heaven. And what we talked about, that's between me and him. But as I sat there and spoke and just unloaded everything I'd been bottling up, he forgave me. I could feel it. Maybe I finally forgave myself. Whatever it was, I felt peace, at least as far as he's concerned.

I didn't wait too long before I found a large branch to spear in the ground and loosen the soil. When it was clumped enough to easily move, I scooped it out with my hands. I could barely see what I was grabbing in the uneven moonlight but I kept on, working my way down for what seemed like hours. Every jab with the rough wood chafed blisters in my palms and tore the muscle in my arms. When the spot was big enough, I sealed the briefcase as best I could in the plastic bag and buried it about a foot and half down. Then I rolled over large rocks and parked them on top.

By then, that large chicken waffle dinner was coming to an abrupt end of it's visit and it seemed intent on forcing itself out regardless of my will or convenience. I don't think any of it necessarily digested as much as it stormed the gates and torched the village. My stomach was churning, screaming for release. I had nowhere else to go anyway, so I figured nature might as well serve my intentions. Like a runny mess of cherries on top, I marked that rock pile as good as any animal in those woods could have. And I can't imagine anybody would have even touched it on a dare.

I tried calling Tim one last time with no answer before I crawled back over to my tree root and lay back, exhausted. I could scarcely make out any stars through the trees overhead. They appeared even dimmer when my eyes became impossible to keep open.

Before I knew it, I was out.

I woke up to the feeling of something lightweight and small dotting my forehead. Then I felt it again. I thought it was a bug at first until I opened my eyes and saw a little kid dressed up in a suit, throwing pieces of twig at my face. I could tell by the expression on his face when I caught him mid-toss, he was about to wet himself.

"Boo," I growled with a sudden movement toward him.

He ran off as he yelled. "Mom! A bum lives here! A bum lives here! And he pooped himself!"

I stood up and hid behind a tree to watch him return to his group by a graveside. There must have been fifty people gathered around a coffin-sized hole when he announced his discovery. Then I glanced down at myself. In the daylight, I looked a horrible mess. I was covered in dirt and sweat and my pants had remnants of shit splatter from that vigorous but necessary evacuation.

I took off. Quickly.

I ran beside the property line until I got to that old familiar part of the fence and climbed over. I dipped my filthy hands in the flowing stream water as I passed, then found the ride I'd dumped near the trail entrance. Hard to believe it hadn't been taken, but there it was, waiting for me. A stolen bike built for kids too young to grow pubic hair.

You know, not even for a moment did I consider running away. I never thought about turning around and digging up that briefcase, using a rock to crack it open like a rich kid's piñata until hundred-dollar bills came pouring out. I didn't think about the money like that. I never saw it as my share, even though it *was* roughly one-third of the take. I needed to find Tim and make sure he was alright. I wanted to know what happened. And I guess part of me wanted to go after Colt. Whatever drove me, I wasn't ready to skip town and leave anyone out to dry.

There was this little Mexican boy named Ely who always hung out in front of Tim's building. There was something just off about him. It wasn't like he was retarded or had Downs or nothing. He was just peculiar. I was never exactly one to go barbecue with the neighbors, but I think I heard someone say he had some sort of autism when I passed two of the residents swapping dirt.

Anyway, I liked the kid. He was real friendly and well-mannered despite the fact his mom was a drunken whore who let her eight-year old son play outside by himself all day and talk to strangers. Most people would avoid him, assholes even ignoring him when he was just trying to say hello. I'll admit, he could get a little carried away with constant questions but at least the kid had respect, which is more than I can say about the little shit throwing sticks at my face.

As usual, Ely was outside when I got there. He kept hitting a rubber ball across the grass with a wooden tee-ball bat, minding his own business and abiding by the rules of some game he invented.

"Hi, Mr. Roy," he said. "I like your bike."

"Thanks," I said. I dropped the damn thing on the ground and stood up straight to get some feeling back in my legs. I never realized how much age had started to tear me down.

"You want to play with me? You can use my ball," he said.

"Sorry, kid. I got stuff to do," I said.

"You have to see your friends?" he said.

"Yeah, that's right," I said.

I dismissed it as I started to climb the cement steps to the apartment building foyer. Then I stopped in my tracks and turned so I could look around the parking lot. My car was where I left it and that was the only thing that usually concerned me. I didn't see anything strange. There were a lot of empty cars but the building had lots of tenants. I had never paid enough attention to know which ones were supposed to be there.

"Hey Ely, how did you know I had to see my friends?" I said.

"I saw them go up," he said. "My mom lives on the second floor. Mr. Jerry and Jeffy live on the bottom. Mrs. Sharon lives on the second floor too but not with us."

"Yeah, yeah. Was it my good friend? The one who usually walks out with me? Is that who went up," I said.

"No. New friends. Two of them," he said, still paying more attention to the ball as he knocked it back and forth. "You're lucky. You have lots of friends."

"Did they look white like me? Or were they black?" I said.

"Um. Kind of in-between. They looked like me," he said.

It was Carmine's people. I should have just walked away. I was worried about Tim though. I had this vision in my head that they were up there with him, just waiting for me so they could drag us both back and kill us for what we done. Maybe I should have just called the cops, given an anonymous tip that gun-toting illegals were seen breaking into his apartment. That would have been enough to clear them out, but who knows what would happen if police got involved. The thugs might have killed Tim on the spot.

Instead, I took a run from Ash's playbook. I ordered pizza. Three of them. Then I bent down and turned to Ely who was watching me the whole the time.

"You must be hungry. Is it your birthday?" he said.

"No. But I think my friends are hungry. You really like my bike, kid?" I said.

"I really do. Blue is my favorite," he said. "I have a blue bed, blue shoes, bl—"

"How would you like to have it?" I said.

"I sure would. I never had a bicycle before."

Despite his words, he didn't seem too excited as he kept his head down and stared at his ball. Like I mentioned, peculiar kid.

"I tell you what. You let me borrow the stick, the bike is yours to keep."

He looked over and kept eyes on his new toy as he handed me the small bat.

"Thank you, Mr. Roy. It rides really nice," he said as he waddled away, walking with it between his legs.

I waited in the foyer and listened as the delivery guys started showing up, one after the next within a few minutes of each other. The intruders argued with all of them in broken day-worker English. They actually kept the first pie. I guess breaking and entering builds quite an appetite. The second and third guys got sent away with pizza in hand, all pissed-off for making an unnecessary trip. I bought the third one though, and he was really grateful for the huge tip. Then again, he didn't know I paid using cash that I had just taken from his car.

I let two minutes pass before I knocked on the door.

"Pizza delivery," I said. I held the box up to the peephole to hide my face just in case they knew what I looked like.

"We did no order it," he said through the door.

I knocked harder.

"Pizza delivery!"

He opened the door, agitated for the interruptions but completely unaware that I was already at half swing. I clubbed his head twice, splitting his forehead open and knocking him against the wall. Then I grabbed the gun from his waistband before he could reach it.

The other Mexican was delayed in response, dropping a slice of pizza to the carpet before aiming his gun at me. By this point, I had his buddy in a choke hold with a pistol pressed against his temple, using him as a shield. The knocks on the head had really dazed him. He hardly even struggled as the blood from the gashes flowed over his eyes.

I believe I called the other gunman *Cheech* or made some threat about blasting salsa all over the walls. Things just happened so quickly, some details are hard to recall. Whatever I said, it didn't have the effect I was looking for. He didn't think twice as he raised his gun up and blew a hole through his friend's chest. The bullet went clean through and grazed me, tearing a cut across my arm. I dropped the limp body and ducked into the kitchen, grabbing the small bat on the way.

He came around the other side of the kitchen and already held his gun pointed at me before I knew he was there. He had me.

"Drop the piece," he said.

I did. Both the gun and the bat.

"Some loyalty you got," I said.

"He screwed up. That's what he gets," he said. "Where's the money?"

"The bedroom," I said.

"*Mierda*. It's not here," he said. "We already tore this place apart."

"Not the money, asshole. A key. The money is in a storage locker. You need the key to open the locker," I said.

"Get it. Slowly," he said.

I stood up and walked toward my bedroom. He followed steadily but kept his distance as I pushed open the door that no longer seemed to offer sanctuary in the trashed apartment. Everything had been tossed and disheveled. Even the fancy door handle from my bedroom door was missing. Of course that stood out as odd, but I was too preoccupied at the time to worry about it.

"It was right here. It might take me a minute to find it now," I said.

"What are you waiting for?" he said.

If there was a key buried under all that mess, I didn't know about it. I was looking for something else. Anything else. A pencil or scissors or a hammer—any object that was heavy and blunt or hard and pointed. I wasn't going quietly. As I scanned the room, I couldn't see anything useful scattered about the pile of tossed furniture. Nothing except the cigar box that held my brother's ashes.

I tried to buy a little time so I could think.

"You'll never find the money. You're going to need me to show you where it is," I said. "We could split it, you know. You could walk away a rich man."

"You can show Thiago. Hurry up," he said.

I knew what that meant. The gorilla had assumed control of the zoo and he had given the order to find us. More importantly, he wanted us back alive. This bean-eating scrap with a gun in my face must have seen me as an opportunity to climb the ladder through new leadership, at the very least earn a pat on his waterlogged back. But killing me wasn't on his immediate agenda.

"It's hidden in here," I said.

I held up Ash's box and opened the lid revealing the dust that was once my brother. He looked inside. That change in focus was all the opportunity I had. But it was all I needed.

I threw the ashes in his face and quickly grabbed the barrel of the gun. He had the trigger but I controlled where it fired. Two shots blasted in the brick as he tried to wrestle the gun away while gagging on the gray haze. He was still moving blindly when I twisted his weapon to point toward him. He wouldn't let go though. Neither would I.

I used my elbow to dig in his neck and force his face back against the door frame. Then I used my foot to slam the door shut on his head as hard as I could. I pressed my knee against it, squeezing it like a vice against his jaw, pinching his ear against the hard wood but that bastard wouldn't let go. He starting kicking and punching and clawing, trying to twist his way free. This wasn't a fight of honor. This was survival. His fingers found their way to my face and he tried dig his nails into my eyes. That just pissed me off. I tilted my head up enough to bite deep in his finger, hard enough that I heard a crunch, then I punched him in the throat. Finally, he let go of the weapon.

I didn't shoot him though. There was already one dead greaser attached to that gun and I wasn't about to plant my print on the trigger. I maintained my hold on the barrel and cracked his head a few times with the butt of the handle. He covered his head as he coughed and gagged, trying to regain control of his breathing.

"Where's my friend?" I said before I spit out the metallic flavor that filled my mouth. There was no way to tell whose blood I was tasting.

"Your friend is dead," he said as best he could with a barely-audible, raspy voice.

I couldn't tell if he was boasting a fact or giving a threat. I didn't believe him regardless. I dragged him by the foot toward the balcony that overlooked the alley.

"I won't ask you again," I said.

Then I grabbed him by the ear and forced him on his feet so he could see just how high up we were. I pulled so hard I thought it might rip off.

"You're a dead man too," he said. Then he busted my lip open with a head-butt.

See, I didn't actually intend to do it. Once he started fighting again though, it was a reaction based off instinct. I ducked one punch and gave a hard elbow to the back of his head. That knocked him off balance. He was so light and his momentum was already heading that way, he just kept going. I didn't toss him. I didn't try to stop him. He grabbed for the rail but he just had too much speed behind him. No possible way he could get a good enough grip. And over the balcony he went.

I didn't see him fall and he had already landed before I could react and look over. He must have been in a pretty awkward position on the way down judging by the sharp, hellish bend in the middle of his calf. He wouldn't die from it, but he wasn't dancing away on it either.

I could hear sirens in the distance and I knew that was my cue to dash. I quickly reclaimed Ash's cigar box and scooped up as much of his remains as I could. I don't know what made me pause. I guess overhearing conversations about digital forensics and cybersecurity had made their way through my thick skull. At any rate, I grabbed Tim's laptop on the way out. I didn't have a clue if their was any evidence on the damn thing or how to get rid of it if there was. I just knew he used it for research and I was trying to protect him.

I made my way to Ash's car in the parking lot, smelling like pig-shit and looking even worse. I threw the computer under the seat without a thought, then put the key in the ignition and prayed the old dog still had some life left. It cranked right up as if it were aware of how much I needed my old reliable friend. Without delay, I drove off with my brother beside me once again, knowing I might be going to battle to save Tim if I could even figure out a way to find him. I just didn't realize I had the compass right under my ass.

11
Family First

I guess I really didn't even understand the root of my feelings at first. Of course I was pissed at the thought of Audrey's life being taken for no reason. She wasn't an innocent, sure, but that don't mean she deserved to die, not in my mind. Being Carmine's wife just wasn't enough to justify it.

But it wasn't her death brewing my blood as much as the thought that Colt was the one who'd done it. I had focused so many negative feelings on him from the get-go and I tried to hold onto them. I really did. As much as I resisted though, he got me to drop my guard and I actually started to like the asshole. I never proved it with a laugh or admitted it with words, especially to his face, but I thought he was amusing. And I started to trust him. That's why I was so let down. He fooled me when I knew better.

I didn't intend on going after Colt until I could talk to Tim but he had disappeared and I had no idea where he'd gone. Had the position been reversed, he wouldn't have gone up and faced the gunmen in his apartment. I came to believe he had probably sniffed them out early just like I did, except he made his way to safety. I wouldn't blame him for running. Tim was a thinker, not a fighter. Not like me. And I wasn't going to just sit idly by with my thumb poking my prostate while Tim was gone. I convinced myself that maybe Colt even knew where he was. That's how I rationalized going after *him* first.

I started checking off everywhere I had seen Colt go or heard him talk about. He wasn't going back to his apartment. He stopped hanging around in his usual dives. I reckoned maybe he got his hands on the money from the locker and skipped town.

Then I remembered one time Colt was whining to Tim about his grandmother. I didn't know her name or where she lived. The only thing I knew was that she refused to stop walking to buy her own groceries even though she had some kind of trouble getting around. That and he called her Grambo.

During his little rant, he specifically mentioned Kiper's which stood out because I had a teacher with the same name, the only person who ever tried to convince me to stay in school as a kid. And it wasn't real common, neither the teacher's name nor the motivational support she tried to give.

With only a single business listing in the phone book, it was easy enough to find. *Kiper's Deli* was a small ma-and-pa corner market, a straggling remnant of the old-time, when local businesses were more prevalent than big chains. It only survived through the years because the neighborhood had gone to pot around it and larger grocery franchises refused to gamble on setting up camp. It was an oasis in a food desert and the regular patrons, like Tim's grandmother, kept the owners afloat.

Having grown up in a black neighborhood, I can't say I was afraid of the hood but I wasn't exactly at ease. I sat in my car for hours, staring at Kiper's front door in the rear-view mirror for any old brown-skinned lady with a walker or cane or wheelchair. I didn't know what I was looking for exactly. I just knew she lived somewhere around there. I guess I was running on desperation and gut instinct, hoping I would recognize some sign of Colt when I saw it.

Then I saw it.

Too much daylight had been wasted and, in more ways than one, the streets were getting a bit dark for my taste. My hand was on the damn ignition when I happened to glance across the way. From around a corner, Colt came strolling with two other black guys, talking and laughing loud enough to wake up the vagrant junkies.

I pulled the pistol out from under my seat and watched where they headed. I wasn't going to confront him out in the open. I wasn't making that mistake again. If I got arrested for attacking another black dude, I have no doubt that *hate crime* would be stapled to the bill of charges. Besides, the one hulk by his side looked massive enough to crush a bear's ribs.

I got out and followed them from a distance, doing my best to not seem so Caucasian but I stuck out like corn in shit. My body reeked with a sticky odor and my clothes were soiled and tattered. I easily appeared to be homeless, an appropriate display I suppose because at the time, that's exactly what I was. At least nobody gave me trouble as I strolled along. Hell, even the dealers were ignoring me.

Colt entered a brick row home toward the end of the block as the two others walked on. I counted the houses in from the end and maneuvered around to the alleyway behind them. It was easy to see him through the upstairs window as he took off his shirt in the bathroom. I didn't hesitate. I crept up to the back door and pushed it, only to feel the deadbolt prevent an easy way in. I was frustrated though. And tired. And out of patience. I used the gun to crack out a small square of glass in the door, enough to reach through and unlock it. Then I quickly went in before anyone could react.

The kitchen floor was crunchy with broken glass but there was no screaming or cries for help, only music. Horrible rap music, the same crap Colt was determined to shove in the ears of everyone in his proximity. I figured it had masked the sound of my entry, enough that nobody was alerted anyway. The thumping bass and synchronized profanity were attacking me from above so that's where I was heading—through a dimly lit hallway toward the steps that led up. At least until I felt the crack of metal against my skull.

"You sumva bitch! Get da hell out ma house," she said.

I put my hand up over my crown and turned around to see a quarter-ton ebony woman winding up again with her quad cane.

"You come up in here, I'll crack ya ass so you don't forget," she said as she released her rage in another full swing. I can't even lie about it. That hurt like hell.

I grabbed the four-footed end of the cane and tried to push her down on the couch where she'd inevitably have a hard time getting up. It was like trying to topple a rhino. She stumbled backward a few steps but maintained her balance on the two thick, chocolate-colored logs that seemed to melt into her slippers. Then I pulled my gun and pointed it at her. I didn't want to hurt her. I just needed her to back off.

"Colt!" I yelled. "Show your face or bad shit is going down!"

"You think I'm afraid of you?" she said. Then she charged me. I mean she literally put her head down like a bull and tore at me, gray hair first.

I ducked out of her reach and ran up the steps. He was already gone, running like a scared little girl and leaving his grandmother to fight his battle. The prick didn't even take a second to put on a shirt. He had jumped out of the bathroom window and was climbing down an old trellis when I looked out. I wasn't going to risk following him down that same way until I heard the stairs creak from supporting the plus-sized predator lukewarmly on my trail. She was slowly making her way up, taking breaks every other step to catch her breath and mumble profane threats in my direction. I shook my head and gave my own curse as I hopped out right behind Colt.

He was easily a good half block ahead. For the life of me, I couldn't figure out how he was able to run so damn fast with his pants drooping down below his ass. But there he was, gaining a lead with every step and slapping the lids of metal trash cans as he passed them.

I thought he was going to disappear when he ducked down an alley toward the front of the housing but losing me is not what he was trying to do. As soon as I turned that dark corner, I felt hands as big dinner plates wrap around my neck. It was the same mammoth I saw walking with Colt earlier. He slammed me against the brick wall and emptied the air from my lungs with a punch in the gut. Then he grabbed my wrist and banged my hand against the wall until I dropped my pistol.

And from the darkness Colt came strolling back, his bright red boxers hanging out of his jeans, proudly on display like a patriot's flag. He held his arms out and his head up with a smug grin on his stupid face.

"Yo, what I tell you? I knew he be coming," he said.

A third spade came running around the corner and stopped in his tracks when he saw us. Then he walked to the other side of me. That's when I spotted a glimmer of light briefly reflect off the gun in his hand.

"You owe Big and me each a c-note, yo," Colt said to him, laughing. Then he turned to me. "See, Toke here thought you were long gone but I knew your pasty-white punkass would be coming up at me. And you just won me a hundy for it."

"Go to hell," I said. At least, I started to before the giant squeezed my throat and slammed my head against the wall.

"You couldn't just take the money and run, could you?" Colt said. "You dumb, yo. I would have run. Toke would have run. Big would have walked but he still been gone."

I wasn't even the one who insulted his weight but Big dug his meaty fingers into my windpipe all the same. My first thought was maybe those kinds of jabs were constant. If any tension existed between them, maybe I could capitalize on it. I turned my eyes to look at the huge arm extending from my neck.

"You can have every cent of the money if you let me go and break Colt's neck right now," I grunted.

"Save your breath, white boy. We's family," Big said.

I had all the luck of a legless rabbit.

Colt looked around for prying eyes before he stepped closer to me.

"Right now, you could be kicking back somewhere, getting lit from top shelf hooch and laying into some fine hooker ass with all four inches of white man's fury. Naw, that ain't good enough for you, is it, cowboy? You gotta come back, all vengeful and shit," he said.

Toke reached forward and handed the gun to Colt by pressing the grip of it against his arm.

"I ain't even blaming you. You pissed, I get it. Doesn't mean you ain't gonna pay for it though."

"You going to murder me too? Go ahead and do it," I said. I was looking for an opportunity to get one last lick in. If I was going down, I was going make sure his face would never be the same.

"Naw, nigga. Killing you be like ripping up a paycheck," he said. "You worth a helluva lot more than the lonely Benjamin that this boy owes me. Now you gonna tell us where you hid the payday."

"I ain't telling you shit. You'll never see that money," I said.

"Oh, we will. Because if we can't beat the answer out of you, we going another direction," he said.

"And what's that?" I said.

"Turning your nilla ass in for the reward," he said.

"Reward?" I said.

"Fifty large is a nice consolation prize," he said. "And while you spending your days trying to forbid the affections of a lonely cellmate, we going to keep looking for that money. And we'll find it too, with or without your help."

"What reward are you talking about?"

"Don't even tell me you ain't seen your ugly mug posted all over the news," he said.

"I've been busy," I said.

"Damn right you have. Seems you wanted for kidnapping," he said.

I scoffed as much as I was able with limited breath. I couldn't believe he could be so stupid.

"You got to be out of your mind. You turn me in, you might as well go dressed in orange yourself because you'll be right there with me," I said. "You'd get more years than I would."

"How the hell you figure that?"

"I know about the blood on your hands," I said.

"I ain't the one who capped Tim if that's what you trying to pin on me," he said.

"Tim's dead?"

"You the one shacked up with him. You didn't know that?"

That felt like a harder punch in the gut than the one Big had actually given me.

Colt put the gun up to my face and pressed it between my eyes.

"You give up the money, you get a chance to run. You don't, you can test your luck with a jury of your inbred peers," he said.

"I'd rather watch that million dollars burn than give it to you."

I could see a change in his eyes right then. "What?"

"You heard me. Do your worst. I'll never give it up. Not to you."

Colt opened his mouth to say something else but stopped without letting out a sound. Then he got a real strange look on his face. Unexpected confusion. He stepped back and lowered the gun so he could look down at my clothes.

"You still wearing the same rags you was when we pulled the job?" he said.

I was so caught off guard by the subject change, I didn't respond with words, just a confounded stare.

"That was three days ago," he said.

"So?"

"And you hid the money?" he said.

"Where you'll never find it," I said sharply, completely missing whatever he was seeing.

"Where did you get the money?" he said.

"You know where I—"

"I swear I'll cap your bleached-flour, cracker-ass right here," he said putting the gun back under my chin. "Answer the damn question!"

"From the job, asshole!" I yelled.

"When you was creeping inside the coffin?" he said.

"Yeah. Where else?"

"You didn't go try to buy a car or nothing? Just hid the whole lot?" he said.

"Every cent of it."

Colt appeared in painfully deep thought as he took a step back. I was sure he was going to pop a bullet in my face. I was waiting for it, prepared for it, unable to prevent it while having a behemoth's hand still wrapped around my neck. It was a full minute of silent thinking before he turned around and started cursing and kicking a nearby dumpster. Then he picked up a trash can and threw it as far as he could. His yo-boy homies looked just as confused as me. Once the tantrum subsided, Colt bent down and picked up the pistol I was forced to drop so he could take the clip out before tossing it down a storm drain. Then he turned to Big.

"Let him go, cuz. This nigga ain't worth shit," he said. Then he turned to me. "You best read a paper or something and correct your look. That face is gonna get you got."

Big let go as he pushed my head, not trying to cause pain, just belittle me. Then the three of them started walking away.

"Where are you going?" I spoke to deaf ears. That just pissed me off.

I'm man enough to admit that I always had bigger balls than brains. I never knew when to walk away. But I needed answers. And if Colt had them in his head, I was getting them even if I had to crack it open to look for them.

An empty bottle rolled around in the alley beside my feet as I stood. I picked it up by the neck like a club and took off running toward them. They were talking and Colt's voice carried, easily loud enough to distract them from my footsteps. I didn't hear what they were saying. I didn't care. I was seeing red. Even as I approached them, I hadn't thought the strategy through. I was running on anger and desperation, both having accumulated to a critical point. While I don't always appreciate my prior experiences, the harsh years in prison had taught me how to prioritize a group of foes. The logic had been ingrained in me. Always take down the largest threat first.

My hand swung over as I approached and smashed the bottle on Big's head. The body of it broke away leaving me holding the handle of a jagged round shiv. Colt and Toke were so caught off guard, neither were prepared, both were empty-handed. I jumped on Big's back, lodged my arm under his chin and wrapped my legs around his waist. Then I pressed the sharpest point of glass against his jugular. He fell backward on me, inadvertently becoming my shield while crushing the wind from my chest. I could feel blood run down on my face from the gash in his head. My lungs had trouble regaining air. But I latched on like a dog in heat furiously humping and refused to let go.

"Aim your piece at me and I'll bury this thing in his neck," I said.

By this time, Colt had fumbled the gun from his pocket and held it pointing in the air. He couldn't aim it at me without threatening one of his own.

"Put it on the ground and slide it to me," I said.

"Now you know *that* ain't gonna happen," Colt said. "You came here to kill me. You think I'm gonna hand over my strap so you dust all three of us?"

"I swear I'll use my dying breath to slice his neck open and rip his head off," I said.

His friend Toke stepped forward slightly only to kneel down closer to my level. Every movement was relaxed and cautious and his open hands remained slightly raised in peace. He took a long breath and looked at me, speaking very calmly in a soft voice.

"You *could* do that, for sure. But you shouldn't and let me tell you why. You're outnumbered. You're out-armed. And you're the only one here with a price on his head."

I didn't say a word. I didn't move an inch. Neither did Colt or the jumbo-sized man wrapped in my limbs. I just inhaled deeply to take in air along with his words.

Toke continued, "How long do you think you have before somebody comes by and calls the police? Who has more to lose if that happens? Time isn't your friend, brother. This isn't a stalemate, not by a longshot. We have every advantage."

"If you believe that, why are you talking to me instead of yelling for help?" I said.

"Because I love the man you're threatening. That's my little brother."

"He's not a little anything," are the words that came out of my mouth. What went through my mind was my own little brother and the small bottle of bone being pressed against my sternum. I could immediately relate to his concern although my own response would have been vastly less subdued.

He looked down at his brother. "You cut him open, you're getting either a grave or a jail cell. We'll all be swept in squad cars, tied up for days. And I'll have to go home and tell my mama her baby boy is dead. That's lose-lose all the way around. But maybe there's a way we can all win," he said.

I didn't let go. But I wanted to. I wanted an option out. Tension and muscle fatigue were taking their toll though, making it harder to gauge the pressure I was applying. I hadn't even realized a point from the glass had started tearing a small puncture in his skin.

"Keep talking," I said.

"You want information. We need information too," Toke said. "Maybe we can help each other out."

Colt scoffed behind him, divisive with every breath. "Don't even, yo. We don't need his ass."

"Shut up, Lester," Toke said abruptly.

"Lester?" I said. I could tell by the look on his face that me just knowing his given name was enough to get under his craw.

Toke faced me again, his expression seeming as genuine as any I'd ever seen. "How about it?" he said.

"I ain't so confident I can trust thugs," I said.

He snickered quietly through his nose before smirking. "Thugs? Dude, I'm finishing up my Bachelor's, trying to get into grad school. The only reason I'm not there right now is because I'm trying to protect certain extended family members that can't seem to quit diving head first into deep shit."

Colt rolled his eyes and sneered. "Whatever, man," he said.

Toke lowered one of his hands and put it on his brother's arm.

"And Big? You know why we call him that?" he said.

"Because you ain't that creative?" I said.

"It's short for *Big Baby*. He works for a florist making arrangements. And once a month he dresses up like a clown to make balloon animals for kids at my grandma's church. He isn't a banger. He's a teddy bear. Look at him, man. He's crying right now," Toke said.

Sure enough, I could see tears rolling down his cheeks and onto my arms. That's when it started to sink in that I may have been the biggest piece of shit out of all of them.

"Even *if* all that's true, I'm thinking we got some trust issues," I said.

"No doubt. But understand this isn't what we wanted. Me and Big didn't know nothing about anything until yesterday. We were just trying to protect our cousin. There was never any intention to *really* hurt you. Still isn't. We let you go, remember?" Toke said. "Show some good faith, brother. Just put the edge down so we can all walk away. Together."

I looked back at Colt and the gun he had lowered down by his leg.

"You going to put that steel back in your pocket, Lester?" I said.

He didn't even get a chance to answer before Toke interrupted.

"He will. And he isn't going to shoot you. If he tries, I'll jump in front of the bullet myself. I promise you that, man to man."

For a moment I paused, but in truth the decision was made without much deliberation. I released my arm from around Big's neck and lowered the broken shard of bottle in my hand, keeping my eyes focused on them the whole time as we stood up. Then I shook my legs hoping to get some feeling back into the testicles that were shoved up inside my body when that giant slab of beef fell on me.

"Now what?" I said.

"Now we go somewhere to talk. Somewhere inside. Hanging around out here at night isn't a great idea. And being seen with you is just plain stupid," Toke said. He looked at the small gash on Big's head. "Before we go, I need something."

"What's that?"

"Your word. You don't attack any of us, we won't attack you. No more violence, no matter what. Not with us."

I looked at all three of their faces, unsure I could really believe any of it. I took the chance regardless.

"I can give it if Lester can," I said.

"Man, you better cut that shit out," Colt said.

"Step up," Toke said to him. "Swear on a truce."

Colt put the gun back in his pocket. "You ain't got to worry about me, dog. I ain't doing nothing. Dirty-man be the only murderer here," he said. Then he turned to walk away.

I didn't argue. I didn't call him a liar. I was covered in filth and quite honestly, just too tired.

"You got my word," I said, not understanding fully why he needed that vow. But I made it with every intention to keep it.

And together we walked, saying nothing worth anything, but at least doing it peacefully. I still kept my eyes open.

12
Cards on the Table

I could see hate in her stare the second I walked in the door. At least mistrust. I can't say I blame her. It was only minutes before that I was waving a nine-mil in her face.

"Is my eyes playing tricks or did you bring back the crazy fool I done chased off?" Grambo said, sizing me up and down like I was a frequent-flying Arab with a knapsack.

"It's alright Grams. It was just a misunderstanding, that's all," Toke said.

"And what y'all think you doing up in here?" she said.

"We're just talking. Working it out like you always tell us to do."

"Yeah, and I guess this is part of the misunderstanding too?" She examined Big's head gash giving me evil glances every few seconds. Toke had taken off his own shirt to apply pressure to the wound. It was more of a small cut really. Hardly worth mentioning except that it made me feel uneasy to see her inspecting it.

"No, Grams. Rodney hit his head getting off the bus."

"Hm," she said. She wasn't naive.

Then she turned to Colt who had plopped himself down on the couch and kicked his sneakers up.

"Lester, get ya damn feet off the coffee table. This ain't no day spa. I swear I'm going to bust ya ass," she said. "You done bringing noise in my house, boy?"

"Yeah, Grambo. We all solid again," he said.

Then she turned to speak with me for the first time. Her expression changed when she looked in my eyes. Her tone changed. She had every right to want to hit me again with that damn four-footed cane. But she didn't hint that she felt that way. Instead, she sounded concerned, civil, even sweet.

"Tonight ain't going to be no more misunderstandings, is there, mister? You ain't going to hurt none of my boys."

"No ma'am," I said.

"And you plan on staying here for a spell and talking through whatever this is without no more ruckus?"

"Yes ma'am," I said.

"Then you need to clean yourself up before you plant yourself on my furniture. Ya smell like hay that done moved through a horse," she said. "Lester, get the man some clean clothes."

"He ain't holding my gear," Colt said.

"Did I stutter, boy? And get him a towel, show him where the washroom is before I smack the sass out your mouth," she said before she looked at me again. "Leave your clothes outside the door and I'll give them a scrub for you."

"Really, you don't need to do that," I said.

"Honey, it's best for everyone around you that I do," she said.

Colt huffed as he nodded for me to follow him to the upstairs bathroom. I cleaned up, washing off several days-worth of sweat and blood and dirt. Then I put on the ridiculous outfit Colt had picked for me: baggy, over-sized gym shorts and a t-shirt with some rapper superimposed over a pot leaf. I swear he did it for giggles. Their grandmother was right though. After I smelled like soap, I realized just how much stench was clinging to my clothes.

I had no idea what to expect when I came back downstairs. I could hear some minor commotion coming from below but I didn't pay it much mind. Then I started to have a moment of doubt, second guessing the trust I put into people I didn't know, leaving myself vulnerable in unfamiliar terrain. I crept real slowly down the steps, peaking around the corner to see the living room empty. I could hear them speaking just above a whisper but I couldn't make out the words. These weren't the kind of folks that ever talked softly which made me even more suspicious. Of all the thoughts I had in my head though, I definitely didn't expect to walk in on what I got.

"...and guide them in peace and understanding as they commune together. Amen," Grambo said, perching her face up with her eyes shut tight.

The four of them sat around the dining room table holding hands. And at one end, in front of one empty chair at the head of the table, there was a large bowl of thick stew with a block of cornbread and an iced tea.

"The boys weren't sure if you had eaten," she said. "Go on and sit yourself down."

I didn't know what to say. This old woman obviously didn't have much money. She could hardly walk. She had a strange man break into her home, threaten her grandson and show not a single redeeming quality. Still, when given the chance, she let me clean up and went out of her way to offer me nourishment without asking for anything in return but my dirty clothes so she could wash them. It was the nicest thing I'd ever seen. I couldn't express proper gratitude to her in words, not while still in the shock of it. I did the best I could at the time.

"Thank you," I said.

"Ain't no trouble. It's the Christian thing to do," she said. "Now don't make me whoop your ass like a woman of the world."

Big had a bandage on his head over where I'd hit him. I probably should have apologized but even then, I wasn't entirely sorry for it. I mean, he did have me gripped around the throat. Instead I quietly sat down in front of the place setting and looked around at the others while their grandmother went into the kitchen to clean up.

"So. Who starts?" I said.

"You do," Toke said, keeping his voice down. "Try the gumbo and tell Grams how good it is."

"Are you kidding?" I said.

"Please, man. It's her family recipe. She lives for that," he said. "We can't talk with her around and she won't leave us alone until you do."

I stirred the dark brown liquid to see pieces of sausage and pepper and unidentifiable chunks of white and yellow stuff. It was thick despite being steaming hot and looking like sewage water. Then I saw Grambo peak her head out of the kitchen for just a second before vanishing back again.

"Just take a slurp of the damn soup and tell Grambo what's what," Colt said.

I scowled at him for a moment before I put the spoon to my mouth. I tasted it again as they all awkwardly watched me like I was about to multiply it and feed the masses. It was spicy and greasy and smelled a bit like feet. It really wasn't my taste but it was edible enough. And I hadn't realized how hungry I'd gotten until a little food touched my lips. Then my stomach demanded more.

"Ma'am?" I said loud enough that she could hear me over the running water.

She hobbled out from the kitchen and looked at me.

"This is best soup I've ever eaten," I said.

She smiled wide, her wrinkled face scrunching up to show her gapped teeth.

"I'm glad you like it," she said. "Well, boys. I'm going to bed. Make sure you decide who's gonna fix my window. And for the love of God, let an old lady have a peaceful night's sleep."

Then she walked toward the steps and began her ascent while we waited. The others obviously didn't want to discuss anything important in front of her. They wouldn't even engage in small talk with themselves. It seemed nobody could really focus on anything but the large issues at hand so we sat in silence, waiting for her to fight gravity against twelve steps. I finished all the food within reach in the same time it took her to get halfway up. It was like watching an elephant climb a ladder. Finally she made it to the top.

I started right into it. "OK, first off, why did you—"

"Tsh," Toke said. He put his hand up as he looked toward the steps. We could hear the floor creak as she moved around upstairs.

I couldn't help but roll my eyes.

"She's on a different floor. You really think she can hear us?" I said.

"Grambo ain't got much that works a hundred percent but her ears be like mutant powers. I swear she got sonar, man," Colt said.

After we heard a slew of mattress springs cry for mercy above our heads, Toke looked at me and nodded. I huffed to show my impatience before I turned to Colt.

"Why'd you do it?" I said.

He was reluctant to open up. "It was Tim's idea," Colt said.

"It was Tim's idea to rape and murder Carmine's wife?"

He got an appalled look on his face. So did the others. You'd have thought I soiled myself.

"What the hell, man? I ain't murder nobody," he said. "Didn't rape nobody neither."

"If you didn't, who did?"

"I don't know. Maybe the same dude who capped Tim. Which we thought was you."

"Why would I hurt Tim?" I said.

None of them gave an answer although they all had one. There was something they weren't saying. I could tell by the way they looked at each other.

"How do you know Tim is dead anyway?" I said.

Big spoke up, never taking his hand off the bandage that covered the cut on his scalp. "I went to his apartment yesterday when Colt couldn't ring him. I saw them carrying out his body in bag. One of the neighbors said it was the dude who live there."

"Only two people stay there and you're here," Colt said. "No genius needed to figure you killed him."

"First off, I ain't the one who sent that bullet flying. And that body *wasn't* Tim's. It was one of Carmine's people. They're after me," I said.

"Ain't just you. I saw some *cholos* sniffing around my place too," Colt said. "How you know Audrey got clipped?"

"Tim told me. He also said the money we got from the job was tainted somehow. I'm still fuzzy on what that means though," I said.

Colt just looked at me with a blank gaze. He didn't want to tell me the truth.

"I wouldn't put too much weight into anything Tim told you, yo," he said. "He screwed us. Screwed us both. I'm sure of it."

I didn't want to hear that. I wanted to reject it with everything inside me.

"You're the one that never came and picked me up after the job. Why should I believe anything that comes out of your mouth?" I said.

"Because it don't sound like you know a damn thing about the little girl," he said.

"What little girl?"

Toke picked up his phone and zoomed his finger across the small screen. After a few seconds he turned it toward me so I could read it. It was my face, my description, my name right under a wanted bulletin in connection to an abduction. Above that was a link to an Amber Alert with an article about the reward being offered by the wealthy parents for her return.

"What the hell? I didn't do this," I said.

"And I didn't touch Audrey," Colt said. "Like I said, we both getting screwed."

"I don't get it. Why would they think I kidnapped a little girl? I don't even know her." I tried to think of any connection I could possibly have but my mind was shooting blanks. I just knew I had absolutely nothing to do with it. Not a damn thing. I promise. "If this is what I'm wanted for, it's easy enough to fix. I'll turn myself in."

"You shouldn't do that," Colt said. "They pretty confident you did it. That means they probably got physical evidence you was there."

"But I wasn't there," I said.

"Then something you touched was planted. Maybe they found a couple of your gray, shriveled-up pubes in her room. Who the hell knows?" Colt said. "Either way, you go in and they throw you in a cell for even a little bit, how long you think before they tie you to the Moreno job? Or one of his people gets to you on the inside?"

"Why do you care?" I said. "You worried I'm going to spill your name?"

"Hell yeah, I'm worried! I ain't trying to go to jail, man," Colt said. "Why you think we ain't turning your ass in and cashing the check?"

"You were going to turn me in an hour ago. What changed?"

Colt sat back for a minute and just stared at me. Nobody answered. That's when I looked over at Toke and noticed one arm had crept under the table at some point during the conversation.

"Show me your hands," I said as I wrapped my fingers around the handle of the semi-sharp butter-knife in front of me.

He slowly slid his chair away revealing a gun in his lap aimed directly at me. My immediate thought was that nothing changed for them except that I had allowed myself to be confined in their space, more easily controllable. It seemed they decided to turn me in after all. I started feeling like a rat caught in a trap and I was mentally prepared to gnaw off my leg to get away.

"We need you to stay chill," Toke said.

"And you think pointing a gun at my dick will do that?" I said.

Toke remained very calm as he spoke. "You promised no more violence. I just want to make sure you keep that promise. I'm not holding this because I want to use it. I'm holding it because I don't want it to be used," he said. "Tell him, C."

But he said nothing.

"Tell him!" Toke said.

Colt wouldn't even look me in the eye when he spoke. It's like he was talking to the table.

"You never had no money," he said.

"What are you talking about? I made the switch in the hearse and the money never left my sight," I said.

"And I made the switch in the junk truck before the bag ever got to you," Colt said. "You never had no money."

"You were hiding in Carmine's truck?"

"In a big box surrounded by scrap metal," he said.

"So what was in my bag? The one I risked my life swapping for a bomb," I said.

He was cautious in his delivery, slow in his response. Colt had seen my temper before. And I never took my hand off the knife.

"Newspapers and phone books," Colt said.

"Phone books?"

"Twenty pounds worth," he said.

I was taken aback. Angry. Hurt. I never felt so used and worthless.

"Why would you do it?" I was nearly growling out the words.

"Like I told you earlier, it was Tim's idea," Colt said. "The job needed three people. It could have been possible with two, but three helped make sure we ain't have no trouble. Tim didn't want to split the cash three ways though. And he said we needed a pigeon."

"I was a patsy the whole time? All those days we pulled jobs together, broke bread across from each other, talked about our personal shit and you were setting me up to play me?" I said. I was having trouble not raising my voice. Hell, I just barely refrained myself from leaping over the table and choking him.

"Man, don't act like we was boys. I didn't like you, you didn't like me," he said. "I saw it in your eyes with every damn word you said to me. You got no respect, you racist prick."

"Race got nothing to do with it. I didn't like you because you're an asshole."

"Keep telling yourself that. You white people all alike. First time you saw me, first thought popped in your head was I'm a criminal, just because I'm black," he said.

"The first time I saw you, you were dealing drugs in a bar," I said. "You *are* a criminal, Lester."

"Whatever man, you know what I'm talking about."

Big slumped over on the table with his hand still holding his head. Toke just sat there and patiently listened. I think his more immediate concern was not waking his Grandmother whose snores had become so powerful, the room was vibrating.

"So let me just get this straight. Was I being set up to get killed or just catch the rap for the whole job?" I said.

"Tim said as long as you didn't find out we made the switch, he knew you'd take a beef before you'd rat us out," Colt said.

"I'm flattered," I said.

"And because you didn't have the money, you wouldn't do no real time, maybe a nap in county if they tried to soften you up but nothing major. You were just gonna to be a diversion until we could relocate," he said. "He told me you'd be fine. Broke, but fine."

"So what happened?" I said.

"Tim was supposed to cut the chain off the warehouse locker for the two-mil we'd got from Audrey. And we was going to meet up, split it down the middle. But when we met, he didn't have it."

"Why not?" I said.

"He told me you got to it first. You had busted open the case, saw the stack of yellow pages and figured out you been duped. Until you just threatened to burn the *one million* you never had, I thought you'd stolen the two large from the locker," Colt said. "I knew your cornfed ass wasn't that bright."

"And he warned you I'd be coming for you," I said.

"With both guns blazing like Wyatt fucking Earp. He said you done killed Audrey."

"Why would I do that?"

"To tie up loose ends, kill off witnesses so you could keep the money," Colt said. "He told me that probably included us."

"And you believed him? You think I'd cut her down in cold blood?" I said.

"Oh, you Father Dirty, patron saint of morality now? You ain't above suspicion. You *did* do time for murder. Plus, he fed me some bullshit about tigers and leopards that get a taste for blood after they kill a person. You know how he do. It was very convincing."

Toke chimed in, breaking the silence he'd held as he listened and caught up to the details like me. "What about the million you switched with Dirty?" he said.

"Tim said it was too dangerous to spend right away. We hid it in a storage unit so things could cool off. I have the only key," Colt said.

"You're certain you have the only key?" I said.

"Positive. I'm the one who bought the lock," Colt said. "I was with him the whole time so I know he didn't mess with the money while it was in the back of the van."

"If he trusted you with the only key, he had something up his sleeve," Toke said.

"I don't see how. Guess we'll find out tomorrow morning when the gate opens," Colt said.

I couldn't focus on the money. It wasn't the highest of my concerns.

"I'm still confused why I'm in the paper for kidnapping?" I said.

"I don't know, man. I honestly know nothing about that," Colt said. "My guess is Tim's the one trying tie up loose ends."

"Which would include getting rid of you. Maybe *that* was my purpose all along," I said.

"Maybe. Or maybe I'll be pinned for Audrey's murder. My prints was all up in that shit, all over that room," Colt said.

"And there it is. *That's* why you're not turning me in. You've never been arrested so even if they find prints, they won't have an ID to match it to. Unless I point them in your direction," I said.

I think he started to feel a little vulnerable, like I had uncovered the leverage I didn't know I had. I know he wanted to discourage me from using it.

"You turn me in, we can forget the cash," Colt said. "They start scouting for Tim, they *will* find him first and we'll lose any shot of getting the money back. Our cabbage will be funding po-po banquets for the next decade."

Toke listened intently, not saying much at first. Until that day, he had almost nothing to do with any of this. But he was smart. And he didn't have the worry of being prosecuted for something he didn't do or killed for something he did. Without that fog in his eyes, he could see a little more clearly than we could and notice things we didn't.

"That woman hasn't been on the news," he said.

"What woman?" I said.

"The wife, Audrey. The Moreno story has been playing non-stop. It's huge. You'd think they would talk about her too, but they haven't," Toke said.

"Maybe they ain't found her body yet," Colt said.

"Or maybe she's not dead at all and police have kept her kidnapping under wraps," Toke said.

"Why would they do that?" Colt said.

"What if Tim had another partner he never talked about, one who could give him inside information, get rid of her own husband and collect huge cash, all the while thinking she'll avoid suspicion by playing an innocent victim," Toke said. "Maybe she's a suspect and they want to find her before reporters let her know that they're onto her."

The suggestion of it seemed like an unfunny joke.

"No way she could be that good of an actress," I said. "The tears, the crying. That's like gold statue award-type shit."

"Tim *was* adamant about not hurting her or getting in her pants. Hell, my instructions was to be nice to her," Colt said. "What if they were having an affair and we helped get rid of the husband and buy 'em a long honeymoon?"

I wasn't buying it. No matter how much sense it made.

"He had a girlfriend though. Remember him talking about it?" I said.

"The sex machine. Yeah, I remember. Talked about it so much I think I tapped her," Colt said. "Doesn't mean she really exist. Or that he wasn't talking about Audrey."

"No, I saw the girlfriend in her house. I followed him all the way over to Howard County one day and saw him spying on her. It wasn't Audrey," I said.

"Howard County?" Toke said. "What part?"

"I don't remember. If I heard it I could probably—"

"Elkridge?" he said like he was psychic. "Somewhere on Bonnie View Lane?"

I sat calmly and stared at him, nearly forgetting he still had a piece pointed in my direction. "Yeah," I said. "How is it you know that?"

"The little girl, the one you're accused of stealing," Toke said. "That's where she lived. Says so right here online."

"How much you want to bet that's who he was really looking up at child services?" Colt said.

Toke put the gun down on the table and slid it in the center. Then he leaned back.

"I think you both have bigger enemies than each other. You boys definitely been played," he said.

There seemed no denying it. My desire to kill one Judas had quickly been replaced by another. I had no idea where to turn and there was still so much confusion hanging over my head. I only knew of one way to clear it up. On that I was determined.

"We need to find him," I said.

"We?" Colt said. "If Audrey's alive, I'm in the clear. I don't need to do shit. You the one that need to find him."

"No. Dirty's right, cuz," Toke said. "Just because this guy didn't get you fitted for a murder charge, doesn't mean he's not setting you up to fall for something. There's no telling what else he has planned."

It was difficult to even process all of the information, much less formulate a strategy in the tremors of Grambo's non-stop snoring. I rubbed the vial of ashes through my shirt, the same way I always did to calm my nerves when beer wasn't available. I was still wishing I had beer.

"Is there anyone else who might know something? Anyone else who knew Tim like you did?" Toke said.

"Nah, man. Not that I know," Colt said. "He kept us in the dark."

That darkness provided cover for all his planning. It allowed him to show us only what he wanted us to see, glimpses of a plan that won our loyalty and secured our involvement. He teased peaks behind the curtain, enough to show picturesque snapshots of revenge and money and freedom, a promise of a better life and lost family restored. He controlled access to shadows. He guarded the unlit vault.

But nobody is perfect. And I knew no matter how careful, he had to have missed a single light somewhere. I just had to find it and flip the switch.

13
The Lesbian

I didn't have much option but to be glued to Colt's side until we had it all sorted out. He'd already proven a willingness to screw me over and I'm sure fidelity was the last thing he expected from me. We weren't letting each other stray very far from our periphery. Big and Toke still tagged along. I guess they wanted to make sure I didn't take the first opportunity to crack open their cousin's skull. Maybe they were hoping to see some of that money too. First thing we did was head to that storage facility and we were there at 6 a.m. sharp when the main gates opened.

We walked to the small compartment that Tim and Colt had rented in the middle of a long row of identical units, distinguishable only by an engraved number-plate on the front. Everything was locked tight with patrolling security guards and 24/7 camera surveillance in place to deter theft. My guess is Tim felt those things would give Colt a false sense of safety and simultaneously keep him from creeping back by himself. It didn't seem like there was any way the lock could be cut off or picked without getting someone's attention. All looked well intact and Colt's key still worked without a problem.

I was feeling a little camera-shy seeing as how I was a man more sought after than I'd ever been. Fortunately, the werewolf stubble consuming my face was a huge departure from the picture being plastered in newspapers. I even popped the lenses from a pair of Grambo's old reading glasses and wore the frames with a wool skull-cap like a hipster in a college band.

As Colt raised the rolling door, a fart-cloud of musty odor wafted out to greet us. Dust stirred up so thick, light was visible in distinct bands around the threshold and twinkling particles looked as big as snowflakes. He said everything appeared just like they left it. Most of the space was empty aside from a pile of old comforters in one corner and a broken wood pallet in the other, remnants of the previous tenants.

"It's right here," he said as he walked toward the blankets.

He yanked them up expecting the worst. But to our surprise, it was still there. The briefcase lay on the ground, untouched since he'd dropped it off. By the awkward smile he gave to the others, I think Colt immediately started to regret telling me anything as his hope in personal riches was just about restored. Then he tried to open it.

"It wasn't locked when I had it," Colt said.

He spun the little numbered dial and tried again but it wouldn't open.

"The code ain't working," he said.

"Maybe you forgot it," Toke said.

"I know the damn code," Colt said. "Just let me think."

I pulled the tire iron out from the trunk of my car and jammed it in the seam where the edges met. Then I beat the thing on the ground until I ripped the latch from its hinge. After that, the other side popped right off. With it laying flat on bottom, I lifted the lid to find tightly-fitted blocks of hundred-dollar bills wrapped in paper bands lining the entirety. It was beautiful.

I could hear nearly orgasmic hums of excitement from the others behind me until, almost in unison, we each bent down and picked up a stack. The chunks of perfectly sized bills were blank, off-white paper, the top bill only printed on one side. Completely worthless.

"Maybe the mob guy ain't give you real money," Big said.

"Nah, yo. I checked it. Flipped through it and it was all legit," Colt said. "Tim must have come back. No other way."

"He gave you the only key, right?" Toke said. "If he trusted you with that, I doubt he needed to come back. I don't think he ever let a dollar travel through that door."

"I'm telling you. My eyes were on the take the entire time. I had it in the junk truck. He picked me up and I put it in the back of his van myself," Colt said. "We drove it right here together. And then we rented the storage unit together." He was doing his best to save face, defend his street smart sensibility. He didn't need to though. We were all just as gullible at some point.

"Why the back of the van?" I said.

"In case we got pulled over. He said a cop might see it and get suspicious," Colt said. "The only time he even touched it was when I was unlocking the door to the storage. He pulled it from the back of his van himself."

"Well, then he pulled out a different case than the one you put in," I said.

"Nah, man. It was the only case. The back of the van was empty," Colt said.

"You *thought* it was empty. He probably had another case set up under a panel in the back seat or the floor board, maybe in the space where the spare tire is supposed to be. And he set it up with fake bills in case you wanted to see it before you locked it up," Toke said.

"The same way we inspected the first two million. Looking without touching," I said. "How much you want to bet no money ever made it in the warehouse locker either?"

A distant thought abruptly returned and jolted Colt's brain into a semi-adequate functionality. He bent back down and fondled a thick lined pocket inside the lid of the briefcase. I didn't even realize the pocket existed until he poked through with his hand and felt around.

"Damn," he mumbled. Then he glanced up at us before turning his head to hide his face. "You right. It's not the same case I had in the junk truck," he said.

"How do you know?" Toke said.

"I saved the burner phone," Colt said. "It was here in the pocket."

"Why didn't you destroy it?" I said.

"It was a nicer phone than the one I have, man. I was going to get a new SIM card and re-use it," he said.

"You cheap bastard," I said, practically fuming smoke from my nostrils. "You were supposed to walk away with a million bucks and you're so worried about a couple hundred that you save a piece of evidence that ties us to the crime of the decade?"

He was without words. I had plenty more for him.

"You at least threw away the SIM card though, right?" Toke said.

Colt still didn't answer, not verbally anyway. He only held a pathetic, defeated look on his face and stared at us through pitiful eyes.

"Please tell me you threw away the SIM card," Toke said again.

"I, I was going to. I just forgot about it after he told me Dirty was on to us," Colt said. "I was distracted."

"That buries you. You realize that, right?" I said. "If anyone finds it and connects it with the slum fireworks display we set off, those are your finger prints on it, your sweat, your DNA. You opened it, you set it up for service, you talked on it."

"I know, I know," he said. "I fucked up, alright."

"And God forbid Tim finds it and figures out what you did. He could have that damn thing express delivered to the Feds right before he charts off to hide on some island in the south pacific," I said.

I kicked the lid of the briefcase closed and slammed it against the side wall. It didn't help none. I just wanted to vent my frustration. We sat there for a good minute, saying nothing and stewing in our own brand of despair. But I guess a glimmer of light is easiest to catch surrounded by pitch black.

"What if he didn't find it?" Colt said. "What if he ran with the bag just like he got it and didn't find the phone? I never powered it down and it might still be on. With the screen off, that bitch probably got some juice left."

"So? You wanna call him?" Big said.

"Nah man. Maybe we could use it to track him like he was doing us. GPS should be working on it," Colt said. "I turned the sound off so he won't even know."

"You know how to do this?" Toke said.

"No, but I know someone who does," Colt said.

"The lesbian?" I said.

He nodded.

Then I grabbed the case full of play money and held it shut under my arm before we headed out. It too was evidence and I wanted it destroyed.

"I hope you're all comfortable in your own skin," I said. "She ain't a fan of clothes."

It's a pitiful thing to be so desperate that you have to rely on the luck of an idiot's mistake. But that's where I was. I felt like I was trapped in a snake pit, one that I'd jumped into with a simpleton's smile. Bitten once with no way to tell how many vipers still surrounded me, all I could do was reach for a single tattered rope to pull myself out. My sole chance for redemption. I was grateful for it, even if it was only dangling there through

Colt's lack of good sense. I never admitted that to *him* though. I reckon that would have encouraged stupid behavior and we'd already had enough of that. I focused on the task ahead, happy to have some measure of renewed hope. Even if it meant I had to get an eyeful of male nudity.

For the entire ride to Claire's apartment, I had to listen to three grown men cry like toddlers over the prospect of seeing each other naked. They almost blamed me like it was my rule, as if I was excited about being surround by more bare black skin than salmon in a seal pond. I quickly shot down that idea. And I made it crystal clear that I was going to punch someone in the throat if they didn't quit whining about it.

When we pulled up to the pizza pub underneath her apartment, I nearly had one foot out of the door before Colt stopped me.

"Yo, yo. Red hoopty," he said.

Two guys sat in a sedan looking toward her place from the end of the block. The window tinting kept the inside of the car too dark to see their faces but it was strange enough that we were spooked.

"What do you think?" I said. "Police or Mexicans?"

"Police would already be dragging her to a windowless room," Colt said.

"Mexicans would already be grilling her up in her apartment," I said.

"Who said they ain't? That wagon could be two dudes lighter than when they came."

"It doesn't matter who it is," Toke said. "Neither of you can go. Everybody involved has both your mugshots taped to their dashboard."

"I don't care. We need her," I said.

"I know," Toke mumbled as he zipped up his jacket. "I'll go. Just call me if you see any movement."

Big looked over at his brother and shook his head. "You ain't going alone."

They grabbed each others' thumbs in a bro-like handshake or gave high fives or *something* to show their unity. I'm not sure. I didn't see. I only heard the slap of skin and didn't care enough to turn around toward the back seat to watch them jerk each other off in celebration of a solid kinship. It's not that I wasn't appreciative of their help. I was just more concerned with that strange car and the situation at hand.

As Toke and Big got out to go after Claire, I watched her apartment window. It sat one floor higher than the buildings on either side though they were all connected, bricked together in city block fashion. There were no signs of life. But my eyes stayed on it, waiting for trouble to show itself. I had no intention of running away. In truth, I was eager to stomp it out.

There weren't a whole lot of words between Colt and I after they left. Not initially. It's hard to make small talk with a traitor who intended to screw you out of a better life and leave you to face the wolves alone. And I suppose it's equally uncomfortable to be on the opposite side of that table, to sit with a man who knows you done him so wrong. I wasn't about to make it easy for him.

"So, you met Claire in her apartment, huh?" he said.

There was a long pause before my response. I was deciding whether or not to even give one.

"Yup," I said as short as possible.

"I only met her when she was setting up the cameras for Tim," he said. "I ain't ever seen it up there."

I was silent despite his obvious grabs at instigating small talk. That quiet lingered for a full minute or two. Then he smiled and gave out a slight laugh, more a quick burst of wind through his nose before he opened his big mouth to try again.

"You know why lesbians are bad drivers?" he said.

I hardly even acknowledged him, giving the briefest scowl before watching the window again with clenched jaws. It was enough of a warning signal that he just stopped trying to be pleasant.

The scouts in the car hadn't moved and there were no signs of activity from our perspective. I looked at the clock on the car radio and decided that I'd only give fifteen minutes before going in and tearing through anyone that stood in my way.

"I really didn't know about the kid," Colt said. "I mean, I still don't know nothing. If he set you up to do time for something like that, he ain't say nothing to me."

"But you were going to help him grift my cut after I risked my life for the both of you," I said.

"I was blinded by Benjamins. What do you want from me? I know it ain't no excuse. I tried not to chill with you much because I knew what was up when we started," he said. "But more we was talking and hanging together, serious, I felt bad about it."

"Not bad enough to warn me though. And then, knowing he was bending me over, to be stupid enough to not think he wouldn't do the same thing to you?" I said.

"You right. You right about all of it," he said. "If I could do it over, I wouldn't let myself get played. And I wouldn't leave you out to freeze."

I faced away from the apartment to look him in the eyes as I spit my venom. "I'd have to be some kind of stupid to ever trust you again and I'm not. So I won't. Once this is over, you're dead to me."

"I don't blame you. I wouldn't believe me either," he said. "I'm still sorry. Take it or leave it, whatever. That's on you. But I just need to tell you for my own peace."

I didn't want to hear it. No way would I ever count on him again. No way I'd give him another chance. Hell, I didn't want to work with him to begin with.

We watched people going into the bar but nothing looked too far from normal. Just young white guys with plaid shirts and thick-framed glasses and lumberjack beards. Then one of the two strangers got out of the car and stood next to the building closest to them. We still didn't know which team he played for, but I'd have bet the house that English wasn't his first language. He leaned against the brick and lit up a cigarette, keeping the majority of his body hidden behind a newspaper box.

"I still can't believe Tim dicked us over." I'm not stupid. And Colt was persistent. He couldn't just sit there quietly and watch the Mexican bystander like I was doing. Maybe he figured out he had a better chance of survival with me than against me. Maybe he was afraid I'd hurt him myself. Whatever the reason, he kept trying to bond. I played along for my own reasons.

"How did you get hooked up with Tim anyway?" I said.

"He bought some herb off me," Colt said.

"Weed?"

Colt nodded.

"I thought he hated the stuff. He was always on your ass for lighting up," I said.

"Yeah, no kidding. I'm thinking those was good faith sales to prove he ain't no narc before inquiring about the full range of my offerings."

"Like the roofies," I said.

"Among other things, yeah. He eventually asked if I wanted to make some quick cash and we ran a few short games. Then I told him about my pops," he said. "I ever tell you why they call me Colt?"

"I figured so you could tell girls you were hung like a horse."

"Nah man. They figure that out on they own."

He smiled, like we were exchanging jokes and becoming buddies. But I was serious. That sounded like the kind the lame strategy he would run.

He continued, "It was my pops. The man loved to play the ponies. Every Saturday, he'd go the track and take me with him and we'd watch races all morning. I used to help pick out who he'd bet on. That's what he let me think anyway. So one time we was there, he looked down and he says, 'Boy, you my little colt,' right before he won a fat stack. Most cash he ever won in a single day. That was it and ever since, I was Colt," he said. "Pops told me I was his good luck charm. Me and his pocket rosary."

"He sounds like a decent guy," I said. It made me think of the kind of dad I wished I'd had, the kind I wanted to be.

"He was the best. Raised me all by himself after my moms left," Colt said as his smile quickly subsided. "He hit a long string of heart-breakers though and wasn't long before he couldn't cover his bets. He owed his bookie, the bookie owed Carmine Moreno, ergo my dad owed Carmine Moreno."

"Carmine killed your dad?" I said.

"Not personally but couple of his people did. He came home with a broken hand one day, broken leg the next week. A month later they found him in a dumping ground, the same one where we parked the hearse that you were hiding in. He was all kinds of beat up, had two bullets in the back of his head and a racing-form stuffed in his mouth. All over three thousand dollars. That's what he owed. Anyway, I told Tim all about it and after that, he told me his plan to get Moreno."

I hated him. I hated what he'd done to me. But I could relate to him in a lot of ways. And I felt bad for him as much as I couldn't stand him. Probably the only thing worse than having a bad father, is having a good one and losing him over something so trivial as money. Against my wishes, I could feel my guard dropping again, even if only slightly.

"Why didn't you ever tell me about your Carmine connection?" I said.

"Tim told me not to, thought you might catch on if you knew," he said.

Another light clicked on as I listened. All of the secrets hiding in the shadows were coming to surface even if too late to really be helpful. It wasn't until then that I even suspected it.

"He didn't bump into me by accident, did he?" I said.

"He said we needed someone who was personally committed, who had motive beyond the coin," he said.

"Seems he needed two people like that," I said.

He nodded before looking out the window, no doubt concentrating more on his past than anything his eyes were seeing. "Why they call you Dirty anyway?" he said.

I almost lied to him, nearly gave him the same pile of shit I'd fed everyone else who'd ask me my whole life. Somehow though, I felt like having screwed me over, he owed me. And I could tell him the truth without worry of ridicule because after everything, he wouldn't dare. I guess I also figured he might not feel quite as bad about his own father's absence.

"I didn't have real parents. We were always broke. Raised myself pretty much since I could walk and you know how it is being a kid. Without some guidance, hygiene ain't exactly a priority. So every time police would nab me doing something stupid, which happened more times than I can count, they'd say, 'we picked up that dirty kid again, caught that little dirty bastard.' It didn't become a thing until cops said it in front of the other little shits I went to school with," I said. "I was probably nine years old, maybe ten."

"Po was calling you a dirty bastard to your face as a kid?" he said. "Cold."

"Yeah, well. In fairness, it's nicer than what I was calling them to their face," I said, smiling for the first time in days.

I never took my eyes off of the Mexican who stood leaning against the building, obviously waiting in the wings for something. He abruptly threw his cigarette down, then he pulled a phone from his pocket and put it directly to his ear. I didn't find it none too alarming at the time.

"So go ahead. Tell me."

"Tell you what?" he said.

"Why lesbians are bad drivers," I said.

"Oh," he said. "Because they're women."

I didn't respond. Not even a little. I couldn't.

"You ain't get it?" Colt said.

But my eyes were fixated elsewhere. I pulled the gun from inside my shirt and stared straight ahead. Then he turned around and saw what I was seeing.

"Call them back. Now," I said.

The man against the building had put away his phone and pulled a black and gold bandanna out of his pocket to cover the bottom half of his face. So did his buddy after he'd gotten out of the car. From around the opposite corner, two more Latinos showed up wearing ample displays of red fabric. They nodded at each other from across the block. They knew each other.

"They flying gang colors, man. If they Carmine's people, why they tagged?" Colt said. I could hear the phone ringing through Colt's earpiece, but Toke wasn't answering.

"Diversion. Something's going down," I said. "They're pinning it on the Bloods and Kings."

If they were going in after Claire, I couldn't just sit back. Assuming they were just going to use her to find Tim, she could wind up with a bullet in the head. And I wasn't going to let that happen. *We* needed her.

As I slid out of the car, I saw Claire climbing through the window—not the one that overlooks the road, but one that directly accesses the neighboring roof. She was moving right above the greasers' heads and they had no idea. Toke climbed out behind her. Big shortly after that. I don't know if she had a camera system set up or what, but somehow she'd been tipped off. They knew what was coming. That didn't mean they didn't need more time to get away though. I was attempting to give it to them.

The two punks sporting black and gold were watching the three reds enter the bar. I deduced how this would work. The fake Bloods were setting the stage, going in as if bangers would ever step foot in a joint like that to just get a drink. The two Kings were lagging behind, waiting so that when they waltzed in, it would appear like rival gang members just happened to stumble on each other and trouble would erupt. Maybe a fight, maybe a few shots fired. Anything like that would make kicking down her door or dragging her out less of a concern to any patrons brave enough to stick around.

I was about to ruin their plan six ways to Sunday.

They were waiting there, one watching the door to the bar, the other fixated on his damn cell phone. God knows how much time they planned to give their buddies before they walked in after. I wasn't giving them shit. I moved as slyly as possible and ran through an alley until I came out on the corner behind them. I pulled up my shirt until it covered the bottom half of my face, then peeked around and fired a few shots into the hand of the banger holding the phone. I figured that was his dominant hand and if it could grip anything, it could also hold a gun. I couldn't have that. Without hesitation, I turned and blasted through the kneecaps of the other one. He was no longer a threat, grabbing his legs in agony and screaming for help. The first thug reached for a piece with his only remaining good hand. I wasted no time pushing him down and whaling on him until he stopped moving.

I didn't hear no gun shots come from the rooftop above. I guess adrenaline or focus on my own confrontation had blocked them out. But the aftermath of fired bullets came down force-fully, too overt to ignore. Blood splattered like rain, followed by the thump of Big's limp body. It hit the pavement in front of me, his head cracking open and staining the sidewalk in a quickly drawn puddle of red. He didn't feel that pain though. He was almost certainly dead from the multiple holes in his chest.

The immediate shock of it made me recoil allowing doubt and anger to follow. Without delay, I turned and ran, knowing I'd done my best to give Toke and Claire a chance to escape. I hoped it was enough but I didn't have much time to worry about them. It was only about a half-block away before I ran into the backup crew we never knew was there.

Four more Mexicans jumped me. I tried to fight back but I ain't sure I landed even a single blow worth mentioning. I was simply outnumbered. They beat me until I was laying on the ground, curled in a fetal position trying to protect my vitals. They kicked my head and legs and ribs and back. I was blinded by the blood that was flowing from every natural hole in my face plus a few gashes they added to my scalp.

"*Anda a la puta que te parió,*" one of them shouted.

I don't know what it meant but I guessed they realized my identity. That recognition is probably the only thing that prevented them from stomping on my neck sideways and taking me out with a quick spinal snap. Whether or not that inaction was more merciful is a matter of debate. I remember feeling my body being thrown down on a hard metal floor, then encompassing movement all around me. I was being transported in a van, maybe a truck bed. I was swaying in and out of consciousness, my vision going from blurry crimson to gray to black. I didn't feel any sunlight, only a cold steel floor.

I never expected to wake up.

14
Meet Your Maker

I saw my brother. There was this old lady with him and they were talking and laughing, sitting side by side on a park bench. That's what it looked like from a distance. As I got closer, I noticed it wasn't a bench but a row of rough wood stumps grown through the sidewalk. The old lady hugged my neck and called me *dad*. And I recognized her as my daughter, Nina.

I swatted at large mosquitoes that kept trying to sting us but I couldn't kill them. They were just too fast. Nina pointed out dirty water that was rising from the ground and told me the bugs were attracted to it. I hadn't noticed the muddy sludge until then but it was already at my ankles and getting deeper by the second. So we ran, Ash leading the way.

It got harder and harder to keep up with them and I remember having the feeling that they were actually running from *me*. Dusty water was up to our waist by then. They were so far away, so out of reach. In an instant, something pulled them straight down from below until they disappeared beneath the surface. By then, I couldn't run anymore. The dark liquid was swallowing me too. It was terrifying.

But it wasn't real.

The first thing I saw when I opened my eyes was Jesus. He had a crown of thorns smashed down low on his forehead, his scalp torn to shreds and his mouth warped open as if screaming in agony. His cheeks were gaunt and sunken. His eyes were rolled-back in his head, flowing with tears that looked like blood. Then again, the whole painting was cast in scarlet. Variations of brown and amber and deep red that created a monstrous depiction of a figure so easily recognizable even if distorted. It was unsettling, probably more so because I recalled that style of the artwork. It was the same kind I saw behind Carmine's desk when we paid him a visit.

I had woken up from a dream into a nightmare.

My right eye would only open partially from swelling. A familiar metallic taste filled my mouth from wounds. I started going through a mental checklist, focusing on body parts in segmented chunks to gauge just how badly I was injured. Breathing was difficult like my lungs were being pressed down with cinder blocks and I was being gouged by a sharp stick with every inhale. My ribs and back were sore and sensitive to movement. God only knows what kind of internal bleeding I had going on. Both hands were tied behind me with my arms wrapped around the back of the chair they sat me on. Wrestling with the rope didn't help. The attempt only dragged coarse fibers against my wrists until they were rubbed raw. The pain was extensive, almost too much overall to focus on any one area. I felt like Jesus looked.

The dim storage room appeared especially dingy through my limited vision. There wasn't very much worth seeing anyway. All the walls in my view were decorated with those hideous paintings, so many that stacks of them remained sitting on the concrete floor, leaning against the walls. They were all different depictions of religious imagery, all in that gloomy chromatic scheme, all focused on suffering.

I heard a door quickly close to my right before I even knew it had been opened. They were checking on me, waiting for me to wake up. And just as quickly as they came, they left the room to relay that information.

I tugged on those ropes in desperation and ignored the pain of them gnawing into the flesh on my arms. I tried slow calculated movements, looking for any give in the knots. Then I tried hard yanks but nothing seemed to get me any closer to freedom. I arched my spine and bucked, throwing my shoulders back wildly but that only succeeded in hurting my head as I cracked it into another skull.

Until I heard the impact grunt, I thought I was alone. The way my body was locked onto the chair, I couldn't turn to tell who was behind me. I had little doubt that they were bound up too.

"Hey, can you hear me?" I said.

I received no answer other than a deep, muffled moan. It sounded male though.

"Colt, is that you?" I said.

Before he could answer, the door to my right opened again, slowly making way for that thick tree trunk of a Mexican. Thiago swaggered in and shut the door behind him. Then he hovered in front of me, looking down on me in his best effort to intimidate.

"You look like the rough side of hell. I've seen dog fight losers in better shape," he said. "Where's your friend?"

"Which friend?"

"You know who I'm talking about."

"I have lots of friends," I said as smugly as possible having been beaten half to death. "I'm very popular."

I suppose it's in my nature to be uncooperative and defiant and, when dealing with animals like him, even belligerent. In that defenseless predicament though, I would have been better off to refrain from sarcasm. He wasn't amused.

Thiago looked around for a moment before calmly picking up a long, rusty screw from the floor. He bent down and held my knee with one hand and put the tip of the screw through my jeans with the other. Then he pressed it into my thigh. It wasn't a quick stab. It was a slow and tortuous turn, constant pain as it broke through fabric, then skin, then muscle. The real pain came when he ripped it out. I couldn't help but scream.

"Where is your friend?" he said.

"I don't know. I'm looking for him too," I said.

He inserted the screw into my leg again, this time three inches closer to my crotch. Even through the anguish, I was coherent enough to see where this was eventually heading. I cried out, then stared down at the two holes blooming a stain in the denim around them as they bled. The room spun just a bit and colors began to turn gray. I could feel my head droop involuntarily. My eyelids were wavering, closing and fluttering against my will. It was a struggle to remain conscious. I lowered my head and took deep breaths through my nose until the vertigo diminished. He stood back, allowing me opportunity to regain strength so he could take it away and grill me some more. His feet were the only thing in my view when he stepped forward again.

"I won't let you black out on me," he said as he slapped my cheek lightly, forcing me to look up at him. Then he waved the screw in front of my face so I was sure to see the tiny bits of flesh it had extracted.

"I'm glad Moreno's dead. He was a piece of shit," I said. The words came out as forcefully as my diaphragm could push them. It was still a mumble.

I expected him to beat me unconscious for it. At the very least, knock over the chair I was tied to and kick me for the disrespect. Instead he bent down and looked into my eyes.

"Yes. Yes, he was." he said. "Hell, killing that *maricón* was the only thing you *pendejos* did right."

Then he stood back up and pressed his finger harshly into one of the cuts on my scalp. I resisted letting him know just how much that hurt. He wiped the blood from his finger across my shirt as he continued.

"Where you went wrong was stealing all that money and trying to frame me. You had the *cojones* to leave her body in my warehouse like street trash? You failed just so you know. I cleaned it up myself. No one else knows nothing," he said. "*Puto bastardo.* Audrey didn't need to die."

There was something in his expression that gave him away. I can't even pinpoint exactly how I picked up on it. I guess the bitter scowl spoke just as much as the words it accompanied. His eyes, his vocal inflection, his flared nostrils and the frown lines around his mouth. There in all lived grief, pain from personal loss. The underlying entirety of what he just told me hadn't registered yet though. My thoughts still weren't completely lucid, but the gears started turning.

"That wasn't us. It was Tim. He screwed all of us," I said.

"Tim?" Thiago said. "Who the hell is Tim?"

"The one who did all the talking when we gamed Carmine," I said. I thought for a second that maybe we weren't talking about the same person.

"You don't even know his real name?" He scoffed. "Even your friend behind you knows that."

With my face so swollen and bruised, surprise may not have been so evident. Every thought of Colt and his loyalty were instantly shrouded with doubt. My mind began to well up with anger and I contemplated quickly arching my back to headbutt him again.

"What makes you so sure *you* know his real name?" I said.

I could see the contempt on Thiago's face. He angrily charged toward me but didn't touch me. Instead, his beefy hands grabbed the chair of the other captive and angrily slid it around so we could see other. I fully expected to face Colt and I was thrown for a loop the second I saw white skin. The man was so badly beaten, he was hardly recognizable. Both eyes were swollen shut. Blood completely covered the bottom half of his toothless face. It made me wonder if I appeared just as awful. His big ears and neck tattoo were still in tact though. That's the only way I could identify him.

"Twinkie? What the hell?" I said. "He had nothing to do with any of this."

"Is that right?" Thiago said.

Thiago removed a large knife from his waistband and cut the cloth stifling Twinkie's mouth. Tears started to seep through the tightly compressed slits that his eyeballs were hiding behind.

"I'm sorry Roy. All I did was tell Phil some stuff about you. Carl and Tonto both done time with him. They said he was a prison whore and didn't want nothing to do with the guy on account of him having the itch and all," he said. "I'm so sorry. I didn't know what he was intending."

"You told *Phil* about me? What did you tell him?" I said.

"Just general stuff. Everything I knew, things you done told all of us at the house," Twinkie said. "Your past and family and likes and work habits. No secrets. Nothing he couldn't find out by talking to you anyway which he told me he was doing because he was vetting you for a job opportunity. I'm so sorry."

Tim—or Phil, whatever the hell you want to call him—had cased me, done research like he did for every mark he ever conned.

"How much did he give you?" I said.

Twinkie wouldn't answer that question with anything but weeping. I guess it couldn't have been much. Maybe thirty pieces of silver.

"I thought I was just giving you a good reference," Twinkie said. Then he stared at Thiago. At least, he turned his head toward him. I don't know if he could actually see a damn thing through eyelids so tightly swollen shut, he could have been blindfolded with shoestring. He looked like an oriental kid with

Down Syndrome. "Please, I told you everything I know. Let me go home, please. I won't even go to the hospital and I won't say nothing to nobody. I promise. I just won visitation rights with my kids and I only want to go home and see them, please." He tried to plead his case some more but the sobbing turned his words to gibberish.

"Shh, shh. Relax, little girl. Don't worry," Thiago said as he put his hand on Twinkie's shoulder, oddly comforting him. Then he looked at me. "So this guy really didn't have nothing to do with it?"

I was angry but not at Twink. He was just a chump like the rest of us and there was no need to drag him down any further. I feel like I could forgive him because at least he had good enough intentions. I can only hope he felt the same way about me and my words.

"He wasn't involved," I said. "He doesn't know anything."

"Then he's useless," Thiago said.

As soon as those words left his mouth, he grabbed a handful of Twinkie's hair and pulled his head back. In the same quick motion, Thiago dragged that large blade across his throat, slicing it from one side to the other. The arterial spray hit my face from several feet away. He used the butt of the knife like a pivot point, pressing it against the spine of Twink's neck while he tugged back on his scalp. The poor bastard's whole throat opened up. He couldn't scream, couldn't fight back. All he could do was stare at me with frightened doe eyes. I couldn't tell if he bled out or suffocated, but his life faded quickly.

Thiago almost looked high from it. He had this crazed stare and a smirk that showed he was uncontrollably pleased with himself, all followed by a relieved exhale of satisfaction. It was like watching an addict get his fix. That expression vanished as soon as he became aware that he held it. Or maybe aware that I noticed it.

"That was no man," Thiago said. "If he really has kids, I did them a favor."

He tried using Twinkie's shirt to wipe off the blade but the fabric was already too saturated with blood. So he cleaned it on the edge of the Jesus canvas. Red accumulation ran down the corner of the art and dripped to the floor as he stared at it and shook his head.

"Look at these fucking things. They creep me the hell out," he said. Then he pushed over a stack of those paintings that leaned against the wall. "You know what these things are?"

He looked at me but I didn't give an answer. I don't think he really expected one.

"They're a monument to Carmine's weakness," Thiago said. "It was an insult to have a Colombian ranked over us to begin with, especially since it only happened to fulfill some favor between the bosses. But him ordering us around like we're his *mayates? Besa mi culo.* I don't care how long he lived in Mexico. He wasn't Mexican."

I couldn't tell if he was letting the gravity of the situation simmer in my head or if he was merely savoring the feeling of power and control that killing gave him. Maybe he was still letting me recuperate before tormenting me further.

"But the worst part about it, Carmine had no backbone. I found that out a long time ago when he was first made. That fool wasn't across the border a month when he demanded I show him the route our drivers were taking. Didn't trust me to plan it, no. Big man had to drive it himself. It was a clean truck, too. Should have been no pressure, no stress. Easy. Just driving an empty delivery truck."

Thiago cut the ties from Twinkie's body and dumped it on the floor while he spoke. The semi-detached head twisted so awkwardly when it thudded against the cement, I half expected it to come fully undone and roll away. With the chair turned around rearward, he slid it in front of me and sat down, straddling and leaning on the back of it.

"He was so focused on bragging to me what a big shot he is down south, trying to convince me what a hard-nose gangster he is, he drives too fast, stops paying attention. And what does he do? BAM. Runs over a little boy on a tricycle. And I mean *over* him. Popped his head open like a crushed melon," he said with a laugh.

Thiago wouldn't put down the knife. He waved it to express and emphasize his words.

"Big boss Carmine Moreno froze up, sat behind the wheel all panicked. Meanwhile, the kid's mother is running over and screaming for help. So who has to clean up his mess? I do. I'm the one snapping the cunt's neck and scraping pieces of undeveloped brain off the blacktop. I'm the one digging a hole to burn the bodies. I was the only one who knew what a coward he was. Nobody ever learned nothing about it but me and him."

Except I knew better. I remember laying in a coffin and listening in on an earpiece while Carmine was informed that his secret wasn't as safe as he thought it was. Thiago had shared that story before. When Carmine was driving toward his demise, maybe he realized then what I was just figuring out while I sat in that chair.

Thiago continued, "From that day on, he showed how weak and superstitious he was. He started buying these hideous things from a priest in some Colombian monastery. Supposedly the dude paints them with blood from his own stigmata. You believe that? And Carmine put one of these abominations in every room to ward off evil or some shit. From day one, he couldn't ever make tough calls and after the accident, he got even softer. He couldn't keep our people in line or our competition at bay. That's where I come in. That's what I'm good at. I built our reputation. I gave us credibility."

Thiago stood back up. He was done bathing in the afterglow of his slaughter and was preparing himself to come at me again. With a quick kick, he slid the empty chair so it toppled over after hitting Twinkie's head. The blade in his hand slowly came forward toward my eye and he kept it there, waving it inches away. I didn't flinch.

"He was a businessman. I am a warlord. I control the green lights, I decide who lives and dies," Thiago said. "And now, you're going to tell me everything you know. I want my money. I want Philip DePoe's head."

Thiago didn't realize how personal those words were to me. He was making a threat; I heard a confession. Carmine never gave a go-ahead to have my brother killed. Thiago did. For that alone, he deserved to die.

Maybe it was the adrenaline from hearing that revelation or watching a man get executed, but I'd woken up. The clarity of my thoughts gave birth to an idea, possibly the only shot I had for escape. Even now, I'm still not sure how I added up the pieces so quickly. But once it clicked, everything else fell into place.

"What time is it?" I said.

Thiago snickered.

"You got somewhere to be, *esé?*" he said.

"Yeah. And you're going to let me go," I said. "I've already signed your death warrant."

My confidence threw him off. If I learned anything from watching Tim—or *Phil*, rather—it was how to sell a lie. I didn't wait for Thiago to even ask.

"See, I've already confessed," I said. "I wrote down the whole thing, all the facts I knew for certain along with anything else I ever suspected. Ain't just about me either. I included everyone. All your information is in there too."

His expression changed though he didn't look overly concerned. Not yet.

"You confessed?" he said.

"I detailed how you were working with Phil, how you were secretly plotting to kill the king, hoping to claim the throne for yourself. You wanted his money. You were sleeping with his wife. I'm assuming she ended the affair and rejected you. Were you getting revenge on Audrey too or hoping to get her back after Moreno was dead?"

He didn't give an answer. I wasn't expecting one. As I revealed all the things I'd deduced, acting as if I'd known all along, I realized even the threat that my fraud represented might be enough. It wouldn't matter if I was correct about every aspect. Hell, it wouldn't matter if I was right about any of it. The fact that I *was* right only made it more convincing.

"You're the reason Phil knew about Audrey's money stash and Carmine's secrets. You were his trusted right-hand and you influenced him to go along with the plan to use the police. You set him up to die. I may have gotten Phil's name wrong in my confession, but yours is absolutely correct."

"There ain't no proof," Thiago said. The hand holding the knife slowly began to relax and drop by his side.

"You that confident in your cleaning abilities? Audrey wasn't supposed to get hurt, I know. But she died in your warehouse and all it takes is one drop of blood. It was pretty stupid to let Phil use it to keep her hostage. You wanted to be the one to rescue her though, right? Maybe that would have won her back."

"If I do time, I do time. Even if a pig sniffs up something, I got a lawyer who—"

"Lawyer?" I said. Then I snorted out a condescending little laugh before I coughed up a wad of bloody clots. "You ain't ever going to see the inside of a courtroom. Your bosses over the border won't trouble themselves with evidence or a trial. Once my letter ties you to Carmine's death and you're exposed as a traitor, it's over, *amigo*. You think your organization is run by reasonable, forgiving men? Or your people are so loyal to you they won't pull the trigger when the order descends from above? Mutiny is a capital offense but you already know that. Why else would you have worked with someone so far removed from your usual crew? Nobody knows about this but you and me and Phil. At least not until they get a hold of my letter."

He tried to remain calm and maintain a look of indifference. But he couldn't, not completely. As soon as I saw a hint of concern on his face, my confidence began to grow. It only got easier to sell the hoax.

"And where is this letter?" he said.

"In an email. After I realized Phil had played us all, I wrote down the whole spiel as an insurance policy in case anything were to happen to me. It's scheduled to automatically send itself to a dozen or so reporters, a few news stations, police, FBI—pretty much anyone who might be interested in spreading the gospel. And everyday that I survive with my freedom, I log on and postpone delivery for 24 hours," I said.

"So it hasn't been sent?" he said.

"Not yet. But I'm the only one who can stop it and I have no idea how long I've been here," I said. With body language in mind, I paused for just a moment to straighten up my posture and lean forward as much as could. "If that email gets delivered and I go down, I'm bringing the house down with me and you're living in it. The clock is ticking. So I ask you again, what time is it?"

"I think you're lying," he said. "I think you're trying to hustle me." But those were just his words. The fact that his knife wasn't cutting into my skin told me he wasn't so sure. Even still, I could feel my heart beat faster from him calling my bluff. I needed to insert some ambiguous truth so he could see a genuine expression of honesty. I learned that from Tim.

"Well, if you're fond of high stakes gambling, wait 24 hours and let's see if you're right. I really don't care about my life anymore." At that moment, I meant it.

He grabbed my chin and pressed the blade of the knife flat against my puffy eyelid.

"How about we go into that email right here, right now. We can use my phone," he said. "I don't have to kill you, holmes. I can keep you alive and in constant pain until you do whatever I want."

"The more you torture me, the more determined I'll be to make sure that confession reaches daylight. I'll find strength in knowing it means your people will find out what a piece of shit you are. And if you wind up killing me, you're killing yourself too. You can run but you know they'll catch you," I said. "Before you bother making another threat, take a good, hard look at me. I have nothing to live for. Are *you* ready to die?"

He aggressively pushed my face away and took a step back. His eyebrows drooped downward from his forehead as if directing attention to the fierce scowl just below them. Then he pulled a pistol from the small of his back and pointed it at me.

"I guess I better start running," he said.

"There's another way!" I said. In an instant too short to contemplate anything, survival instinct rerouted my mind from the rotten hand that life had dealt me to an involuntary reaction in the interest of self-preservation. I couldn't passively accept death. My brain was saving my ass. I had turned my head to the side and shut my eyes completely. I didn't think I'd even get that sentence out before hearing gun shots ring in my ears or feeling slugs riddle my chest. But he didn't fire. I slowly looked up to see him standing there, waiting for me to continue. "You want Philip DePoe. I can find him. You want the money, you can have it."

"You can deliver both?" he said.

"I can," I said. "But I need the lesbian. And I need you to call off the dogs so I can track him down without having to dodge bullets."

He hesitated a reaction as he contemplated his next move.

"And what do you want out of it?" he said.

"My life, obviously. Other than that, I just want my name cleared. That starts with finding Phil. The police want me for something that I didn't do and I think Phil knows why," I said. "Let me go and I won't do nothing else but chase after him. And once I get my hands on him, I'll give him to you. Any money he still has, that's all yours too."

"You expect me to just let you walk out of here?" he said.

"If you're smart. We have a common goal that you're under pressure to reach and I can help," I said. "Mutual interests can turn enemies into friends."

"I don't need friends," he said. "I need to turn in somebody's head for Carmine's death. If you don't find me DePoe, I'll take my chances not having the money and turn in yours."

I didn't know how to respond to that. It looked like I might live to see another day and I was almost afraid to say anything to ruin it. But before I could get too excited for my impending freedom, he reminded me that nothing comes without a price.

"You now have another task to do every 24 hours. You're going to call me and check in, update me on your progress," he said. He walked over and looked at Twinkie's body, the cadaver resting face down on the ground at the shoulders and knees with the ass jutting in the air like a pyramid. He lightly pushed it with his foot so it fell over, easily twisting the loosely connected head in an unnatural direction. "This crybaby liked to talk and he told me all about you. I know you have a young daughter. What's her name again? Nina?"

I didn't answer. I simply clenched my jaws in anger.

Without a response, he continued, "If you don't call or you run or you steal my money or that letter ever gets out, I'll stop hunting Phil long enough to find your daughter. I'll bring her back here and I'll make a woman out of her myself, *papi*. We'll all take turns, days on end, breaking in every hole on her body until she learns how to please a wide variety of men. Then she'll spend the rest of her life turning tricks to help pay back your debt."

I didn't trust him with the dirt from the sole of my shoe but I believe he made threats with the truest of intentions. And I knew right then and there, somehow, I was going to kill him.

15
Free Lunch

I t ain't that they wantede to hide where we were going but where we came from. That's why when his lackeys drove me away, I was blinded by a cloth hood that wasn't removed until the van door slid open and they tossed me out on the sidewalk. It was a surprisingly quick release. Thiago made sure of that. I guess he bought into the threat of imminent exposure more than I expected.

The afternoon sun strained my pupils beyond their pace to adjust making it impossible to plan my footing accordingly. With my legs sorely stiff from the beating and my wrists still loosely bound together behind me, there was no chance of breaking the fall with anything but my face when I hit the concrete. Yeah, it hurt, but I was already in so much pain, another abrasion was hardly noticeable.

I rolled over and looked at the street while the van sped off, chirping rubber against the asphalt as it rounded a corner. And behind me, a muscle car full of Mexican gangsters watched me struggle to a sitting position and wiggle my hands free. The thug glaring from the passenger side window nodded his emotionless head upward as if pointing behind me with the thin strip of hair on his chin.

It wasn't until the hooker came over and helped me up that I realized I'd been discarded in front of a strip motel, *The Nomad Inn*. It was a cesspool, the kind of dump that charged by the hour and included amenities like bed bugs and gonorrhea.

"You OK, baby?" she said. That was before she looked at my face and gasped. She took a step back, horrified at my appearance but not enough to stop staring.

That little bit of interaction got the attention of her pimp, some greasy-haired douche in a track suit like he was sponsored by Nike. The skin-peddler stormed over from near the motel's office with a chip on his shoulder bigger than his balls though smaller than his mouth. He wasn't a tough guy, but I wasn't even in good enough condition to fight off a grade-school bully.

"Hey asshole, we got standards here and you're distracting my customers," he said in his trashy Eastern European accent. That's all the threat he was able to say though before a loud whistle got our attention. We all looked over at the Mexican in the passenger seat of the car, scowling and shaking his head as he watched us. "You got a problem, *Chicano?*" the pimp said.

There were no more words between them. The thug only responded by raising his arm above the edge of the door, revealing a hand cannon that rested in his lap. At the same time, we heard the distinctive pump of a shotgun being loaded from one of the other riders in the backseat. *Shick, shickt!* The pimp backed down immediately, grabbing his whore by the arm and scolding her as they walked away.

I looked at the gunman but I didn't thank him. We didn't bond over it and there was no reciprocation expected. He was just following orders and I don't speak Spanish. Besides, when he held that revolver up, I noticed his knuckles were busted and bruised. It's very possible those wounds may have been done against my face only hours earlier. I couldn't know for sure. But if so, my guess was he didn't understand why he was protecting a gringo he'd so fiercely beaten down. Then again, he probably didn't even know why they'd attacked me in the first place. He'd do it again though, or worse, as soon as he was instructed.

The next thing I knew, black hands grabbed my shoulders and pulled me into one of the motel rooms, shutting and locking the door behind me. Colt peeked out through the curtain before looking at me like he just inhaled a fart.

"Nice place," I said.

"Nice face," he said.

My legs began to tremble, so much so I didn't think they'd support me. I flopped down on the most readily-available piece of stained carpet and propped my back against the wall.

Toke sat in a fluffy chair in the corner, leaning forward against his knees with a pistol dangling from his hand between them. His eyes were red and glassy. His nose sniffled every few seconds to keep snot from dripping out. Otherwise, he stayed quiet.

Claire was on the bed, keeping her body in place and turning her head only once to look at me. She appeared just as deflated, silently stewing in deep thought over whatever tension I'd interrupted.

Nobody talked at first. We just sat there and listened to the sounds of rhythmic sex and overacted orgasms from adjacent rooms. But some people don't know how to shut up and enjoy a moment of peace.

"How did you find us? And why ain't the *Pachucos* killing you?" Colt said.

I didn't want to answer. I wanted to shut my eyes and rest. But I knew I didn't have time for that. Colt wouldn't allow it anyway.

"They won't hurt us, for now. I made a deal," I said. "But we have to find Tim."

"You made a deal?" Colt said. "What kind of deal?"

"The deal is, we give them Tim or we die," I said.

Colt reacted predictably. Whining is the only response I'd expect from him.

"What you mean *we?* I didn't make no deal," he said. "I plan on getting my black ass out the city and they can deal with that."

Claire perked right up.

"That's a super idea, brilliant even, and one I've been pushing for hours," she said, directing her derision at Toke. "If we can walk out that door, we need to do it right now. These guys are no joke. We'll each go our own way and—"

"We can't leave," I said.

"The hell we can't. You want to take your elephant-man-looking ass back for round two, be my guest. I like my head the way it is," Colt said.

Claire started to say something else but the rising anger blocked out my sense of hearing until it culminated as a fist into the wall. The hotel was such a poorly built joint that I didn't even hit sheet rock, just paneling nailed into studs.

It was effective enough though. They both stopped talking as I got back up onto my feet.

"How long were those gunmen outside?" I said.

"I don't know. Maybe an hour?" Colt said.

"Why'd they wait an hour? You think they were afraid of the herd of hooker witnesses? Or they were stymied by the duck tape holding the lock in place? These animals have no qualms about breaking down doors and executing people in the street," I said. "Do you have any idea how close you came to being slaughtered?"

None of them answered. They just stared.

"Now you listen to me. I just went through hell to give us all a stay of execution. Running won't save you. You ran once, they found you quick. They'll do it again. If you skip town, you'll just be passing on the burden to your friends and family until they catch you," I said. "What do you think will happen to your sweet Grandmother when they question her to find you?"

I pointed to my face.

"This isn't my fight," Claire said. "And I won't be leaving anybody here that can't fend for themselves."

"You don't think this is your fight?" I said.

"No, it's not," she said. "Tim was on the level with me. He only screwed me out of the one payment, the last one. After seeing all this, I'll give him the benefit of the doubt and say he just couldn't get to the bank to make the drop. I've got no reason to be a part of this anymore."

She may have been right. And if Tim never screwed her over, it was because he knew how valuable she could be. I needed her most of all.

"Why were the Mexicans after you?" I said.

"I don't know," she said. "I've done a few jobs for them before but they were all through Tim. They knew about me but never met me. They must have somehow found out my name, where I lived."

"Somehow? I'll tell you how. Tim made sure they knew. Like it or not, you're a loose end. He was working with one of the Mexican captains and they know everything about you."

If a lie is what it would take to save my daughter, so be it. I would have partnered up with the devil himself to concoct a story that would secure her help.

"How do you feel about rape?" I said.

Claire tried to act tough but her lips quivered as she spoke. "I've survived it before," she said. She was nervous already.

"Not like this," I said. "When they mentioned you by name, they called you a *free lunch*. It used to be just an MS-13 term but the other gangs adopted it to show they were just as strong as the Salvadorians. You familiar with it?"

She shook her head reluctantly.

"Mexican gangs go through two stages of initiation now. First the jump-in, where a couple of bangers will beat a recruit for a few minutes just to see how tough he is. He can't resist or cover himself. He just has to take it. They call this an *act of love*," I said. "You think I look bad? This was just a kiss."

Toke was still zoned out, rocking in place and staring at the pistol in his hand like he was oblivious. But Colt and Claire were listening intently. I had them hooked.

"Assuming the recruit survives, they'll take him out a few days later for his reward, the *free lunch*. They'll troll the streets, find a girl by herself and drag her off somewhere secluded. Then they'll hold her down and take turns raping her. And each man, right as he squirts his personal blend of felon seed inside her, he bites her, takes a chunk of flesh right off of her body. Some gnaw the face or lips, some the shoulder. I've heard a few will chomp a nipple clean off. The real animals will swallow it to prove what hardcore men they are, the way hunters drink deer blood. She becomes the free lunch," I said.

Claire's eyes became glazed and a tear leaked out of one side.

"That's not even the worst part. To demonstrate his loyalty, the recruit gets the honor of raping her one more time, but not with his limp dick. They want to make evidence nearly impossible to find, so the last thing that goes up inside her is a sawed-off shotgun. By the time they're done, half of her body is nothing more than a stain."

I don't think the devil could have come up with much better. Sadly, the only lie I told about the ritual is Claire being marked for it.

"I can't help you even if I wanted to," she said. "Like I already told these lunks, repeatedly, I don't have PIN codes to the phones needed to trace the one Tim has on him. I don't even have the phone numbers anymore."

"You didn't keep them?" I said.

"What the hell do you think? I keep them written in my diary?" she said. Then she looked over at Colt. "He activated the phones. If he doesn't have the numbers, why should I?"

"You're smarter than us. We just hoped maybe you'd have some way of tracing it," I said.

"Well, I don't. I made it habit of being very careful and that included not keeping evidence of major crimes."

"I thought you didn't know what we were doing with them," I said.

"I knew you weren't using them to socialize," she said. "I've always stayed blissfully ignorant on purpose. For my clients' protection as well as my own. This is how I don't get caught. This and not doing business with the most-wanted kidnapper in the state."

"I didn't kidnap no little kid," I said.

"I don't care," she said. "Your fingerprints were found at her house. They think you did it and you're getting a lot of attention for it. That means I no longer work with you."

"How do you know they found my prints?"

Revealing she had any knowledge about my situation was accidental. Her expression displayed her immediate regret.

"My brother is a cop. He's only a uni but he hears things and told me all about it. He wanted to know if I'd ever seen you around," she said.

"What did you tell him?"

She looked at me like I was retarded. "I told him *no*, obviously," she said.

"Thanks," I said, hoping she was being honest.

"Save it. I whistled that tune to cover my own ass," she said.

"Did he say anything else?"

"Like what? He wasn't asking for clues to hunt you down. He was just worried about me, worried I might run into you doing what I do," she said. "He looks out for me."

"I was never in that house," I said.

"You don't have to convince me," she said. "I don't rat."

"Did he say where they found my fingerprints?"

"No!" she said, snapping with the harmless aggression of a pitbull pup. Claire was getting frustrated and out of patience. She wasn't concerned about my innocence or my fate. It wasn't her problem. That's why she answered before even thinking about the question. Fortunately, after having a few seconds to cool down, her memory caught up with her emotion. "Actually, yeah. He did mention it. They found your prints on a door knob."

It only took a moment to figure it out. "A knob or a lever?" I said. No doubt, it was the one gone missing from my bedroom door at his apartment. Tim had taken two minutes in the middle of an abduction to switch them out. He planted my presence at the kid's house.

"I don't remember," she said. "They also found the stun gun used to knock the kid's mother out when the girl was taken. It had your prints too." It could only be the one we used to hit Audrey, the one I trusted my mentor to destroy afterward.

"This was all Tim. I think he stole that kid from his own girlfriend," I said. "I'm not sure why. Maybe they stole her together."

"I don't care," she said. "I can't help you and first chance I get, I'm gone."

Toke stood up and growled at her, "I told you. You're not going anywhere until you think of a way to help us." He was angry, almost foaming at the mouth. He gripped his gun firmly and looked at her with such hate, not pointing it at her, but waving it as an extension of his arm. It wasn't until then that I looked down at Claire's hands and noticed she was bound to the bed frame with zip ties.

"What's going on here, college boy?" I said.

"She's not leaving until she thinks real hard for a way to find this prick. I want him to pay for starting this whole thing. I want the Mexicans dead. They killed Big, man. And she don't even want to give it no second thought. Well, she's not leaving until she does."

I looked over at Colt. He held his hands up and shrugged his shoulders, apathetic and impotent as always. Then I took a deep breath and a minute to clear my mind. My face was throbbing and my head pounding. The last thing I wanted to do was play babysitter but I needed to defuse the situation before more problems began to pile on top of the mountain we already had. That meant making sure the gun in his hand remained dormant.

"This ain't you," I said. "This ain't the way to go about it."

"She wasn't going to stay any other way," Toke said. "She made that clear from the start."

"What are you going to do? Keep her bound up here? Hole yourself up in this Petri dish until she remembers a bunch of numbers?" I said. "If she can't help us, are you going to kill her?"

Toke's lip started to shake. The grief for Big was skewing his judgment and he was lashing out, eager to execute vengeance on anyone he could place blame. I didn't know what he was thinking. Maybe he figured I would pull the information out of her once I got there, me being the ex-con murderer and all. This wasn't his wheel house and his broken heart blinded his eyes. He wasn't really thinking at all.

"You're upset about your brother. I can relate to that better than anyone. But she's not being uncooperative because she's stubborn. She doesn't have the ability to help us and if leaving is what she wants, we'll need to let her go."

Toke stared at the wall and bobbed his head back and forth. I don't think he'd ever felt loss so personal before. He didn't know how to handle it. I was almost afraid the dangerous end of that pistol might find a new target, possibly even the head of the person wielding it.

"Look at her. She's somebody's daughter, somebody's friend. You hate the monsters who killed Big. Don't become a monster to her people," I said. "Cut her loose."

I gently slid the pistol out of his hand, watching his tears flow more heavily as he relinquished control. With little thought, he pulled a small folding knife from his pocket and set it on the table beside me. Then he flopped back down in the chair and buried his face in his hands so he could weep in limited privacy.

I ripped through the zip ties with the small blade and stared down at her face. She wouldn't look directly at my injuries, instead keeping her focus on the knife. I could see anxiety through her reluctance. And it was hard not to notice the nervous droplet rolling down her cheek.

"Do I look that bad?" I said.

"You don't look great," she said, still avoiding more than a quick glance. "How do you feel?"

"Like reheated dog poop," I said.

I don't know what made me edit my words like Claire was a little kid. I guess the leaky-eye reminded me of her feminine side despite her liking vagina as much as the rest of us. And I suppose part of me felt bad for giving her that whole rape speech. Whatever the reason, she smiled ever so slightly after hearing it.

Toke had demanded assistance at gunpoint and I had tried to scare her into cooperation. I really believed she was powerless to help from that point. At the same time, I needed to use every tool at my disposal before labeling her a dead-end and I still had one left that I was obligated to try. I'm not sure why it was the hardest option for me to utilize. I guess it made me feel vulnerable to put myself on display. But I was desperate. So I told her the truth.

"They're going to get my daughter. If I don't find Tim, they're going to steal my little girl and sell her for sex. She's only twelve," I said. "Please, if there's anything..."

I didn't cry. I don't know that I looked defeated or brokenhearted. I'm not sure my face was even capable of it. But I felt a surge of emotion I hadn't felt in years as I let those words escape my lips. I'm sure it showed.

Sadness trickled down her face from her brow to her lips, her whole face drooping like a wilted flower. She could think of nothing to offer, but I think it was the first time that day she genuinely wished she could. As a habit, I stubbornly refused to remember how much power there is in sincerity. A natural consequence from living a dishonest life, one of many occupational hazards. But for all it's strength, it did no good. There was no water in the stone. She opened her mouth to form words before she softly shook her head without offering anything but hollow breath.

"Then get out of town. Change your name. Avoid major cities for a while," I said.

"Thank you." She didn't know if she could leave or not, but I wasn't going to stop her. If she couldn't help, there was no need for her to be dragged down too. She threw her backpack over her shoulder and headed toward the door.

I disappeared into the bathroom and stared hatefully at the unrecognizable figure in the mirror. This was the first time I saw the hideous tribute to violence that my face had become. One eye was so swollen, it looked like a second pair of lips with the other appearing only marginally prettier. My nose was pushed off to one side and my cheeks were dominated by bruises. The entire bottom half of my face was painted with blood that had flowed from every natural hole in my head along with a few that were bestowed. I then understood the multitude of a gasps I'd received. Even after cleaning off as much blood and grime as possible, I still looked like a Halloween mask.

It really surprised me to find Claire still there when I walked out of the bedroom, scribbling on a scrap of paper. I guess my last humble plea for an innocent child prodded her conscience to rethink over any information she had.

"Did they really threaten your daughter?" she said.

I nodded.

"Do you think Tim really stole that missing girl?" she said.

I nodded again.

"I don't suppose you have a passport for Carlos," she said.

"What are you talking about?"

She shook her head briefly. My confusion wasn't unexpected. "I'm pretty sure Tim Prose isn't his real name," she said.

"I've already figured that out."

She continued, "See, most of what I did for him was forge new ID's—driver's licenses, passports, that kind of thing. I don't know what his real name is, but he used two other aliases. I thought it might be helpful to have them." She handed me the paper with a list of five names and waited for me to read it. "The bottom three names were passports I made at his expense, but they didn't have his picture."

I read the names but they meant nothing to me.

"Whose face was on them?" I said.

"*Carlos Esposito* had your picture," she said.

"And the two female names?"

"Both were little girls," Claire said.

Toke chimed in, "You didn't question why he'd buy fake passports for little kids?"

"He told me they were his daughters and I didn't question it," she said. "Blissfully ignorant, remember?"

It didn't make complete sense. Part of me wanted to keep believing that this was all a misunderstanding and he would clear it up if we could just find him. But I knew that wasn't true. The evidence overwhelmingly pointed otherwise.

"He was supposed to help me get my daughter back," I said. "If he made one for me, maybe one of them had Nina's picture."

"Possible," Colt said. "But if he made one for you and your kid, it wasn't to help you. It was to frame you."

I was already wanted for kidnapping. If cops were to question a witness who'd seen me visiting his apartment, they would search the bedroom where I'd slept every night. And they might just find planted passports indicating my intent to flee the country with a stolen kid, mine or otherwise. He could make sure I was buried in evidence and all of us, police included, were distracted enough to allow him time and room to escape.

"How much would you bet that he got plane tickets in that fake name too?" I said.

"That's a safe wager," Claire said. "If he wanted them found, he would have bought them online and left the browsing history overtly evident on his computer. I could check if you had it."

My mind was zoned out in such deep concentration, her words didn't register. Not at first. She adjusted her backpack and put her hand on the door to leave.

"Then again, if you had his computer, I might be able trace that burner phone," she said. "I'm sorry I can't help you. Believe me, I don't want to have to run and start my life over, but—"

"His computer?" I said. "You can trace the phone if you get his computer?"

"Probably. Unless he did complete reformat," she said.

I suddenly felt stupid to not think of it before.

"Where's my car? Did you bring my car back?" I said, looking at Colt.

"Yeah, it's across the street. But I ain't driving it back to that apartment. Last we heard, Tim's place was swarming with pigs. You know they got a couple of blues sitting on it," Colt said.

"That computer probably already in lock-up, tagged as evidence."

I think I smiled. I would have anyway had the swollen tissue around my mouth been able to move.

"I don't need to go to his apartment," I said. "I just need to cross the street."

16
Sanctuary

I had never been to a city coffee-house before that day. And after going, I don't think I'll be visiting again in my lifetime. We stood out like lepers from the college kids and business polos, all scrambling to overpay for oddly-shaped cakes and pretentious candy-lattes. I caught a few eyes on us, like they were trying to figure out the nature of our relationship. The whole atmosphere pissed me off. It's not that I minded squatting amongst hypocrites who were all just as afraid to sit in close proximity as to offend their liberal live-and-let-live doctrine by admitting they didn't want our group of misfits there. I rather enjoyed making them uncomfortable. I just didn't want to pay for the experience. Charging as much for a coffee as a couple of beers seems just as criminal as anything I ever done.

But we weren't there for a caffeine buzz. We just wanted access to free internet and electrical outlets. So we sat in a corner as isolated as we could.

"Here they are," Claire said as she dug into the digital records on Tim's laptop. "Two tickets for Carlos and his daughter to Hermosillo International in Mexico. That's you."

"Never heard of the place," I said. "What's there?"

"Drug wars mainly. But it's probably a good choice for someone looking to disappear. Combined with that fake passport, he was building a strong foundation to screw you bloody," she said. "And only slightly more buried in the folder archive, two more tickets to the same place under one of the aliases Tim used."

"If he made it to Mexico, we'll never find him," I said.

"My guess is those tickets are just to throw off anyone chasing him. I highly doubt he actually went south," she said.

"Why do you say that?"

"I recovered some files he recently deleted and there's some language audio lessons in there," she said. "He was learning French."

"We're not going to find him if he made it to Canada either," Toke said.

She continued clicking and zooming around the screen quicker than my eye could keep up. It might as well have been witchcraft for all I understood about what she was doing.

"Can you just find that phone?" I said.

"First off, it wouldn't burn your tongue to say *please* every once in a while. Give it a whirl. Second, I know you think this is a magic box filled with all of the answers to life's mysteries but it's not a genie bottle. I can't just rub the side and have it shower wishes on you."

"I only meant time ain't exactly in my favor," I said. "It was a request for the focus to be on finding the burner phone. *Please.*"

"There's a decent amount of thought and effort involved here if you want it done right. I need to sift through hundreds of files and directories, some of which are hidden, download and reinstall software, then configure everything all in the right order so nothing gets overwritten," she said, keeping her eyes focused in front of her for the entire rant. "If you're that bored you can go get me another coffee as gratitude."

"Yeah, and if you going up, I'll take one of those little fudge cupcakes," Colt said, loud enough to be heard by neighboring patrons. "Them bitches look tasty as shit."

A mother holding her young son tossed a disgusted look our way before getting up and moving to a table on the far side of the room. I would have been more worried about being recognized but having vagabond-style scruff and the face of an armless boxer, I bore little resemblance to the aged mugshot being plastered all over the news.

"What's the matter with you?" I said, restraining the throw of my voice. "This ain't no damn tea party. I should shove that cupcake up your ass."

"Excuse me for trying to enjoy the fruit of our surroundings while there ain't a gat pointed at my face. Why you got to be a dick about it?" he said.

Claire pulled her head up from the screen and slapped the table.

"You two can bicker all you want but go do it away from here. I need to concentrate," she said. "If you won't get me coffee, at least give me quiet."

I had to bite my tongue and wait patiently. Claire could have easily played ignorant. None of us would have known any better. Silence should have been an easy request to satisfy. I owed her as much.

All I could do while I sat there and watched is think about Nina. I recycled memories of that tiny baby and conceived a little girl on the verge of becoming a woman. I imagined how she might be dressing up dolls in her room or playing in the yard. But grim, mental renderings seized my thoughts the way a group of cold-blooded gangsters might invade her house. I visualized them waving a gun in Nina's innocent face, their hands covered with blood splatter from the foster parents they'd just murdered. I saw them in my mind's eye grabbing her by the hair and viciously dragging her from the safety of her bedroom. The scenario only played out worse from there.

"He deleted the applications we used but not the setup log. No surprise he didn't find it. It's a hidden file in the system folder," she said. "This is exactly why you don't leave your IT person in the dark."

"Can you get what we need from it?"

"Already did. I have them, all of them. Twelve phone numbers, twelve PIN codes," she said. "How many phones are we looking for?"

"They all been destroyed but the one," Colt said. "Hopefully the battery still got juice."

"Simple enough then," she said. "I'll ping every number. If we get a response, GPS should give us a location."

"And if there's no response?" I said.

"Then I truly can't help you," she said.

She entered the first digits and we watched the on-screen cursor become a tiny rotating circle indicating the search in progress.

No Connection Found In Network

She plugged in another number. Then another. Then two more.

No Connection Found In Network

We watched each one go through the same process of searching and not coming up with squat. It became more discouraging with every negative reply.

It was two more attempts before we got a hit and the search opened a new window in the browser. Contained within it, a map of the United States scaled out to show both coasts. Every few seconds the graphic would zoom in until it finally displayed a small street map with an address.

"This can't be right," she said. "This is only forty-five minutes away. Pennsylvania."

Colt shook his head. "Five days on the run and he that close? Hell naw. Tim must have spotted the phone and tossed it out."

"More likely he ditched the whole case," Toke said. "If he found the actual phone, he would have broken it and we'd get no signal at all."

"Unless he threw it in the back of someone else's truck or under the seat of a taxi or something. We could be tracking a ghost," Colt said.

Every theory seemed viable. I didn't care. "We have to check it out, regardless," I said. "Let's go."

"We all going?" Colt said.

I stopped myself from standing mid-movement to pause and stare him down. I want to say it was an expression of frustration or disdain, but there was an equal amount of confusion.

"Do you have somewhere else to be, kid? Some appointment more pressing than saving your own skin?" I said. I couldn't wrap my head around his mentality but I wanted to wring his neck for being so spineless.

And Colt looked at me like I was the asshole.

"I'm going," Toke said. Then he turned to his cousin. "We got to try to make things right. For Big. You should feel that debt more than anybody."

Claire chimed in as she continued to stare at the screen and punch keys. "I'll go too. At least to see what you find in P-A. I was planning to skip town anyway and there's safety in numbers."

"Guess you ain't ever seen what an Uzi do to a crowd," Colt said. "Just saying, it probably just the empty briefcase, right? So the four of us going on a road trip to look at some bag and scratch our heads in Quaker country?"

"You don't know what we'll find," I said.

"But I know what will happen if we play with fire for too long," he said. "I'm sorry about your daughter man but you can't protect her. You ain't even know what she look like. You better off to call the cops and give an anonymous tip or something."

I wanted to reach across the table and slap him. Partly because he just aggravated me with his callous apathy, partly because I had no valid argument.

"We got another hit," Claire said.

"What do you mean?"

"Another phone number got a hit. There's two phones active," she said. "This one is pinging real close to the first."

My eyes immediately went to Colt and his with me. I needed him to verify the statements he already made or confess something new. We leaned forward to speak as softly as we could and still hear each other.

"I destroyed both of mine and the two cameras in the hearse are gone," I said. "Carmine was holding one and we used one to trigger the bag. That's six."

"I burnt up the pair in the junk truck and Tim lit up the SUV remotely," Colt said. "That was on the news so I know those four are toast."

I popped my fingers out after eliminating every one like a third-grade kid doing math on his hand. "That leaves the one you decided to save and the one Tim was using."

"He was supposed to burn it. Why would he keep it?" Colt said.

Claire closed the laptop and slid it in her backpack. "Why would he need to destroy it?" she said. "It's not directly connected to his personal information, just the crime. He didn't think anyone would be able to trace it. Hell, he didn't figure in a hundred years you'd even think to try."

"That ain't his style, though," Colt said. "He was too careful."

I almost hated to agree with him but I had no choice. Like the people in his life, Tim would only keep that phone for one reason. He still needed to use it.

It was well into night when we reached the cemetery. That's where the first GPS signal led us. It wasn't a grand resting place. There were no stone walls or iron gates. It wasn't organized with rows of expensive granite markers, no statues. It was a graveyard in the simplest terms, cluttered with as many untamed trees as plain headstones, each looking like they were intruding on the space of the other. The carvings had eroded away too much over the years to be legible, especially under the glow of the cell phones we used like lanterns.

Checking out that location seemed logical since it was the first one we encountered, the closest one to the road really. It was a random, flip-of-the-coin decision, not an intentional delay. I swear on my life. Had I known what was going on, I would have given my right hand to get to you sooner. As it were, we were blind and ignorant of the nightmare you endured. So we did what seemed reasonable at the time and followed the only clues we had.

"The coordinates lead right about here." Claire stood in front of a large dogwood tree and patted on the bark. Above, I could only see silhouettes of limbs and branches wrapped in moonlight.

"You think he hid the money in a tree?" I said. Tim obviously wasn't sitting up there or anywhere else around us. Wasn't hard to deduce we were close to the phone that Colt had stowed away in the briefcase.

"No. I'm just telling you where the GPS reads. But depending on signal strength and satellite position, it's not always one-hundred percent accurate," Claire said. "It could be anywhere around here."

"Anywhere? How far off are we talking?"

"Twenty, thirty meters maybe."

"Is that for real or you just spitting numbers?" Colt said.

"It's a guess. An educated guess," she said. "Do I look like I launch satellites for a living?"

I looked up at the tree and wondered, just for a moment, if he really would have climbed the damn thing to hide the cash up above. It just didn't seem reasonable. Then I looked around at the area surrounding us and listened to my thoughts come out of Toke's mouth.

"We're in a graveyard," he said. "Only makes sense that he would bury the money. Probably right in a grave where anyone with half a conscience wouldn't bother it."

"So how we find it?" Colt said.

"Look for freshly moved dirt. He'd want to be able to dig it up quickly so the bag would only be six inches, maybe a foot under the surface." Of course, I was using my own experience burying a briefcase to make that assumption. Had I been thinking it through completely, I should have remembered exactly what I had done in the same position a few days earlier. Then we might have found it.

We decided to start at the tree, each on a different side. In a coordinated manner, we circled around the roots, slowly spiraling outward as we searched for any indication of a recent dig. The four of us followed behind each other, all of us rechecking areas to make sure nobody missed anything. Thirty meters away from the tree meant there was a sixty meter diameter to scan. And the farther we got away from the center, the harder it was to keep track of what we'd checked. We had a lot more ground to cover than time to properly do it.

I could tell Claire was running short on patience. She surely had regrets over hitching a ride with us when she could be in train station waiting for an escape pod to whisk her away from the whole mess. I can't say I blame her. That girl was smart though. I really wanted to tap her brain for all the help it could give. And aside from her chosen career path, she was trustworthy in an honor-among-thieves kind of way. I didn't want her to leave. Luckily, we were out in the middle of no man's land and I held the keys to the only ride at hand. Claire was stuck with us. Frustrated or not, she helped us search to speed things along if for no other reason.

No matter, after the better part of an hour with a handful of people scouring the area, we found nothing.

Toke stopped to look over the large plot of land we'd covered and compare it to the vast amount we hadn't. "What direction is that other signal coming from?" he said, staring at one particular spot in the distance.

Claire looked at the compass on her phone and pointed directly where he remained faced. "Somewhere that way."

"Look at those trees," he said. "I think there's a church over there."

In between branches that formed a window to the sky, the silhouette of a sharp object protruded up in the distance. It was a steeple.

"If anything is here, it's not going anywhere tonight. Let's check that out," Toke said.

Colt kicked a pile of brush that hardly moved as his foot disappeared inside of it. "We shouldn't do anything but find those papers first. You don't know he ain't coming back for it tonight."

"I don't care about the money," Toke said.

"You should care. We find that cash, we have leverage against the Mexicans *and* Tim," Colt said. "It's one step closer to freedom."

"He's not wrong," Claire said.

I knew he made a reasonable point. Believe me, it was hard to admit even in my thoughts. At the same time, I couldn't bring myself to trust Colt. Not completely. Not again. I couldn't be sure exactly what he'd do with the money if he found it and I was determined to keep an eye on him. That's why I suggested to do things like I did. "When we find Tim, I'll make him show us where he hid the money. Then the Mexicans can have both."

"You want to hike? Get to it," Colt said. "Me and Claire are gonna hunt for the stash."

"No, you're coming with me," I said.

"Hell I am," Colt said, holding a grimace like he'd taken undeserved offense.

"I ain't asking," I said. "Claire can look for the money."

"Are you insane? I'm not staying here alone," she said.

"I'll stay with her," Toke said. "We'll keep an eye out for anyone and do another pass in the opposite direction. A different perspective might help."

It's hard to believe that those two came from the same family tree, aside from the obvious physical similarities. He wasn't a criminal at heart like his cousin and, very unlike Colt, he became easier to trust with every interaction. I admired Toke's persistence despite his motivation being fueled by personal vengeance. Maybe even more so because of it.

Colt finally relented. He knew I saw him as a rat. My old brain wouldn't let go of his treachery so easily and I was determined to keep him close. Together we started walking toward the direction of the signal, the same path toward the building Toke had spotted. Darkness made it difficult to see much through the trees and brush. That also meant Colt and I were well hidden. We kept a steady pace, making our way down thin paths and not saying much about anything. I preferred it that way. Occasionally we'd hear a stick crack from a nocturnal critter going about its nightly prowl. We'd stop and look around, make sure it was nothing before we pushed our way through to the base of the steeple and the building attached to it. We were being cautious, unfortunately at the expense of time.

The church was dilapidated, completely abandoned decades before if appearance was any indication. Smaller batches of gravestones surrounded the exterior, most of which were much bigger and more ornate than those we'd searched earlier. Both cemeteries were part of the same plot of land, though separated by a decent amount of wooded property. I suppose the politically religious wanted to keep the social classes distinct even in death.

The affluent families of the congregation probably thought being buried closer to the building made them closer to God. But I couldn't help notice their headstones had worn away just as much.

I stopped for a moment to look the place over and get a lay of the land, decide on an attack strategy. A van was parked on the other end of the building, barely visible from our vantage point. I reckoned he was inside, probably hiding with his girlfriend, makings plans to escape in whatever paradise they chose. I wanted to hurt that man. And before I knew the truth, I wanted to hurt *her* to hurt him.

That's when we saw Tim. Phil. The man whose identities were a hundred and none. We hardly recognized him at first as his beard had grown fuller than my own. Not to mention he was wearing eyeglasses for the first time I'd ever seen. I doubt they were truly prescription but I can't say for sure. Turns out, I hardly knew the man at his core. But there he was, walking out of the church and toward his van.

You know, there was a day in the very beginning when Tim was grooming Colt and me to be his disciples and unwitting sacrificial lambs. He stopped us before getting out of the car right at the site of game we were about to run. "Keep your eye on everyone around you, including each other. Don't make a move until the right moment," he said. "Timing is key, so lock it up."

I should have known that's why he picked Pennsylvania. Being there was just an attempt to keep timing under his control. Through the chain of events that would eventually lead to us all to drop even further down that rabbit hole, the two of us approaching right when we did was probably the worst timing possible for everybody involved. We were too far away to catch him, too close to remain unseen.

Once we were spotted, he had no reasonable option but to jump in the van and flee. So he did.

My first instinct was to run back, grab the others and hop in our car to chase him. We had walked so far though, his head start was too enormous for us to even know what direction he blew once he made it to the street. I still remember the deer-in-headlights look on his face when he saw us walking out from the trees. Tim hesitated, if only for a second. We found where he'd been hiding and we caught him with his gloves down. Now we needed to see what he was forced to leave behind. That's the only reason we went in the church at all.

It was still a functional building in most regards. Walls, doors, carpet, even pews mostly remained present if not entirely intact. Moonlight painted the main floor through stained glass in distinct beams as it bounced off particles of floating dust. The colorful patches of soft illumination settled in the smoke from candles that had been extinguished minutes before. The view was dim going inside and only got darker the further we ventured.

Both of us searched under the seats and behind closet doors. The idea occurred to Colt that we'd probably find at least part of the money. Tim would have kept out some cash for traveling expenses he figured. I was hoping more to root out clues to where he was heading or a smoking gun that could help clear my name. I thought I'd give anything to find one. But at the darkest end of the spectrum of predicted outcomes, I never imagined coming across what we did.

"I got something," Colt said. "Check it out."

I didn't answer him, didn't even change my focus or look in his direction. At that point, he hadn't seen what I found.

"Yo, Dirty. You hear me?" he called again.

We walked up to the front of the room intended to be a sanctuary though I'm sure that's the last label you'd give it. That's where you were. His *girlfriend*. The one Tim had professed his love about so adamantly and repeatedly to Colt and me. The girl I'd threatened in my thoughts before I knew what it meant.

You were laying on the platform behind the pulpit. Still blindfolded. Gagged. Naked.

He left you bound up in such a way that every bruised limb was spread out as far as possible from your body. The position itself left little doubt as to what he'd been doing. A small amount of the blood on the floor between your thighs removed it completely.

I don't know how much of this you remember. They say younger minds are much more effective at blocking out emotional trauma that stems from sexual abuse. For your sake, I hope they're right. You were only six at the time.

When my brain finally deciphered the image that my eyes were feeding it, I contended with a surreal disbelief that refused to let my feet walk any closer. *You* were what he wanted. And this is what he wanted you for. The realization struck me that we had helped him break into social services to find you. Our assistance had facilitated your capture. Our dedication to revenge funded his escape.

I was consumed by a wave of guilt and horror for my unintentional part in any of it. My body was stunned to momentary paralysis. I could physically feel self-loathing wash over me, triggering every nerve ending from the hair down to full attention. For the first time since I can remember, probably since I was a little kid no bigger than you were when I found you, I cried. I fell on my knees in front of the church altar and I bawled like a woman in hiding, profusely but silently.

I mourned your loss of innocence. Then I mourned the loss of my own.

17
Contingency

Startling you was the last thing I wanted to do but I couldn't look at your naked body for a moment longer. The loud clanging you may recall came from me pulling off the communion tablecloth along with the serving trays that sat on top of it. That velvet decoration was the closest thing at hand to a blanket. I covered you up to your neck but you didn't flinch. We untied the cords wrapped around your wrists and ankles but you didn't move. Not at first. The purple fabric shifted on your chest as your lungs inhaled slow, shallow breaths. You were obviously alive, just not responsive.

I was as gentle as I knew how to be while removing the gag from your mouth. Your teeth were so deeply sunk into the rubber ball, my hand shook with apprehension as I pried it away for fear of causing more damage.

"Mandy? Are you OK, Mandy? Can you hear me?" Of all the things Tim lied about, I'd come to find out that your name surprisingly wasn't one of them. But you wouldn't utter a word no matter what I said to you. I suppose my voice ain't the most comforting. And your mind was somewhere distant.

The only thing I didn't remove was your blindfold. I tell myself I didn't want you to be scared having to see my mangled face. Really though, I think I was afraid to look at yours. I didn't want to see pain in your eyes. Or maybe worse, to see a vacant stare with no emotion at all.

"What do we do?" Colt said.

"I don't know."

"Should we call Toke and Claire?" he said.

He picked a horrible time to willingly yield to my lead. I was Helen Keller behind the wheel, swerving on the shoulder and barreling toward a cliff.

"I don't know."

You slowly turned your little body on its side and curled up into a fetal position. Then I sat down on the nearest ledge and looked at you, as if waiting for an answer to present itself.

"What did you find?" I said.

Colt looked down at his hand as if he'd forgotten he had something there. Then he gently set it down on the floor in front of me. A backpack shaped like a plush teddy bear. Colt reached down through the unzipped head to pull out some of your clothes and dolls, followed by a small stack of hundred dollar bills, maybe seven grand worth.

"That ain't all," he said.

He carefully pulled out a brick of homemade C-1, the same explosive we'd gifted Carmine. It wasn't armed, but had with it all the pieces to make it so. Wires, blasting caps, electronic switches.

"Did you get him more clay?" I said. "After the first batch?"

"Nah, man. Just the six blocks we used up on Moreno," he said.

"Six? Try four." I said. "I helped him load up four pounds in the briefcase."

Colt looked down as he shook his head in subdued but obvious contempt. It seemed like every time we kicked over a rock, we uncovered more of Tim's deception waiting to crawl out. "Maybe he's got the other brick stashed around here somewhere."

But I didn't give it much thought. My mind was preoccupied with all the stories he used to tell us about his girlfriend. Countless times he would his share sexual escapades, distorting details to get the approval and justification he wanted until he probably even believed them. While I tend to reserve that aspect of my life and refrain from listening to others, Colt would encourage sex stories, thriving on the depravity. Too often we'd visualize the memories he'd share if not vicariously live through them. Of course, we didn't know his history at the time and how intertwined it was with yours. We certainly didn't know you were a kid.

I picked up one of your toys to look at it. It was a doll dressed in a brightly colored outfit with a small image of a sun on the sweater. Her hair had been brushed to a mangy mess, worn out by too much attention. There was something so pure about a little girl practicing love on an inanimate object and giving way more than was needed. Definitely more than deserved.

Then I stared at you, lifelessly curled up on the floor in front of a table that had a scripture carved on the front: DO THIS IN REMEMBRANCE OF ME. It was phrased like a command from God. And it resonated with me.

"I'm going to call the police," I said.

Colt looked skeptically concerned. "That ain't the way to go about this, man."

"It's over," I said. "We need to get her help."

He got a little closer, keeping his voice down so you couldn't hear. Maybe he grew half a conscience and didn't want to scare you. Or maybe he simply didn't want to incriminate himself any further in case you were listening. "Look, I ain't trying to sound like a dick but you got to inject some reality back into this situation. Having this little girl *might* clear your name with the cops. But you don't even know if she can talk enough to tell them the truth. Meanwhile, Tim's on the run and he knows we on to him."

"The cops can go after Tim with my description. It'll be better if you back me up but I'm willing to take the heat alone if need be."

"Oh, and you think they'll just up and chase him? Man, they after you with cuffs in one hand and a noose in the other. If this kid don't talk, what you think they gonna do? They ain't gonna listen to you," Colt said. "And then what happens with the Mexos? The money?"

"The money has to be buried back there somewhere. The Mexicans can kiss my ass and search for it themselves if they want it so badly," I said.

"Even if they believe you, they ain't going to swallow that pill," he said. "We need to find that cash before we do anything. We need to find it fast."

"All you ever cared about was that damn money, you selfish son of a bitch." I stood to my feet, moved by anger and sadness and frustration. "If we do ever find the stash, I won't let you take a dime from it."

He scowled and got even closer, puffing out his chest like a Silverback trying to establish dominance. "I don't want to touch it. This ain't about being rich no more. This is about our lives. You may not give a shit about yours anymore, but I do. Toke and Claire do," he said. "And I bet Nina does. If you end up taking a fall for this little girl, what happens to your own blood? You think the state will care enough about a pedophile's kid to keep a squad car parked outside her house? Ain't like you got public opinion on your side."

I was out of answers. My thoughts were clouded. And, fuck, I hated when he was right.

He took a deep breath and relaxed his tone before he continued. "Look at her, man. She ain't in any pain. She ain't going nowhere. She's sleeping. Let her rest."

"That asshole might come back," I said. "I'm not leaving her here. Not alone."

"Don't leave. You *should* stay," he said. "But the loot really is the key to getting out of this. And Tim could be on his way to get it right now. I need to warn my cuz and go back to help them look. I just need to know you ain't doing nothing stupid while I'm gone."

I had to bury emotions, fight my own convictions. I had to withhold help from you. And it was killing me.

"Watch your step," I said, plopping my body back down to slump on a pew. I hung my head and stared at my shoes, trying to avoid looking directly at you. "He might have the last clay rigged out there somewhere."

That was hard enough, to idly sit on my hands and do nothing. Colt's pat on the shoulder may have been well-meant but it was ineffective. The only reassurance I could digest was self-granted, that at least I was keeping you out of further harm's way. But even that was short-lived. A rocky-bottom floor still awaited the impact from my fall.

As soon as Colt reached for his phone to call Toke, mine began to ring. In the few seconds it took to dig the damn thing out of my pocket, my mind had built hope that they had found the money and were calling to let us know. I wanted to hear news that we finally had everything we needed to escape the whole mess. We could start setting things right, and get you to someone who could help you recover. That's what weighed on me most heavily at the time.

Then I looked down at my phone and saw Tim's number.

I answered the call using every ounce of restraint I could muster to not scream my words through the microphone. "You sick bastard."

"We're all sick in our own way, Dirty," Tim said. "Just a bunch of animals hand feeding whatever disease afflicts our minds. At least I know what satisfies my cravings."

"I am going to find you."

Colt moved a little closer so he could hear Tim's response through the phone pressed against my ear. "I don't doubt that at all," Tim said. "In fact, I'm going to tell you where I am. And you're going to come to meet me."

"What makes you think you ever get to call the shots anymore?"

"Because I have something you want," he said.

"What could you possibly have that I'd want?"

There was no background noise, just silence until his wretched voice traveled through the line, uttering words that winded me like a punch to the gut.

"Nina," he said. "I'm looking at your daughter right now."

I couldn't respond right away. My jaws clenched and I shook with anger but words couldn't come together to express my hatred effectively.

"It's just her and her foster mommy at home right now. It's actually a real cozy place," he said.

"I don't believe you," I said. "You're a liar."

"Probably the best there ever was but I swear *this* is truth. Haven't you asked yourself why I stopped in Pennsylvania?" he said.

I was seeing red. Adrenaline was pushing my thoughts quickly in every direction, too fast to organize into any kind of strategy.

"Contingency. I was so sure they would have picked you up by now. Had that happened, the heat would have dispersed enough that I could be out of the country and out of your life," Tim said. "But I had to protect myself in the off-chance you showed up. And there you are. So here am I."

"If you touch my kid, I will hunt you down and invent ways to keep you in pain."

"I don't want your kid, Dirty. I want my kid," he said. "She's special to me."

"You think I'll give up this girl?" I said. "I'll cut your throat first."

"A man craving steak will still eat burger when he's hungry. Do you understand what I'm talking about? One of these girls is coming with me," he said. "You think that over. I'll call you when Nina is in my van."

Then he hung up.

I shouted and screamed and kicked over tables. I threw any object I could pick up and broke stained glass. Then I bent over to catch my breath and look at you. You hadn't moved. You didn't flinch. You were a shell of a human being at the time, your mind lost in hiding.

Colt didn't try to comfort me, didn't try to intervene. He didn't know what to say because he didn't know what I was thinking. He couldn't relate. But my hands were tied just as much as yours were when we found you. I didn't see any other option that could keep me from sinking to more despicable levels. To take down Tim, I had to be as cold-blooded and conniving as him. I had to be willing to destroy something personal.

"Do you remember how to wire the explosive?" I said.

Colt was reluctant to respond back. "Yeah. What you got in mind?"

"I'm going to kill him," I said. I picked up the brick of C-1 along with the blasting cap and started wiring them together.

"How you plan on giving him that?" he said. But I think he was already starting to see where my thought was headed.

I looked down at the fuzzy teddy bear backpack and then at you.

"By offering him what he wants," I said.

Just like everything involving Colt, we argued about it. We only had a twenty-minute window to come up with something. But by the time we got the call, he agreed my horrific plan was the best option, maybe the only one. I called Thiago to get him in the area on standby. I didn't want that asshole more than a few minutes away. At the same time, I couldn't have him knowing our exact location. We gave Toke and Claire as much information as they needed to help, but not so much that they had a chance to protest. And once again, I'd find myself trapped in a car, next to an explosive wired by my own hand. It was my idea though. I wanted my enemies to die and my daughter to live. I was prepared to give my own life to make that happen.

Your little body could stand when I stood you up and you would walk when prodded to do so. But it was painful to watch. You were like a zombie, aimlessly wandering ahead on unsure legs. I could hardly bear making you move knowing what you'd been through. So I carried you, laid you down in the rear seat of Ash's car. Then I strapped the teddy bear sack to your back. There was a tiny piece of wire hanging just outside of the head through the zipper, but that was intentional. I wanted to make sure Tim could see it. I needed him to know I wasn't playing around. And sitting beside me, in the otherwise empty passenger seat, was a wireless electronic remote that had the potential to end both our lives with the press of a button.

Tim couldn't pick too public of a place to make the exchange. Fortunately, at that time of night in rural P-A, even the most popular areas were vacant. He had me waiting in the empty parking lot of a strip mall grocery store. I thought he'd pull up nearby but Tim was always so careful. He knew he'd created a dangerous enemy though he only saw me as a brute, some mindless gorilla safely kept impotent so long as it's caged.

When he finally arrived, he parked in an adjacent lot a hundred feet away on the opposite side of some black iron fencing. I drove my car until it was facing his van through the barrier but I kept a distance just as lengthy on my side. Then I waited for him to make a move.

Only a moment passed before he rang my mobile. I was feeling so much hatred, I didn't want to give him one word more than necessary so I extended no verbal greeting. I just put it up to my ear and waited for Tim just start talking.

"Any recommendations on how we do this?" he said.

Too many times, I'd watched him ask people what they wanted or how they wanted things done under the guise of courtesy and respect. They'd lay out their cards on the table and, at that point, he knew their mindset without showing his own hand. Of course, he'd accept their idea on the surface to give them a sense of control, then subtly twist it into whatever he wanted from the start.

"Nope," I said. I wasn't allowing him an inch to work with.

"Well, maybe it's best to not bring the girls out into the open. Let's just trade vehicles," he said. "This van is certainly worth more than your clunker but I'm willing to part with it to make the switch easy."

He had to know I wouldn't go for that. This was his first pitch. He was testing me.

"So I can drive around in a wagon you just used to steal a kid? I don't think so."

There was a breathy pause as he tried to read my face from a distance. Then he threw another foul.

"Fair enough. Well, then how about we each walk to get our girls at the same time? I'll get mine, you get yours. We'll cross opposite ends of the fence to keep our distance from each other."

I had to examine every idea very carefully and keep a sharp lookout for all the ways he'd be able to screw me. There were plenty.

"And what's to stop you from blasting that last chunk of C-1 once I step inside the van to get my daughter?"

He smiled. Cocky son of a bitch.

"If you know I have the last brick, then I can surmise you found the other. So I could ask you the same question."

"You could ask *now* but not ten seconds ago because you didn't know that I found it. I bet that makes you feel pretty uncomfortable. A strange feeling that maybe even got you wondering what else you don't know," I said.

"Mind games aren't your strong suit, Dirty."

"Maybe they ain't yours either," I said.

He put the phone in his lap and stared at me through the wrought iron fence that separated the two asphalt lots. His smile had slowly shrunk away. He was starting to get frustrated.

"The only other method of exchange I can think of is for us to carry each others' kids to each others' cars. Can you find any fault in that?" he said.

"If I had to register a guess, I'd say you have that explosive strapped right to my daughter's body," I said.

"You think I would use a kid to Trojan horse a bomb?"

"Why not?" I said. "That's what I'm doing."

He was thinking hard, like a chess champion mulling over the board trying to plan his next move. But I wasn't playing the same game. Giving you up to that sick bastard wasn't even a choice in my mind. I was only pushing him to exhaust his options until he backed himself into a corner.

"I think you're going to reject every idea just to be difficult," he said. "So, why don't you just go ahead and tell me what you suggest?"

"I suggest we talk face to face like men," I said.

I was pulling him from the comforts of the familiar, making him look in the eyes of a dangerous victim he'd screwed over so completely. Tim never had to do that. Face the betrayed. He was always lounging in the shadows by the time his marks realized they'd been duped if they ever realized at all. Not this time. My trust in him knew no limits before his elegant castle of bullshit buried me as it crumbled. I wanted him to see the hatred in my expression. I wanted anxiety to cripple his thoughts. He knew

I was after blood. But that would take patience to get him where I wanted and for a time, I was willing to settle for messing with his head and stealing his focus.

Besides, I needed to get away from the car.

"You have a gun in your lap, no?" he said.

I paused briefly before I lifted a nine-mil above the dashboard so he could see it through the glass. No point trying to hide it.

"Let me show you what I have," Tim said. He raised his clenched fist up toward the windshield. His fingers were tightly wrapped around a metal grip that extended out a couple inches on either side. "Do you know what this is?"

I knew but I didn't reply. So he explained.

"It's a dead man's switch. If I die and release my grip, a spring will close the circuit as the lever opens. And the explosive that you so astutely presumed to be in my possession *will* kill your daughter. Do you understand?"

I pressed the button to end the call. Then I turned around and looked at you still lying in the back seat. Your eyes were open for the first time since I found you. It was a blank stare but a sign of life nonetheless.

"Give me a full two minutes," I said. You might remember me saying it, but I wasn't expecting anything from you.

I slid the phone in my pocket as I got out of the car. Then I walked toward the fence with the gun in one hand and the bomb detonator in the other, both visibly evident by intention. He reluctantly did the same. During that long walk, a dozen scenarios went through my head. I wanted to end this as quickly as possible. But there was no way I could kill him, not without risking the life of my little girl in the back of his van. That is, assuming he had her back there at all. I had to fight my instinct to attack.

We finally came in close enough range to talk in a comfortable volume. Then we stood in uneasy silence until the one who could tolerate it the least offered the first words.

"I assume Colt is somewhere in the darkness with a rifle in hand?"

"Assume whatever you like. Makes no difference to me," I said.

His eyes didn't really even scan around us. I suppose he felt it unnecessary to care if anyone had him in their sights. That switch in his hand was a security blanket in his mind. And as long as he held it, I would be his protector.

"I think it's safe to say we're not going to shoot each other." He let the pistol in his hand rest limply as he extended it away from his body.

"It's a safe bet," I said. "For now."

"Then how about we put them away to ease our tensions?"

"I feel more at ease having it pointed at your skull," I said.

"On good faith then? To prevent mishaps from over-zealous emotions."

I held the electronic switch up so he could see my finger on the red button as I lowered my weapon. It wasn't as fail safe as the rig he set up, but a threatening reminder nonetheless. Then we tucked our guns away—me in my belt, Tim under his jacket in a holster like Doc Holiday.

"So, now we're face to face. Are you going to propose how we end this stalemate?"

"This ain't no stalemate," I said. "This ain't no game."

"You're arguing semantics? Let's just make the trade and part ways," he said.

"We'll be leaving soon enough," I said. "For now, we listen."

He finally began to look around as the idea set in that there was more happening than immediately apparent. "You wouldn't have been stupid enough to call the police, would you?"

"I don't talk to police. You said so yourself."

"Then what are we listening for? Tell me now or I leave," he said as he took a step backward.

Couldn't have been more than five seconds before my hip blurted out an ear-pleasing bell tone. I pulled the phone from my pocket knowing exactly what the message would be before the text even arrived. And just as I opened the picture attached to it, *his* phone began to ring.

"Go ahead and answer the call," I said. "It's important."

After a moment of befuddled hesitation, he raised it to his ear keeping a sharp eye on me.

While I couldn't hear the words Colt used to break the news to him, I imagine the dialogue relied heavily on the use of profanity and the term *yo*. But the look on Tim's face showed me that however the message was relayed, it effectively shriveled any confidence in his own leverage. He stopped listening for a moment to view the photographic evidence we'd both been sent. And I felt content to watch him squirm as he looked at that image—a briefcase full of cash sitting next to a grave. After all, once the money was found, Tim no longer held all the cards.

"Now we can talk," I said.

Tim's eyes shifted on the ground in front of him as he quickly tried to conjure up a new strategy on the fly. But he was entering the castle I built. And he had no response.

I walked a few steps closer to him as I spoke. "Obviously, the deal has changed. I'm taking my daughter. And I'm taking this other little girl too."

"Don't overlook the calamity I keep confined in my fist, Roy," he said. "What's to stop me from letting my palms breathe this crisp night air and send that little angel to heaven?"

"Your life," I said. "That van turns to flames, suddenly I've got nothing to lose. And gun to gun, I think the advantage is mine."

"I'm going to need more incentive than that," he said.

"I figured you might." I slipped the phone back in my pocket and confidently took a couple steps toward him. "I ain't just taking the girls. I'm buying their freedom. In exchange for both of them, you'll get your share of the money—the one-third we originally shook on, less fifty grand to each of these kids for the hell you put them through. Consider it asshole tax."

Tim looked in my eyes to judge my sincerity as he weighed his options. I suppose a shootout with a convicted murderer seemed less appealing than walking away scot-free with a few hundred grand in his pocket. "And that'll make us square?"

"Square? Not by a long throw," I said. "But I won't put a bullet in your head if that's your worry. Neither will Colt."

"And he's already agreed to this?" he said.

"He's knows exactly what we're doing."

18
Penis Fencing

There was no debate. We were traveling on my terms. The possibility that his van could have been seen fleeing the scene of Nina's abduction made it too risky to use. That was the only argument I needed to force him to do it my way. I wasn't budging on that condition. Just as critical in my mind, I had no idea what surprises Tim had in the back of that van and no interest to find out. Ash's old car, on the other hand, had been registered in a fake name and was stashed with everything I needed. It held only one secret but not from me.

Despite what might be considered the preferable position in the situation, I felt helpless as I looked over my shoulder and saw the fear on Nina's face. I'd thought of her many times over the years we'd been apart. Not once did I consider her anything but my daughter despite being no more familiar to her than any random Dick off the street. And finally seeing my pretty little girl, riding in the car with her, I wanted to tell her I was her daddy but it wasn't the proper time. She'd been estranged from me since before she stopped tapping the breast. My memories of us together were hazy, but Nina's were nonexistent.

I can't imagine the confusion and terror raging inside her head. Tied up, not being able to speak while in the back seat of a jalopy driven by the man who'd kidnapped her. The duct tape

Tim had used to cover her mouth had to stay on for her own good. I couldn't have her screaming when Colt inevitably startled her and I had no chance to warn her about him. I'm sure it provided no comfort to look at her side and see you, a younger girl who'd clearly been through the wringer so completely that you maintained a state of unrelenting indifference. Nina had to wonder what the hell happened to you and fear that she'd be next to go through it.

For the record, in case you don't remember, I wouldn't let Tim touch either of you once I could prevent it. I'm the one who sat you up in the back seat and put a jacket over your body. I transitioned Nina from his van to the seat beside you. I wouldn't even let him buckle your seat belt. He wasn't getting near either of you. Ever again.

I stared at the bag Tim had strapped to Nina's chest, knowing full well I couldn't restrain the bomb inside if Tim got the notion to release his grip from the detonator. I looked straight in her fearful eyes and spoke out of promise anyway. "It's alright. It's going to over soon. I ain't going to let nobody hurt you." It was a sincere gesture, at least in desire. But I guess those words were little consolation from the battered stranger firmly holding a gun, even if I did have it pointed at her captor.

"It's really hard to concentrate on driving with that cannon in your hand. You think I'm going to jump out of the car?" Tim had one hand wrapped around the steering wheel and the dead man's switch in the other.

"Precaution," I said. I kept my answers at a minimum. I didn't want to engage him.

"Against what? You can't shoot me," he said.

Not yet. But the same wouldn't hold true for anyone else who might be helping him. There was no telling what other tricks he had up his sleeve and I wasn't taking any chances. I didn't owe him the explanation though. So I didn't give it.

Tim made it clear he was opposed to driving us but it only made sense. He knew exactly where he'd hidden the money and I wanted to keep my eyes on every move he made. The gears in his head were always running. I had to have the brakes handy. Even as he drove us back to the woods, he continued trying to pull my strings.

"Do you think you can trust Colt with all that money?" Tim said. "He's probably halfway out of the state by now."

I was determined to not allow him inside my head and just as conscientious to not let him know that he'd lobbed a softball. His suggestion was impossible after all.

"He'll be there," I said.

"How can you be so sure?"

"Because he's real eager to see you again."

I wanted him to be the one who remained unsettled. Hard to say if it had any affect at all.

"I thought you hated Colt. The entire time we worked together, you never trusted him. And you weren't wrong to feel that way. He was *so* eager to betray you," Tim said. "If you only knew the cold things he would say about you."

"He made a mistake. He owned up to it," I said. "He begged for his life. Begged for forgiveness."

Tim made a face like I just proffered him religion. "That's a lot more forgiving than I expected you'd ever be."

"Maybe you don't know people like you think. Way I see it, I can't get too mad. He was just following the lead of a backstabbing traitor," I said. " And I was duped by the same shit-heel."

"Colt was an idiot. A means to an end. I never could stand listening to his ghetto-trash nonsense," he said. "But he was easy to manipulate, easy to train. Like a circus chimp with a mental capacity too small to see his impending fate at the glue factory. That's the only reason I used him."

He was finally starting to say things that were pleasing to my ears. I didn't want him to stop. I wanted him to keep on with all of his bad mouthing. Because everything I could hear, Colt could hear. So I prodded him.

"If he were in this seat instead of me, I'd expect you'd be giving him the same exact speech, only with my name."

"But he's not smart enough to be in that seat, is he? That's my point. He's brainless. You're different, Dirty. It's why I kept you closer. You can think things through. You had honor. You were loyal. I always respected you," he said.

"You framed me."

"I knew you wouldn't go back to prison. The door handle that I swapped out, it would have been rejected evidence. It wasn't even the exact model those people had before. Same with the stun gun. I was just buying time," he said.

"You set me up. You stole from me. Knew I could be killed or locked up," I said. "And you didn't give two shits about any of it."

"That's not true. I saved a burner phone so I could call the cops and anonymously admit guilt, proclaim your innocence. They would trace the number and know it was one used in the crimes. I was going to make sure you went free, just from a safe distance."

"I think you saved that phone to frame Colt, maybe even get him killed. But it don't matter no more," I said, glancing at you in the back seat. You'd hardly moved from the position I'd placed you and it was making me angrier by the second. Then I stared at Tim with evil blazing from my eyes as I leaned in and quietly unleashed my hate. "Had I known about your repulsive appetite, your sick lust, I would have plunged a knife in your throat the moment we met. And I think God would reward me for erasing His mistake. Like putting down a rabid dog or correcting a miscarriage that He forgot," I said, shifting back in my seat. "Or flushing His toilet."

We drove for a few minutes in quiet, our bitter exchange succumbing to the hum of the tires kissing asphalt. Street lamps were sporadic at best. It was getting harder to see your faces in the backseat with the glow of moonlight doing next to nothing to illuminate the inside of the car. Nina looked as if she was resting her head against the seat cushion from what I could tell. I like to think my presence helped calm her nerves some, but it could just as likely have been the vibration of that old engine relentlessly soothing her to accept whatever fate awaited.

I saw Tim look at Ash's cigar box lodged between the dashboard and the windshield in front of me. I thought he'd make some derogatory remark but he never did. I guess he reckoned better than to blow on the fire for fear of the sparks hitting his eyes. Then he scoffed under his breath and settled into a head-shaking smirk. Everything he did made me want to hurt him. But I couldn't. Not yet.

"You got something you want to say?"

"Penis fencing," he said.

It was hard to not slap that damn grin off his face. "What?"

"Remember that nature show I was watching a few months back. Documentary about the flatworm. You walked in on the last half. It doesn't sound familiar?" he said.

I didn't respond. I'd grown way too tired of hearing about anything that had to do with nothing.

He continued despite my obvious apathy. "Flatworms are hermaphrodites. The whole lot of them have both sexes and they battle to see who carries the eggs by sword fighting with their penises. Winner gets to impregnate the other one. At any rate, it just reminded me of us. Makes me wonder if that's we're doing right now?"

"I don't follow," I said.

He glanced over to read my face before he spoke. "Just can't help feeling like we're in a struggle to see who can fuck the other first."

A rare thing for him to show his mindset. It was good to know where he stood.

"You already won that ribbon," I said. He always thought he was so clever, so much smarter than everyone else. Hell, he usually was. But that damn nature show came back to me as he was describing it. And I wanted to get my jabs in when I could. "Do you remember the ending? The ones that wind up alone poke their dicks into their own heads so they can still reproduce."

Tim smiled. He seemed surprised, almost proud that I'd paid enough attention to recall it. Maybe he was just happy I was talking to him, opening myself up to possibly being manipulated. I shut that right down.

"That's what you should have remembered," I said.

"Now I don't follow," he said.

"Worms with no partners end up fucking themselves."

Those were the last words spoken for the rest of the drive.

Tim drove past the road we'd all gone down earlier until we reached a narrow dirt driveway that was nearly invisible from the main road. He moved the car slowly, keeping his high beams lit as they provided the only light in the darkness that swallowed us. At a hundred feet through the trees, we came to an abrupt end at a circular clearing, hardly wide enough to maneuver the car. Tim turned us as much as he could to rest the headlights on yet another section of cemetery hidden beside a small wooden shack. The structure looked decayed enough to collapse from a solid belch.

"What is this place?" I said. Several calf-high piles of rocks marked off certain spots like primitive shrines. Other mounds had tiny headstones, most broken to pieces, some smashed to rubble or crumbled by bulging tree roots. It was unfit ground to bury a surly dog.

Tim scanned the area around us, not answering right away. His vigilance didn't cease even as he spoke. "They call it *Bett des Vergessenen*. It's where the church buried orphans. Where is Colt?"

"I don't know. He should be here somewhere," I said. I reached over and took the keys from the ignition so he couldn't drive away. Then I opened my door.

"Where are *you* going?" He was losing more control with each passing moment and it was making him sweat. Not giving any answer didn't help calm his nerves but that wasn't my concern.

I got out and called for Colt in the darkness, but he wasn't out there. Only seconds passed before Tim stepped out as well, though he kept his mouth shut. His eyes kept bouncing around, trying to detect any danger as he tapped on the hood of the car with the dead man's switch. I don't know if that was anxiety or him trying to remind me that he wasn't defenseless. It was hard to not find some pleasure in the uneasiness on his face.

"What's in the shack?" I said.

"Groundskeeping supplies probably. Gravedigging tools maybe. It's a sexton's shed," he said as he kept looking all around like someone was going to jump out at him from the shadows. "Something's not right. Where the hell is he?"

I walked toward that rickety structure and Tim tagged along ten steps behind to keep an eye on me. I didn't trust him enough to keep my back toward him, but I knew he wouldn't trust me to go alone. If I wanted him to follow, I had to lead with confidence. We ended up fifty feet away from the car, standing directly in the bright headlights. Between long looks at me and wakeful scans of our surroundings, Tim never stopped glancing at the car doors to make sure nobody got near them. The high beams blinded us to the girls inside but he made sure they weren't leaving the vehicle, with or without help. That was good enough for what we needed.

I again started calling Colt's name, knowing full well he wouldn't come. I was just distracting Tim. Covering up stray sounds. Buying time.

A moment later, my phone sounded out.

"What is it?" he said. He almost sounded panicked.

I pulled out my phone and looked at it, never relaxing the grip of the gun in my good hand. "A text," I said. "From Colt." It read just as simply as I'd hoped: *It's done.* That didn't surprise me none. I was waiting for it.

"Well?" Tim walked closer but wouldn't dare stand beside me. We weren't allies any more.

I hung my head and growled as I shoved the phone back in my pocket, a fraudulent exhibit of disappointment.

"What did it say?" Tim demanded again in agitation.

With a deep breath and a sigh, I relayed the message he needed to hear. "It said: *I took the cash I deserved. You bitches can fight for the scraps. See you in Hell.*"

I could see the fury on Tim's face as he made a fist and pointed at me with his free hand.

"I knew it. I told you he couldn't be trusted!" He turned and moved toward one of the small mounds of rocks that sat off by itself, cursing under his breath the whole way. On his knees, he used his free hand to hastily cast the stones aside one by one until he uncovered a round flat of wood hidden beneath it. "We have to track him down," he said. "That was our money!"

He flipped the wooden cover to reveal a hole lined in mossy stonework, a well in a previous life. Then he pulled on a length of rope that descended inside, backing away until the briefcase and the large satchel emerged out of the blackness.

Tim knelt back down and opened up both bags, one after the other. As he looked inside and saw that they contained every cent he'd stashed away, it finally occurred to him. But by then, it was already too late. I remember the moment the realization hit him. I could tell by the smirk on his face right before he expelled a hollow chuckle. Even in defeat, he remained arrogant.

"You had no idea where it was, did you?" he said. "Now you do. Bravo." He held the switch slightly above his shoulders and waved it at me. "It changes nothing." Still on the ground, the bastard wouldn't look up as he spoke to me. I think he felt ashamed to look in the eyes of an underling who bested him. But he didn't know the half of it.

Tim pressed his free hand against one of the larger rocks to stand up. That's when I shot a hole straight through the meat between his thumb and trigger finger. Then I kicked him in the side to knock him off his feet.

"The deal is changing again," I said. I reached down inside his jacket to snatch the pistol from his holster while he cowered on his back and focused on the wound in his palm. He still clung to that damn switch though.

"What did you do?!" he yelled.

I'd taken his weapon and removed his ability to shoot in case he had another hidden away. I couldn't take the chance of him running though. So I pointed the gun at his knee.

"Stop! Stop! I swear I'll drop this and blow those girls to Hell!" Tim had entered into survival mode but he wouldn't release that security blanket until he was sure his death was imminent. It was the only bargaining chip he had left.

It wasn't enough.

I squeezed the trigger again, popping his knee into a bloody mess as the bullet entered one side and burst out of the other. He cried out in a moment of agony before staying true to his word. It was a rare moment of honesty. Tim held the switch out away from me and spread out his fingers, dropping the device into the well below.

In an instant, I heard the explosion come from behind me. It was a bit louder than I anticipated, but far less climatic than what Tim expected. I never told him Ash's back seat could fold down in the center of the bench, discreetly giving direct access to the trunk between you girls. It just never came up. He definitely didn't think Colt could have been riding in the back with us the entire time, waiting to remove the blasting cap from the C-1 strapped to Nina's chest. But that's how it went. Colt had thrown the glorified firecracker out the window, removing both of you from danger and pulling the rug from under the animal I once saw as a partner.

It was over for him. He knew it. "Go ahead and do it," Tim said. "Put me down." He was whimpering, challenging me to end his misery.

"I already told you," I said. "I ain't going to put a bullet in your head. Neither is Colt."

And I meant it. We still had a debt to pay.

I figured they got lost on the way there for as long as it took. It was an easy turn to miss no matter how well I described it. The whole area was wilderness after all, home to little else but trees and small critters Colt referred to as *hillbilly livestock*.

Toke and Claire had found their way to us though. It was short walk through the woods, close to where they'd been searching though more imprecisely located from the GPS coordinates than Claire had predicted. No matter, the car's headlights acted as a beacon once the gun shots got their attention. By the time they walked up, we had already bound Tim back against a tree further into the forest. I had him standing as best he could, with a rope between his neck and a higher branch that prevented him from sitting. He wasn't getting any pity on my watch. I wedged Ash's cigar box between the small of his back and the tree trunk. That's probably when he realized it's where I had stashed the brick of plastique after I'd found it in the church. On the ground four feet in front of him, I set down the money satchel, diligently repacked to finish the job. It would be impossible to miss.

Claire was too disturbed to stick around. The second she saw him bound up, his mouth duct taped shut using the same piece he'd put on my daughter, Claire had to remove herself from the area. Knowing what he'd done, she agreed with the punishment. She just didn't have the stomach to watch it being carried out. I preferred her stay in the car with you girls anyway. I figured of any of us, her feminine touch might be the best thing to provide solace in the short-term. I don't know where she drove off to wait, but she took you and Nina out of harm's way. That's all that mattered.

I told Toke and Colt to go with you too but, surprisingly, they didn't want to leave me to deal with cleaning up the mess alone. So we waited, together. The three of us stood around our captive, each strategically close to different trees. We tried our best to not focus on his death. No matter how deserved, killing someone always kills part of yourself. And once that innocence is lost, a blackness builds inside you with every repetition. I had become able to numb my conscience and justify my actions. But as I watched them avert their eyes from Tim, I knew they could feel that part of themselves dying. They were grieving.

Morbid curiosity got the best of me while we had the opportunity. I can't say with certainty what drove me to ask. A bit of me wanted to remind them why he was in that position; another part wanted to be reassured that Nina would be unlikely to ever encounter anything so heinous as the suffering he caused. The rest of me was just looking for an excuse to lash out. I walked up to that animal and tore the tape from his mouth.

"How did you meet her?" I asked.

"What are you talking about?" He had to feel death looming over his shoulder. He wasn't shook up though. He was sedated like he'd already accepted his demise.

"Mandy. How did you ever meet that little girl in the first place?"

Tim didn't answer right away. I wrapped my hand around his throat and shoved the barrel of the gun against his balls. I was ready to sever his manhood with the squeeze of a trigger. But just before I could let that bullet obscure his gender, he spilled his guts.

And I beat him for it. Relentlessly.

He could have been trying to get me to kill him before his suffering got any worse. Thinking in that regard, his words could have been lies. But honestly, I'm not sure if any answer he gave would have made much difference. I just wanted to hurt him. Once he got out the whole story, I pounded him until his face was as unrecognizable as mine. I'd like to say he got paid back for what he done to you but I don't think that's possible. As bludgeoned as he was, he didn't get what he deserved. He got off easy.

I pulled the collar of his jacket and wiped off his mouth enough to stick the duct tape back in place. Toke and Colt had long since diverted their attention, not encouraging me or trying to stop me. There was no more condemnation or blame. We didn't even talk about it none. All I could do was join them in uncomfortable silence. I don't think that lasted nearly as long as it felt.

They finally pulled up in an over-sized SUV and pointed headlights our way after spotting us in the distance. Thiago marched over with three of his goons, all walking a few paces behind him like third-world wives. None of them had guns in their hands but I had no doubt the bulges under their shirts were heaters. I kept mine fully loaded in the small of my back, knowing it would probably be needed.

Thiago didn't give no greeting worth mentioning. The three of us watched him lour as he sized us up, one after the other.

Then he shifted toward Tim and inspected the mess I'd made of his face, probably disappointed he was getting sloppy seconds. "You run over him with your car or something?"

Tim was groaning and moaning. His relaxed state of acceptance had transformed into an excited panic when he saw the gangster approach. That's how it looked anyway. But he couldn't say a word with his lips sealed.

"He's here and he's breathing. I did my part," I said.

"And the money?"

"Everything we found is in the bag."

With a nod, he signaled one of his lackeys to inspect the satchel. I admit, I was a bit nervous as he pulled it open. The bills were the fakes, the same ones we'd photographed beside the headstone to fool Tim, the same ones Tim had left in storage to fool Colt. I had my fingers atop my jeans, positioned to squeeze the detonators inside my pocket. I was fully prepared to end my life and open the door to Hell if they got wise. It was dark though and he only had his cell phone light to look at the contents. He didn't flip through the bills. And he didn't go all the way to the bottom to find the last brick of explosive hidden underneath the papers. Once he stood up, I thought maybe we were free and clear.

"Our business is done," I said.

Thiago didn't say anything. He just gave me a cold stare as we started to walk away to the sounds of Tim furiously screaming from under the duct tape. Truth be told, when the email confession didn't even get a mention, I stopped believing we could make it out alive. I don't think they would have let that happen. I figured we'd only count three steps before they'd reach for their straps and send airborne lead in our direction. In actuality, I made it about fifteen.

Toke and Colt were farther away than me, though I don't know exactly by how much. I was keeping my attention on the

Mexican bangers, just waiting for someone to show a piece. I was still too close for comfort but I didn't have a choice. I had to pull the cord. Sweat and blood and struggling jaws finally managed to break Tim's lips free of the adhesive so he could get those words out.

"It's a trap!" He shouted the warning just to screw us, maybe bargain his way to survival.

We all heard it but having been blindsided, the words didn't register in their brains as quickly as ours. By the time they processed the information and pulled their weapons, the three of us had already fallen behind thick trees and stones, whatever was closest. I crushed both buttons as I hit the ground.

I imagine it was the brick of explosive in the satchel that blew one thug to unrecognizable chunks and tore Thiago's legs from his body. They were closest to that one. The explosive in Ash's cigar box seemed to do the most damage though. Before I'd wedged it behind Tim's back, I filled up the empty space with nails and screws I'd found in the gravedigger's shed. His entire body was ripped in two and small pieces of shrapnel coated the area around him. I heard pieces of metal hit trees far beyond where we'd been able to hide.

I didn't wait very long to survey the damage. Any survivors would still be stunned and I couldn't waste the opportunity to get the jump on them. It was a bloody mess. Pieces of flesh and body parts and charred remains were scattered around the trees. And on the edge of the circumference of damage, against the odds, I found the last two rats still breathing. They were pretty badly messed up, both disoriented and shredded from the flying debris. I moved toward the most badly injured and put two slugs through his head. That was as much mercy as I could give him.

Then I stepped over to the only Mexican still clinging to life and slid his gun away from him. He couldn't walk or even get to his feet. He crawled on his belly as best he could going real slow and not getting very far. I was going to finish it right then but I figured he wasn't mine to take.

Toke was squatting down, hovering over his prostrate cousin so he could rip his jeans and examine his leg. Apparently, Colt didn't dive far enough behind cover and caught some of the flak. The makeshift buckshot perforated his calf like a distant shotgun wound. I'm sure it hurt like hell, just not so bad that he couldn't stand up and hobble off with some help. Some might call that karma. I don't know about all that, but if it had to happen to any of us, I'm not sorry it was him.

I didn't walk over to see it right away though. Ain't no way I was leaving that banger to his own devices when one of those devices could be a weapon he had tucked away somewhere I wasn't willing to reach. Besides, I had one more gesture to make, one more wicked act backed with good intentions.

I grabbed the guy by his foot and dragged him a few yards into a more open area. They didn't notice me pulling him until the Mexican started yelling and throwing handfuls of sticks and leaves at me. Then Toke left his cousin and sprinted over.

"What are you doing?"

"Look at his face," I said. "You don't recognize him?"

The thug turned over and started blasting us with Spanish curses. At least, that's what I guessed it was by the tone. I pointed my gun at his face so he'd quiet himself down but that didn't work. He kept on spouting harsh dialogue that meant nothing to any of us. So I pressed my foot in a bloody patch on his pant leg that had been torn open in the explosion until he raised his hands and whimpered.

"No, I don't recognize him. Should I?" Toke said.

"He was the trigger man. This is the bastard who popped Big."

He wasn't of course. That is, he could have been. I had no idea. But I remembered what it was like craving revenge for spilt family blood and feeling worthless for not appeasing it. I knew how it felt to maintain empty space where a brother used to be, to know it ain't ever getting filled again. Not in the same way. And after all of Toke's help, I wanted to pay him back somehow. I figured, giving him some kind of closure would be the best thing I could do.

"Are you sure?" he said.

"Positive," I said. "I saw him do it. I remember his ugly mug."

The guy couldn't speak English. He couldn't plead his case. It wouldn't have mattered anyway. When staring in the face of a swift and final judgment, everyone pleads innocence. But no matter what, whether that crime or another, he was guilty of something. I have no remorse.

"Eye for an eye." I held the gun by the barrel and extended it out in front of him.

Toke wrapped his fingers around the grip and looked at it for a moment before he pointed the business end at the thug's chest. I thought he was going to plug him. The Mexican thought so too. I don't know what little chant that *mico-culo* kept repeating but I know it ended in *Dios* and I know that means *God*. Toke knew it too. That was enough of a prayer that Toke could feel his humanity disintegrate the closer he came to pulling the trigger. He might as well have been pointing the gun between the eyes of his own soul.

Once his lip started to quiver, I put my hand on the hardware and lowered it so he no longer had to make that choice.

"Go help out Colt and let's get out of here," I said. "I'll take care of this."

Now I ain't going to confess what happened next as there's no need to incriminate someone for correcting an injustice. I'll just say Toke, Colt and I walked away by ourselves after every bullet in my gun had been spent.

Toke had tears in his eyes when he handed it back to me. "*Lex talionis*," was all he said. We never talked about it again.

❊

And that's how it all happened. After spending time with you and Nina, Claire refused to have any of the cash. Seeing as how it was there for the taking, Colt and Toke didn't argue about splitting it with me. We could see past the origin and look logically at the alternatives of where it would end up. We saw the possible good that could be done with it. Maybe it's a gender thing.

I know it don't make up for the hell you been through as a kid but I'm hoping you'll take the money in this box. Build something proper with your life. Enjoy it. Let it help you. Maybe it can buy me some kind of redemption for my part in the whole mess, either in your eyes or in whatever God awaits to judge me in the afterlife. In any case, I feel better you having it.

One last thought. In case you get it in your head that you need to know exactly where you came from to know where you're going, I hope you abandon any search you start. Just like the money, origins don't make no difference. You determine where you go by your own decisions. If this money finds you of adult age and breathing like I intended, you can make the choice right now to be something great and to be happy with where you're going, no matter what you've been through, no matter where you came from. But if curiosity gets the best of you—and with you being a woman I suspect it might—I hope you reconnect with my daughter first. Nina can tell you anything you need to know.

I wish you nothing but happiness for the rest of your life. I mean that from the bottom of my heart. Be strong and brave and smart. And Mandy, be good.

Sincerely,
Roy Conrad

Epilogue

After reading the last page for a third time, Amanda flipped it over so she could no longer see the text. She had read the whole thing in one sitting, only taking breaks to get coffee and use the bathroom.

Theodore Kemp watched her walk back and forth when she'd periodically emerge from the cramped room, though they didn't speak. Sometimes she'd have a smile on her face, other moments tears in her eyes. He never considered interrupting her no matter how much grief he would inevitably catch from his wife for coming home late. This was too important. He was sitting back in his chair playing a puzzle game on his phone when he noticed Amanda standing in the doorway.

"I'm finished." The long letter was stuffed back into the padded envelope under her arm. She looked exhausted. "What should I do with this?"

Theodore escorted Amanda to the back of the building where he instructed her to feed the papers, face down, into a high-capacity shredder. In less than a minute, the entire stack was destroyed.

"I'll help you carry the lock box out to your car."

Amanda put her hand on Theodore's arm to stop him before he could walk away. Then she held out several hundred-dollar bills that she'd removed from the fire safe.

"What's this for?" he said.

"Everyone needs a lawyer eventually, right?"

"I've already been well compensated," he said as he pushed the money away. "You don't owe me anything."

She put the folded cash down by her side and stared at the floor as if afraid to speak her thoughts. "I want you to help me find someone."

"Who?"

"His name is Roy Conrad," she said. "I don't know too much about him other than he served—"

"Whoa! Stop right there," he said. "Amanda, if this is in reference to anything you just read in that envelope, you can't be talking about it, remember? Not even to me."

"I remember," she said. "There's no confidentiality because I'm not your client. That's why I'm trying to hire you."

"You don't need a lawyer right now. You need a safe-deposit box for whatever is in that treasure chest you got. The smart choice is to go live your life, enjoy the blessing and don't look back."

"I'll hire a private investigator if you can't help me," she said. "I know that's not what you do, but I figured you might have resources you can use. People you trust."

Theodore looked at the determination in her eyes, trying to decide how to quell it. He wanted to help her. At the same time, he had an obligation to decide what Dirty would want, to find a solution that kept potential backlash for everyone at a minimum. That meant having as few people involved as possible. If he didn't give her guidance, she would seek it elsewhere.

"OK. I'll help you," he said. "But the best I can do is give you his daughter."

❀

It was early when Amanda pulled up to the inner city row home. While she didn't exactly feel safe anywhere in the city, this particular part of Philadelphia included several streets worth of bars where tourists and hipsters would congregate, the same area college kids from rich families would visit to spend their parent's money. It wasn't immune to malfeasance. However, the business generated by the area's vices caused police to constantly make their presence more pronounced. And it took seeing a blue uniform at a nearby intersection for her to even get out of the car.

Amanda double-checked the house number as she approached it. Then she raised her fist to knock on the door but it opened before she had the chance. A heavily tattooed and pierced Asian woman stopped suddenly on her way outside, startled to see she had a visitor at her steps.

"Oh! Can I help you?" The woman raised her eyebrows as if leery of the young girl.

"Nina?"

"No. I'm Sue."

"I'm looking for Nina Conrad," Amanda said timidly. "Does she live here?"

"Can I ask what this is in reference to?"

Amanda held back her words initially, afraid to give away more information than necessary. The reluctance didn't go unnoticed.

"I'm an old friend," she said.

"You look too young to be anybody's *old* friend," the woman said, her tone more suspicious than jovial. She momentarily waited in vain for a response before she turned around and yelled up a staircase. "Neen! You have a visitor!"

"Who is it?" an echoing voice replied from upstairs.

Sue turned her head back toward the door, looking for an answer she didn't have.

"My name is Amanda."

"Amanda!" Sue repeated loudly to the floor above.

Footsteps thumped down the hardwood steps followed by soft voice. "I don't know any Amanda," she said before she descended far enough to see her visitor's face.

Nina was an attractive woman, undeniable even to those who aren't fond of body ink or facial jewelry. Her light skin seemed even more so against her jet black hair and dark makeup. The whites around her pupils shrank between squinting lines of rich eyeliner as she stared at the young girl standing at the entrance.

"I'm sorry. Do I know you?"

Both women stood inside and looked over Amanda as they waited for a response. It was intimidating for a young girl who regularly suffered problems with anxiety. The beginnings of a panic attack crept up on her. Amanda started to think she'd made a mistake. It took all the courage she could muster to continue a dialogue.

"Your father helped me once. You probably don't remember me," she said. "I'm sorry. I should go." She quickly turned to walk away. Her inherent inclination to run was constant and relentless.

"Mandy?" Nina said. "Little Mandy?"

Amanda stopped walking at the edge of the stoop and crossed her arms in front of her chest, taking deep breaths to calm her nerves.

"That is you, right? The little girl from the backseat of the car," she said to the young girl shyly facing away from her. "Of course I remember you. How could I forget?"

Before she knew it, Amanda had arms wrapped around her in a warm embrace. Nina cried as she turned the young girl around by the shoulders and squeezed her. The tears were contagious. After a few seconds, the unchained emotion broke down the awkwardness of someone invading the personal space she'd so adamantly protected. Amanda opened her arms and hugged the stranger with whom she'd shared such a life altering experience. And it felt cathartic.

"This is *her.*" Nina said to her partner. "This is Mandy."

Sue looked almost relieved as she came outside and down the cement steps. "So, you're *her.* I'm sorry if I seemed rude. I thought maybe you were a salesperson or Jehovah's witness or something," she said. "Maybe a crazy, stalker ex-girlfriend."

Nina cocked her head with raised eyebrows as if she'd just received a verbal jab, the way that long-time lovers react when a past argument is revived for reference. Then Sue kissed Nina goodbye before heading off to work.

With her arms wrapped around the young girl, Nina escorted her into the house. Uneasiness began to subside as they sat face to face across a wooden table and two cups of hot tea.

"How did you find me?"

"An attorney. His name is Theodore Kemp," Amanda said.

Nina giggled for a moment before she repeated the name in a mocking tone. "Theodore Kemp: attorney at law." She giggled again.

Amanda looked confused while she waited for the joke to understand the punchline.

"Forgive me. I'm just not used to hearing people refer to him like that. All professional-like," Nina said.

"You know him?"

"Very well actually. By the time I was reunited with Roy, my father, they had become close friends. He was more like family."

"Oh?"

"In fact, he was around so much, I started calling him *Uncle* Toke. That was long before he passed the bar."

All that Amanda had read, it never occurred to her that Toke and the lawyer were the same person. So significant in her past, yet very much a stranger. She already had an abundance of information to process, a backlog of emotions to sift through. And none of it could be shared.

"So Mandy—"

"Please, call me Amanda."

"You don't like *Mandy?*"

"I've always hated *Mandy* ever since I can remember. Just hearing it makes my stomach turn. It wasn't until two days ago that I had any idea why." The roots of many residual quirks that Amanda maintained became clear to her, even if it was difficult to believe how she'd acquired them. But she accepted the truth, knowing it was the first step to overcoming the past.

Nina didn't ask her to explain it. It was easy enough to understand the disdain stemming from distant memories of a time in her life that was better forgotten.

"I take it you just turned eighteen, *Amanda?*"

"Yes," she said. "Mr. Kemp, your Uncle Toke rather, sought me out."

"And gave you a care package he and Roy set up for you," Nina said.

Amanda let a few seconds of awkward silence pass before she spoke. "Something like that."

"It's OK. We don't have to talk specifics. I already have an idea of what he gave you. Let me show you something." Nina got up from the table and came back with a photo album that looked like a discarded relic from the 1970's. "I used to hate my father, you know? I was ashamed when I discovered I was churned out from the seed of a convicted felon."

"When did you find out?"

"A few days after *that* night. They picked him up for kidnapping me because I identified him as being there in the car with us. My foster parents didn't have much choice but tell me about him. Police kept showing me his picture, tried to coerce me into saying Roy was the one who nabbed me but that other bastard's face was stuck in my mind," Nina said. "And I kept telling them, *no*, this man didn't kidnap me. He *rescued* me. *He* brought me back to safety."

"Did he get into trouble?"

"Not for that, no," Nina said. "He told the cops an old associate was trying to blackmail him back into crime and was using me for pressure. With my testimony, Roy was let go for lack of evidence. They even pardoned him for breaking his parole due to extenuating circumstances."

Amanda felt a kinship blossom as she listened. Hearing this other perspective made the past feel more authentic than it had before, like a history that belonged to her instead of an elaborate lie in which she'd been inserted. At the same time, it seemed unreal that it had been kept from her. "They never asked about *me?*"

"Well, the woman who was with them—"

"Claire?"

"Yes, Claire. She dropped you off at a hospital in Baltimore. They didn't want us connected to each other or to anything else they'd been involved in, for everyone's safety. And I was so distraught when the whole thing was over, I never mentioned you to the police. They didn't know about you to even ask my dad when he was questioned, so *he* never brought you up. And the next day, when I told my foster parents about you being in the car, they didn't believe me." There was a subtle pain in Nina's voice that became more noticeable with each word. It's as if she'd been waiting years for this moment.

She continued, "The therapist convinced them, and eventually me after several years of medication and brain-scrubbing therapy, that you were never there. You were some imaginary construct I created to cope with the stress, built from all the news stories I'd seen about you being kidnapped. It was a coincidence, they said, that you were found on the same night and that's why you'd been inserted in my memory. My mind created a calm companion to give me strength and share the burden, as if knowing a younger girl could handle it, then I could too." Nina teared up as she reflected back on the entire experience.

Amanda took a sip from the hot teacup, more out of courtesy than desire. She had little to give in the way of consolation. It was taxing enough trying to fend off her own demons.

Nina spoke softly as she stared down at the wooden tabletop. "Why didn't you talk to the police? You could have verified what happened. I wouldn't have felt like I was crazy."

There was a trace of blame in her words that didn't escape Amanda's attention. It was hard to not take a little offense at such misguided aim. But it seems everyone is found at fault when trying to deal with such an overflowing vat of emotions, especially one left unresolved for years. And that was understandable.

"I don't know," Amanda said. "I don't remember anything from back then."

"Nothing?"

"As I read the letter your dad left me, I started having flashbacks. But they aren't clear. I don't remember being taken or kept or... assaulted. I don't remember being rescued. The whole experience is a blank," Amanda said. "Honestly, I don't have many childhood memories at all. The first vivid ones I have are with my adoptive parents. They've always been mom and dad to me, even after they told me I was adopted."

"I'm sorry," Nina said. Any remnants of anger and resentment she held onto had disintegrated into sympathy for the quiet girl who'd gone through a far worse ordeal, even if it had been erased from her memory. "It's probably better that way."

Amanda looked down at Nina's arm, in particular the intricate tattoo pattern that spiraled up from her wrist and disappeared under her sleeve. Then she put her focus on the book where Nina's forearm was resting. "You mentioned that you wanted to show me something?"

Nina smiled as she lifted her hands from the album. "Like I was saying, I always hated the fact that my father was a criminal. Bothered me for years, almost as much as the thought that my parents gave me away to strangers because they didn't want me. Then, right after I turned eighteen, this black dude walks up to me out of nowhere and says he knows my father. My *real* father."

"Did you believe him?"

"Not at first. But Toke didn't try to get me to go anywhere with him or even try to convince me. He just told me that if I wanted to know about my real father, I should visit some storage locker. Then he gave me the location and two keys."

"How long before you went?"

"About an hour. I'd always been curious about my real dad so I went right away. And inside there was a small safe with Roy's side of the story, a letter explaining why he wasn't able to be my dad. You were mentioned in it, of course. I assume he gave you something similar, otherwise you wouldn't be here."

Amanda nodded her head.

"There were a few more personal items too, things he had saved just for me." Nina began to rub a cylindrical necklace hanging beneath her sweater, a habit she seemingly inherited with the object. "This scrap album was one of them, but I think he'd want you to see it too."

Nina slid the book across the table and opened it so Amanda could view the contents. It was lined with newspaper clippings and yearbook photographs. There was a high school musical program for *Guys and Dolls* where Nina had gotten the part of *Goldwyn Girl #3* along with a torn ticket stub. There were photographs of Amanda playing soccer and an article printed in a local paper when her team lost a county championship game.

The whole album was filled with memories of both of them. They were personal relics he saved as he watched the girls progress in age.

"Toke told me that my dad had kept an eye on both of us for years. Made sure we were OK. He took it upon himself to adopt you from a distance while he tried to be a part of my life as much as he could. And he took every bit of his share of the money and divided it in two, right down the middle. Roy gave you an inheritance like you were his own kid. Then he died a poor man."

Amanda was so engrossed as she looked through the pages, the words didn't immediately register. But once her mind processed the thought, she couldn't help but mourn a criminal she never knew.

"He's dead?"

"About six months ago in a car accident. Head-on collision."

"I'm sorry," Amanda said. It was a genuine sentiment, though not without some selfish basis. Thanking him face to face was no longer an option. And that was half of the reason she'd made the trip.

She let her eyes wander around all of the open rooms within view as they sat in a moment of silence. Paintings, alternating between surreal and macabre, adorned the walls while strange collectibles lined scattered shelves. Overtly sexual statues made from metal gears and stained glass. Animal skulls and jars of what appeared to be hair. And sitting on a chair in the corner, an old baby doll slumped over, its arms tattooed in permanent marker. The design matched the one on Nina's arm perfectly. Or more likely, as Amanda figured, Nina's arm was decorated to mimic a favorite toy left behind by her mother. This might have been done in an effort to maintain a symbolic connection with a woman who'd abandoned her, maybe even establish a rapport should they get the chance to be reunited. Amanda didn't know and didn't think it was appropriate to ask. Besides, the only remaining question that burned through her mind was in regards to her own mother.

"Do you know anything about my real parents?" Amanda said bluntly.

Nina raised her eyebrows and restrained a manufactured smile, as if either hesitant or confused.

"Your parents?"

"Yes. In the letter your dad left me, he indicated you could help me find my real parents if I found myself wanting to meet them."

It had been years since Nina had read those words. And being eighteen herself at the time, she was too involved with her own feelings to consider the past of this young girl. While she knew one day their paths may cross, Nina always focused on questions she would ask, not those she'd be expected to answer. In addition to the money, the letter and a few personal artifacts, Roy had left Nina with a burden. They never talked about it, even after they'd reconnected. It was only mentioned once in the letter, then forgotten until now.

"Find them? I can't help you find them," she said.

"Well, is there anything you can tell me?" Amanda said.

And just like that, Nina recalled that detail of the story her father left behind.

Having to wait there with Tim bound to the tree at our mercy, I just had to know.

"Mandy." I demanded. "How did you meet that little girl in the first place?"

Tim didn't answer right away. I wrapped my hand around his throat and shoved the barrel of the gun in his crotch. I was

ready to castrate him with a squeeze of the trigger. But before I
had to do anything so vicious, he broke down and told us.

I almost regret hearing it.

Mandy's mom was a junky. Just a lost teenager. A runaway.
Tim found her after she started turning tricks and he'd visit her
on a regular basis. It wasn't long before she got herself knocked
up with no idea who the father was. Could have even been Tim
for all they knew. Once that belly started showing, nobody else
wanted to touch her but that didn't stop Tim from seeing her.
And it didn't stop her from pumping herself full of chemicals.
Escaping reality was incentive enough but the possibility of
miscarriage was a bonus in her mind. With Tim's guidance,
though, that didn't happen.

After she delivered Mandy, things got even worse. She was
broke, alone. The responsibility of a kid only fueled her
addiction. And she became so desperate for a fix, she offered
anything and everything. That included her baby daughter's
innocence, no doubt with Tim's prompting. That's when he got
attached to her.

Mandy's mom was eventually killed, stabbed by a drug-
riddled John. Tim was nabbed for some kind of fraud charge.
Once he got out of the stir, he started hunting Mandy down.
And he used us all to do it.

Now, I ain't got the heart to tell that girl about her
beginnings. God knows what that could do to a person. I know
she done been told she's adopted though. I found that out years
ago. She's bound to have a desire to search for her birth parents
eventually. Once that fire takes hold, she may track you down
in the process to help her.

All I know is I've seen the family she's got right now and
that's all the family she needs. I think she's better off not
knowing. At the same time, who am I to decide what truth to
withhold? I can't make this decision alone and I reckon you can

probably relate better to a young girl more than a worn-out, old crook like me ever could. So should that day come, I'll leave the *truth* up to your good judgment.

I love you. I always have.

"Anything at all?" Amanda said again.

"Yes," Nina said. "I don't know how to even tell you this."

"Just be honest. I want to know where I came from." Amanda stared straight ahead with her round, doe eyes.

"Roy told me that your parents gave you up for adoption because they were too young and didn't think they could handle being parents. They tried to reclaim you after you were in the state's system but were killed in the process. It was a carjacking I think."

"That's what he didn't want to tell me?"

"I'm sure he didn't want to make you feel any worse than necessary to explain why he was in your life at all. I know he took to caring about you and what you thought of him."

Amanda nodded and sipped her tea before the meeting lingered into a further release of pent-up emotions. Once lighter topics began to prevail, conversation dissipated into a reminder that the two women were strangers with few interests in common. They hugged and exchanged phone numbers, promising to keep in touch. Both spoke with good intentions, even if deep down they knew true closure meant separation from the whole experience, including each other.

As she watched the young girl walk away, Nina couldn't discern whether her version of the past was acceptable enough to help Amanda move on. But she felt better supplanting a few poisonous facts with more palatable lies. Better for toxic truths to die in peace than turn to cancer.

Roy would find solace in that too. Despite the story Nina had been asked to tell, he actually remained in prison, counting down the years he had left to serve on his most recent sentence. Amanda didn't need to know he eventually returned to crime. He'd rather be dead in her thoughts than give her more reason to think poorly of him. Maybe she wouldn't ever consider him a savior or hero, but she couldn't deny her life was better directly by his hand. For all the bad he was held accountable for, he could hold onto that thought on even the loneliest night.

Nina would affirm that hope next time she'd visit him, a regular routine she'd already maintained for several years. It was more than just gratitude for all he'd done for her. She had come to love him, even respect him. With both desiring to be closer, they would continue to build a relationship and make up for the time that had been stolen from them both. Just maybe, having her back in his life would be enough to save him from himself and keep him clean for good.

A Note from the Author

Being a fiction writer, I don't live in reality. The vast majority of the time, my thoughts are somewhere else getting to know people that don't exist. I'll spend days thinking about these characters, then months obsessing over which words best describe them. I sacrifice health, family time, hobbies, and vacations as I bury my nose in a laptop attempting to craft a world that I hope others will visit. It can be a lonely, selfish life and for many authors like me, most of the time, there is little reward for it.

Now, since you've gotten this far, I'm assuming the story interested you enough to finish the book. I'm deeply grateful that you gave it a chance and I truly hope you enjoyed reading it. Please feel free to contact me with comments or criticisms. If you did find it worthwhile, please recommend it to a friend and rate my book online at www.amazon.com or other online retailers. It's the biggest compliment you can give. Thank you for your support.

Oh, and if you noticed the two signifcant anagrams hidden within the text, I'd love to know. There may even be a little something in it for you.

Humbly and Sincerely,
David Lineberry
ashenpawn@gmail.com

Visit Us:
www.ashenpawn.com
Ashen Pawn Publishing is also on Facebook.